Lost Ground

Ulla Jordan

 **FriesenPress**

Suite 300 - 990 Fort St
Victoria, BC, Canada, V8V 3K2
www.friesenpress.com

Copyright © 2015 by Ulla Jordan
First Edition — 2015

ISBN
978-1-4602-5985-6 (Hardcover)
978-1-4602-5986-3 (Paperback)
978-1-4602-5987-0 (eBook)

1. Fiction, Historical

Distributed to the trade by The Ingram Book Company

Contents

To
Lauri and Maria Vesalainen
who lived through it all

and to
Wolfgang

with love

Berlin 1936

1

Tina would never have stopped at the Hotel Andalusia if her father had been wearing his regular walking shoes. But that morning he'd put on a pair recently bought on the Kurfurstendamm, thinking he would be seated all day at the Olympic Stadium. By mid-afternoon the sun had turned the stadium into a cauldron so they boarded a stuffy tram back to the city centre and walked for an hour through the cool green groves of the Tiergarten park. That was when he noticed the red stain on the rim of his shoe and the blister on his heel. They sat down to rest on a bench and Tina glanced in the direction of the Unter den Linden.

"I see cafés over there," she said. "We could get lemonade."

"The Linden is one of the great streets of the world," he said. "It's a pity the fool Nazis ruined it. Look at those swastika flagpoles! That's where the lindens used to be." He gestured toward the central boulevard. "And they've put loudspeakers in the chestnut trees. It's like the Circus Maximus now."

"Did you come here with Mama?"

"Yes. She loved the Linden. It was one of our last trips."

They sat in silence for a moment. Tina had been ten years old at the time of her mother's death and sometimes had difficulty remembering her.

"When we left the café on the Linden we passed a store with an open market," her father continued. "They had crates of fruit and among other things a crate of peppers. Red, green, yellow, different shapes and sizes. I said to Mama, 'Look, I've finally done what you told me to do when you were angry with me—I've run as far as the peppers grow.' "

Tina laughed. She knew the saying, a mild curse suitable for ladies. "What did she say to that?"

"She said, 'I never said I wouldn't go with you.' And then she smiled that smile—the same one you're smiling now—so wide the corners of her mouth dipped a little and that dimple formed. I called it her pirate smile."

"She was so beautiful."

"No more than you. The boys at the club often teased me, wondering how a dusty old professor landed a beauty like her."

"I know how much you still miss her." She wondered if he would ever marry again. He was still a good-looking man, fit and trim with thick grey hair. If she brought up the subject, he invariably said that when one marries at an older age, once is enough.

"People tell you to put the past behind you." He looked down the street, beyond the banners and the shoppers and the speeding black cars at something she couldn't see. "They don't realize that some things remain forever in the present. Never mind about that. Aren't you glad you decided to come to Berlin? Now that you've finished school it's time for you to see the world. I started travelling when I was your age. Spent my twentieth birthday sampling Congolese tobacco at the Brussels World's Fair."

"Oh! I'm not as brave as that but yes, I'm glad I came. This is a beautiful city. Despite the fool Nazis."

They got up from the bench and headed up the Wilhelmstrasse away from the Brandenburg Gate, past a side street that led to the Andalusia.

"I remember that hotel," he said. "Let's have refreshments there."

The Andalusia had an elegance unfazed by its threadbare Persian carpets or the chipped angels on its rococo mirrors. One wall of the lobby was covered with equestrian drawings, and someone had tried to evoke flamenco dreams with filigreed Spanish wall sconces. While her father made for an armchair, Tina looked for the ladies' room, edging past the guests who milled about under the chandeliers. The chandeliers, Austrian crystal by her guess, lacked the brilliance of those at the Hotel Adlon or the Bristol. So did the guests, although they still glittered enough to make her feel provincial in her plain linen suit, chosen at a designer boutique in Helsinki as her signature outfit for the Games.

None of her travel brochures had prepared her for this, her first trip abroad, her first foray away from her native Finland. Nothing could, she decided. No one is born cosmopolitan. However confident you feel on your own soil, your first step away from it changes you into a wide-eyed child prone to behaving out of character, comparing yourself to others at every turn. She saw a doorway marked *Damen,* and as she walked toward it she thought about the brave little duck. This was a story from her childhood about a duckling who left the farmyard pond and swam down the stream, until the stream widened into a river and then into an ocean bustling with huge ships. In terror the duckling turned and paddled back to the pond, vowing never to venture out of it again. Clearly she was destined to become a pond duck, she decided as she joined a queue of women filing through a gold-trimmed archway.

She squeezed in at the mirror and dabbed on lipstick. Her hair had unravelled into disorderly blond wisps and she tried to wet it back into its lacquered waves. Back in the lobby, she scanned the crowd for her father and found him studying the drawings of leaping horses, speaking to a courtly man with a curving moustache. She knew immediately that this was an English moustache, well-tended and tidy, the kind she had seen in country and garden magazines.

"They're *cartujanos,*" said the Englishman, pointing at the horses with his pipe. "Finest of the Andalusian breeds. Bred by the monks around Jerez, prized for their fire and intelligence. Have you seen Seville? You should. Go there when the Games are over."

"I'm getting too old to be traipsing around the continent," said her father.

"Nonsense! You haven't aged a bit. Same sparkle in the eye, same gold in the eyebrows."

"And you haven't lost your fine manners, Philip. I only came here for my daughter's sake, really. Her friend is competing in the Games. Ah, here she is now. Tina, my dear, meet Philip Taylor, an old friend from my London days. He's a journalist covering the Games."

Taylor suggested a drink in the lounge. Tina knew her father was thirsting for a cognac, but in Finland young women didn't frequent bars, so they stayed where they were, the men rambling on about Spanish horses while she watched the crowd in the lobby. Most of them were newspapermen, rolling in from the stadium, loud and boisterous. She played a guessing game. The one with the unruly forelock—English. The one whose shoulders moved in shrugs—French. The one with doe-brown eyes—Spanish. And so on. She felt a slight irritation that her father had used the word "friend" to describe her sweetheart, Paul, who was a runner competing in the Games. She thought of him as her fiancé, even though he had yet to propose.

Suddenly Taylor beckoned to someone in the doorway. The lobby was awash with smoke and argument but the newcomer navigated through it with scarcely a sideways glance, pausing only to avert a collision with a wayward elbow. He was tall and slightly too thin, but his broad shoulders gave him an athletic air; his face was lean and saved from boyishness by two vertical lines on either side of his mouth. He paid little attention to them, instead looking anxiously at the entrance to the lounge.

"You look a little ragged. Been out working your charms on the ladies of the evening?" Taylor studied him from under black eyebrows.

"Very funny. I do have more finesse than to pick them up off the streets."

"Of course you do. Looked for you when I left the stadium. Couldn't see any sign of you."

"I left early. The noise was getting to me."

"Ducking out early won't get you a Pulitzer."

"I'm not here for a Pulitzer. I'm here because my editor's appendix acted up two weeks ago and I was next in line."

"Come now," said Taylor, stoking his pipe, "don't throw away your chance at glory."

"Glory?" The newcomer's lip curled in a slight sneer. Taylor turned and with a flourish introduced him as Tom Henderson of the Chicago Chronicle.

"And this is Eric Björnström and his daughter Tina," he swept them into the orbit of his hand. "Dr. Björnström was with the Finnish Embassy in London for many years."

"Please," said her father with a smile, "don't call me Dr. Björnström. My doctorate was in history. I don't want dizzy women coming up to me for smelling salts."

The American glanced at them and nodded. Then he lit a cigarette, and again gazed in the direction of the lounge entrance. Tina stood in silence, trying to think of something witty to say, like the sophisticated heroines in American romantic comedies. She hadn't mastered small talk, being either too timid or too outspoken by turns, sometimes within the same conversation. This stranger, who seemed to have taken no notice of her, intrigued her. Though she was inexperienced with foreigners and journalists alike, in her youthful universe men were classified as either frogs or princes. The frogs, whom she did not view unkindly by any means, knew they had little to lose and being boorish or eccentric could do them no further damage. Here was a man whose looks made him a prince but who displayed no interest in his subjects.

"What an exciting life you newspapermen must lead," she finally ventured in his direction.

"It's—" he looked at her and frowned, whether in displeasure or discomfort she couldn't tell. "It's strange what people think."

She was about to ask him what he meant when a stout man standing next to them suddenly swivelled on his heel like a rotating pumpkin and peered at them through eyes circled by layers of weathered skin.

"Knew I recognized the voice! What the devil are you doing here, Henderson?" He spoke with a drawl she knew from American films to be Deep Southern. "Do young pups draw all the best jobs now in Chicago?"

"I hardly qualify as a pup."

"True! I've drunk your Yankee ass under the table often enough."

Tina gasped at the word "ass", a word never spoken in her social circles, and her handbag slipped from her hands and landed on the floor. Its contents spilled out and disappeared into the floral patterns of the carpet.

"Oh, how clumsy of me!" she stammered and bent down to retrieve them while Taylor and her father upbraided the southerner for his language. She said nothing, furiously raking in her cosmetics from the carpet.

"Ah, womanhood," said Taylor. "I remember her as a quiet pretty child. She is a child no longer. These accoutrements of femininity attest to that."

"Tina is a level-headed girl, but young people these days all emulate the film stars."

She glared up at both of them and as she did her eyes met Tom Henderson's squarely for the first time. He too was on his hands and knees, his arms sweeping the rug for her stray hairpins.

"Never mind," he said, his eyes holding hers with a surprisingly mild gaze.

"Never mind what?"

"What they say. What do they know, anyway?" With that they both stood up. He resumed his nonchalance and she composed herself and her accoutrements. She tried to hide her flaming cheeks, afraid that if he looked at her she'd drop something again. Excusing herself, she made for the gift shop. She bought a package of mints, fanned her face with her gloves, and headed back.

The lobby was in motion with guests parading into the dining room and reporters streaming through the doors and doing a shuffle from one group to the next and into the lounge. Barbs and profanities flew through the air like darts but Tom merely studied his cigarette even though some were directed at him. She heard Taylor whisper to her father, "Tom rather sees indifference as a work of art."

Taylor had forgotten about her presence, but her father had not. His pursed lips told her it was time to go and they said their goodbyes. As they waited for a cab at the entrance, she saw Tom Henderson stalk across the now half-deserted lobby. His footsteps echoed on the marble floor and the night clerk nodded to him as he passed. He stood in the doorway briefly and then a red-haired waitress rushed up to him and he disappeared into the lounge. She would have liked to follow him and watch him, and try to reconcile the way he deflected overtures at every turn and the way he looked at her as he scrambled to find her lipsticks on the floor of the Andalusia.

2

The next day was blustery with scattered showers. Tom slept late and when he arrived at the stadium, heavy clouds were rolling in and the qualifying round of the long jump competition was nearly over. Jesse Owens, the American sensation of the Games, fought off a stiff challenge from Luz Long of Germany and made the final round on his last attempt. The press box was jumping.

"What do you think about your boy Jesse now?" Philip Taylor called to him from the British section a few seats down.

"He'll win."

"Maybe not," said another Brit. "Long is giving him a run for his money."

"I'm taking bets," said Taylor. "How much are you in for, Henderson?"

"I'll pass."

The Brits pounced at once. "So the Americans have no faith in their heroes!"

"Shame! No loyalty to king and country?"

Flustered, Tom dug out a few marks and threw them into Taylor's palm. "Screw king and country."

"You don't have a king," said Taylor.

"Then screw yours."

"In a manner of speaking you already have. Your Mrs. Simpson—"

"Screw her too."

The rain began as the competition ended and Owens won his gold medal. Adolf Hitler slumped in his seat and glared at the track, clearly out of sorts. Owens, the burnished bronze American who belonged to a race the Nazis called inferior, was circling the arena with Long, the blond German, arms upraised together in a victory lap. "Oh-wens! Oh-wens!" chanted the crowd, and American flags waved here and there. The press section bounced in excitement.

"Fifty pfennig says the little tramp slaps his knee," said a British reporter, training his field glasses on Hitler's VIP booth, in plain view directly beneath them.

"Going to throw your pfennigs in the hat, Henderson?" asked Taylor.

"No. The Fuhrer can shoot his brains out for all I care."

"You've seen too many Tom Mix films."

Tom grinned. That was what he liked about Taylor. Many of the English reporters didn't admit to even a passing acquaintance with the popular culture of their American colleagues, and exchanged asides about Ascot and Wimbledon as if to affirm their superiority. But the very first night at the Andalusia lounge, when they happened to share the same table, Taylor had rambled about Coca Cola and the World Series. It came as no surprise that he also watched cowboy movies. Tom rarely struck up friendships with his colleagues, even his own countrymen, whose ebullience often chafed on his nerves, but he'd made an exception for Philip Taylor. It didn't hurt that Taylor knew everything there was to know about the athletic events, and could educate him on the finer points of the steeplechase and the marathon.

The long jump pit was being raked and a new group of athletes emerged from the sidelines and took their positions on the track. Tom stood up and stretched his legs.

"I think I'll take a stroll. Watch my notes, will you?"

Taylor shot him a bemused glance. "Your Pulitzer is safe with me."

Tom stepped out of the aisle and up to the concourse. This vantage point gave a splendid view of the stadium itself, a sight that impressed him as much now as when he first saw it. There was no denying its beauty—the red cinder of the track, the brilliant green grass and tier rising upon tier of grey stone. He focused his attention on the starting line. A dozen runners were loosening up in preparation for the first heat of the men's five thousand metres. This was a race he always watched alone. It had been his own distance a lifetime ago in college, a sophomore aching to run in the Los Angeles Olympics of 1932. His heart pounded as the runners checked their shoes, then tensed at the line, ears straining for the commands. The starter lifted his pistol, and bent his knee at precisely the same moment he always did before firing. Crack! they were off, not in a burst of power like the sprinters, but with controlled deliberation, each man engrossed in his own strategy.

The first lap was uneventful but as they approached the straightaway the field was bunched up tightly, much too tightly, he noted in alarm. He saw elbows flailing, heels kicking too close to other heels. Someone's going to get hurt, and the instant he thought it, it happened. Two runners broke out and the rest converged behind them. A thin runner with straw-coloured hair toppled sideways to the infield grass. His ankle twisted ominously as he went down. Tom fixed his glasses on the fallen man, saw the Finnish flag on his jersey, saw his face twist in a look he knew, a feeling he'd memorized—not the knife blade of physical pain, but the implosion of a dream's sudden death.

Watching the runner limp off the field, Tom guessed that the ankle was sprained, not broken. The young man would run again, although that would be small comfort now. He focused again on the runner's face, judged his age to be about twenty-three. Not old for a distance runner, not too old for a comeback.

Back at the press box, he gathered up his notepads and looked around. The reporters were filing out of the stadium in a buzz of high excitement.

"Henderson!" Taylor called to him. "Collect your winnings."

"Later. At the bar."

Tom leaned back in his seat. This act of the playbill would continue long into the night and while he didn't look forward to it, he was resigned to it the way he'd been resigned to garbage detail at summer camp. Not that he objected to the alcohol. If anything, that was the saving grace of the whole spectacle. It was just that he didn't enjoy the company of fools, and by ten o'clock on any given night the majority of his colleagues fit that description, himself included. In truth, by ten o'clock or even earlier, he didn't enjoy anyone's company. This worried him from time to time. He suspected it might signal some deep flaw in his psyche. On the other hand, it might just be sloth, which was a deadly sin as he recalled. Was it really his fault if he didn't care? He could never answer these questions and it was easier to have a nightcap in his room and forget about them, which was his plan for tonight.

Taylor was stacking his notes in a neat pile and sliding them into his briefcase as he collected his pipe and umbrella.

"Going for a stroll, Taylor?"

"I'm meeting my friend Björnström at a café. Care to join us?"

"No thanks. I think you'll be happier chewing over old times without me."

"Nonsense. Come along."

All right, he thought. Maybe they'll have better scotch. And maybe the old gentleman will bring along his daughter, the one who jumped when she heard the word 'ass', whose blond curls wandered across her forehead, and who lacked the irritating Hollywood airs that he saw in almost every woman in the city. In the lobby he'd taken stock of her in his usual way—early twenties, pretty face, long legs, small breasts that didn't quite fill out her fitted jacket. Nothing overly remarkable among the glitterati here. But as they searched for her makeup on the floor, he decided she had the loveliest eyes he'd ever seen, large and clear with thick lashes. Their blue gaze shook his composure for a moment. He could feel it still.

3

Tina and her father returned to their hotel from the stadium just as Paul arrived. When he walked into the room she hardly recognized him, a stranger with downcast eyes who seemed to have lost twenty pounds and all the colour in his face. She'd seen very little of him in Berlin. The Athletes' Village was twenty miles from the city centre and his coaches kept him on a tight training schedule. Now, after his fall in the heat of the five thousand metres, his Olympics were over. He limped into the room and she tried to embrace him, tried to tell him she loved him, but he turned away from her, saying only that the ankle was mildly sprained. He sat down in an armchair by the window, answering questions in monosyllables. Finally, she left him to sit mutely alone.

"He acts like he hates me," she said to her father in the hallway.

"It's not you. Right now he hates himself."

"But it wasn't his fault."

"No. In a way it would be easier if it had been. Then he could try to fix it. As it is, he's sitting there thinking the universe is against him."

"Then what can I do?" she tried to stay calm, although her heart was bursting.

"Just be with him. There's nothing we can do or say right now to lessen his pain."

And so it went for two hours, with them tiptoeing around him and his face setting more firmly in stone rather than softening, his eyes growing more distant.

"Look," Björnström finally said, "why don't you both come along with me tonight? I'm going to meet my friend Philip Taylor at a café. You'll feel better if you go out, Paul."

"No, thanks, I'm fine here," he said. "You two go."

Tina knew the worst thing for him would be to sit and brood, so she nagged him until he stood up and she draped a jacket over his shoulders. The three of them set out along the road beside the Tiergarten. Paul lifted his face to the cool breeze from the river Spree.

"The beer will do you more good than the breeze," said Björnström.

They crossed a small courtyard and suddenly there it was, the café nestling like a glowworm in a chestnut grove. Taylor was waiting at the entrance and the American was with him. Tina touched Paul's sleeve, nudging him forward. Always shy, now he sought the shadows more avidly than ever. From the chagrin on Tom's face, it was clear he recognized Paul from the track and she regretted pressuring him to come; she hadn't foreseen the effect the reporters would have on him, people who had witnessed his humiliation. She tightened her grip on his arm.

"This is my daughter's friend, Paul Salmi," said Björnström. "Paul was to have run in the five thousand metres, but he had an unfortunate accident in the heats."

"How is the ankle? It was the ankle, wasn't it?" Tom asked.

"Just twisted." Paul replied in serviceable English, offering no further comment.

"Here's to a full recovery," Tom said. After a slight hesitation he added, "In fact, I have some personal knowledge of what you're going through."

They looked at him in surprise. "It's a long story," he muttered, and they could almost see him trying to pull back his words. A chill set in but before it could take hold, Taylor wheeled toward the entrance and led the way inside. It was an old-fashioned kind of café with a rose-entwined trellis around it. They sat near the edge, where the scent of moss mingled with the roses.

"An idyllic spot indeed," said Taylor in his Shakespearean way, cradling his pipe. The waiter brought jugs of frothing beer and a glass of wine for Tina. He lit the tea candles and they flickered over the checkered tablecloth.

They chatted as acquaintances do, about the city, the weather, the Games, the Nazi spectacles. Tina sensed a feeling of closeness unusual for a group of acquaintances. Taylor knew her father, it was true, but Tom was a total stranger. She saw a change in him from their first meeting at the Andalusia; now his features softened and unfurled like a stream breaking free of winter ice. Only once did his eyes turn cold again, when Taylor asked him about the "personal knowledge" of disaster on the track that he'd mentioned. He answered tersely that as a runner in college he'd taken a bad fall while training for the Los Angeles Olympics, and then because of the stock market crash, his family couldn't afford to send him back, and he went to work for a newspaper in Chicago. Or was it Toronto? He spoke so quickly she didn't catch every word.

At intervals she tried to draw Paul into the conversation without success. He drank mug after mug of beer in silence and neither she nor anyone else had the heart to press him to talk. They'd all seen his Olympic dream shattered and they hesitated to step into the debris, instead circling it like a smoking train wreck. Every now and then Tina stroked his arm, even though he rarely looked at her. She silently searched for words of comfort to offer him, words that wouldn't ring hollow. The worst of it was her suspicion that it was her duty to join him in his gloom, but gloom was a solitary place and the night was too bewitching to throw into a black hole.

The café had filled up now, not with tourists but local people, with a few brown shirts sprinkled here and there. Some of them cast curious glances at their table, foreigners that they were and in evening clothes. Waiters scurried about with trays of beer and sausages and three gypsy violinists strolled the aisles, men with obsidian eyes and crimson vests. They paused at their table.

"A song for the fraulein," said the lead violinist, and they struck up a melody.

"*Otchi Chornya*," said Taylor. "Dark Eyes. One of the finest Russian tunes."

"My eyes are blue," she said.

"Never mind," muttered Paul.

"So you've been listening after all," she whispered.

"Ah, the Russians!" Her father lit a cigar and ordered cognac, infallible signs that he was on his favourite topic. "They've been at our backs for a thousand years. You worry about Hitler and rightly so, but Stalin has his own plans."

"Whatever happens, we're neutral," she said, and they all looked at her in surprise. She realized the wine had made her bold, and she enjoyed the feeling.

"You're on Stalin's doorstep, my dear," Taylor said, raising an eyebrow. "If there is a war, you'll be in someone's way."

Tom said nothing. She imagined that in America all this probably seemed unreal, stories from the Thousand and One European Nights. He smoked one cigarette after another, and leaned back so far into the shadows of the trellis that she couldn't read his eyes. Once she met his gaze and held it until he looked away. His hand trembled just enough to make him spill a few ashes on the tablecloth. What was he thinking about? A woman back home? Broken dreams? He was a grown man, not a boy like Paul, and she had little experience with grown men.

Now the musicians struck up an Argentine tango and the evening burst into light. She thought of this as the click of life, when everything else falls away in the intoxication of the moment. Not everyone could feel it, but she was sure the American could, despite his nonchalant airs. His eyes flashed when the music took flight. She saw the flash and seized on it as a sign to address him with bravado she didn't really feel.

"Do you dance the tango?" she asked.

"Dance? I used to, in college. But I gave it up."

"Were you good at it?"

"I taught Valentino everything he knew."

"Then you shouldn't have given it up."

"Maybe not."

That was when she first heard him laugh. She watched as other couples got up and danced in the aisles. If Paul's ankle had been healthy, she would have dragged him out there. As it was, she sat and fretted, while Tom leaned back into the shadows again.

"They're playing *La Cumparsita*," said her father.

"The king of tangos," said Taylor. "The continental version is smoother than the Latin. If you heard this in Rio you'd be hard put to recognize it. A splendid piece anywhere. Mr. Henderson here by his own admission is a dancer. Perhaps he can show us his American style."

Tom leaned forward. "I said I used to dance. Past tense. Is this another test of national honour?"

Taylor leaned across and whispered to him. "So why don't you dance any more, Henderson?" His eyes crinkled in amusement. "Perhaps a broken romance, a loss of confidence? Are the memories returning? Proms, sophomore swings, the glances across the room. It's all come back, hasn't it?"

"No. It's simple. If I feel like dancing, I will." Tom stubbed out his cigarette and stood up.

"May I?" he bowed to Paul, who looked at Tina's shining eyes and nodded. Tom guided her out to the floor. He held her lightly at the waist and she felt her body stirring beneath his hand, gliding so softly she felt almost weightless.

"I love the tango too much," she said. "I apologize." She glanced back at the table, where Paul sat nursing his beer.

"For what? Wanting to dance?"

"For pouting because I couldn't."

"Well, then I guess I should apologize for pretending I could."

That made her smile. "It's easy. Just push me and I glide."

He pushed forward with his knee and his thigh met hers, whether by accident or design she couldn't tell. She turned her head a few degrees toward him, brushing his chin with her temple. His fingers tightened around her, and his shoulder curved into hers. She danced by instinct and the pounding bittersweetness of the tango lifted her higher and higher into a private galaxy just above the trellis of the café. She forgot about Paul, she forgot about her father, she forgot about the catastrophe at the track. He guided her up and down the aisles and into a corner and swung her into a Valentino bend so fast her feet nearly slipped out from under her.

"That was very good," she said. "Very good."

"It's coming back to me."

"It's never too late to start again," she said. "What else did you give up after college?"

"All my virtues. I only kept the vices."

She fell silent, mortified. How silly of her to imagine he would confide in her. The dance ended, and he walked her back to the table. She didn't dare look in his face, certain she had overstepped a line of some sort. She leaned against Paul and tried to coax him into eating a plate of sausages. Tom watched her from across the table.

After the tango, the musicians took a break and soon the singing began at the tables, the usual German drinking and marching songs. One in particular was sung over and over again. She didn't know what it was called, but Taylor did. He said it was the *Horst Wessel Song*, and it was a sort of Nazi anthem.

It was about then they decided to leave. The singing went on behind them, drowning out the exquisite silence of the summer night.

4

They cut through the Tiergarten on the way back, Björnström and Taylor walking ahead, Tom walking with Tina and Paul. Wrought-iron lampposts lined the walkway, and in their glow the crowns of the lindens spread out in wide mazes against the dark teal sky. She stopped at a bridge over a creek. "You go on ahead," she said. Neither of them did. They stood wordlessly beside her on the bridge like two forest spirits.

The night began to feel magical and she knew that was mostly from the wine, but the air itself was intoxicating. It was a soft summer night and she ached to draw it all in. There were small noises in the dark, rustlings in the trees. Then she caught the scent of violets and saw a violet patch down by the creek, velvet blossoms in the waterside grass. A gentle slope led to the water's edge and she went down it easily, with Paul calling after her to be careful.

"Don't worry, I'm fine. I'm picking violets."

"I'm coming down to help you, it's dangerous down there. You'll slip and fall in the dark."

"No, you have a bad ankle," said Tom. "I'll go."

He came down to the creek and stood near her on the slope.

"Smell these violets," she said. "And look at the stars! Every star in the universe is out tonight! There's the North Star. Do you see it, above the linden?"

"Yes."

The moonlight filtered through the leaves and dappled his face with shadows, etching his straight brow and mild blue eyes, unexpectedly mild. It was that tender cast of his eyes that made her go on as she did.

"We have a story," she said, "about two children, a boy and a girl, who get lost during a war. They end up far away from home and you think they'll never find their way back, because the countryside is devastated, they recognize nothing. They remember two things about their home: the North Star and the birch tree. There are thousands of birch trees in our country, you think it's impossible for them to find the right one but they do. The birch and the star bring them home."

"Charming," he said, glancing at the star and then at her face.

They started back up but she slipped on a wet rock and lost her footing. He reached to steady her and his arm brushed her breast. His hand on her shoulder was warm, and she leaned into him for an instant. A soft ache passed through her body, a tremor like the shimmering of the night. She stepped back in embarrassment because she was standing close, much too close to him.

"Of course, that's not a birch," she said with a wave at the linden, carelessly, almost rudely, as she clambered up the slope alone. Paul waited and paced on the sidewalk, and she reached for his hand.

What followed was so swift and furious it registered only as a blur in her mind. First she heard shouting and the noise of a scuffle ahead. Then she was running in the dark, Tom already far ahead of her, Paul with his bad ankle limping behind. Her father's voice calling for help and Taylor raging, "Leave off! Unhand me!" Even then the Shakespearean.

When she got there it was all over. There had only been two of them and they fled as soon as Tom arrived on the scene. She rushed to her father, but he was fine; they hadn't touched him at all. Only Taylor had been attacked. He had a cut lip and not much else; in the dark many of the blows had missed their mark. They stood for a moment in shock; Taylor waved off their solicitude. No need to go to the authorities or a hospital.

Her father regained his wits first. "Why did they only attack you, Philip? If it was a robbery— "

"It wasn't. It was mistaken identity. I bear a resemblance to another English reporter here at the Games. It's been noted before."

"So?"

"He's a well-known leftist. And a Jew."

No one spoke. Taylor finally said that someone at the café had probably noticed him and followed him. Björnström muttered that it was time for them to go back home. Paul walked in silence beside Tina and her father. She wanted to touch his face, to cool it, because even in the dark she could feel it burning. There was no use trying to tell him it wasn't his fault, he had an injury, he couldn't have got there any faster. She had needed him, her father had needed him, and he'd fallen short. He'd failed on the track and failed again here. She knew how starkly simple it was in his mind.

5

Later, Tom sat in the Andalusia lounge, deep in a mahogany corner beside a potted palm, nursing his scotch and thinking about the evening. He was sorry about Taylor, of course, but he didn't believe it had anything to do with a resemblance to a colleague. Just a pair of pickpockets who took flight when they realized they were outnumbered.

And Taylor's misfortune was the least of it. He always knew when something had cut deep. It came in like a slow arrow and spread through the soft tissues, finally setting the nerves of the heart to quivering. It was the girl, the rush of pleasure he'd felt on the dance floor, the scent of violets in the night, her voice telling him about the star and the birch. She knew little about life and he knew too much, and he wanted to start again and learn it all with her.

And it went even further than that. He rarely evoked his own memories, but standing on the bridge had taken him back to his boyhood— to evenings on his front porch listening to the sounds from the prairie meadow and the muffled noises of the town beyond, convinced that out there lay all the possibilities of life, if he could just walk far enough into the night to find them. And then running through the fields in the summer twilight until he collapsed in the cool grass as the stars came out and the scent of the neighbours' woodsmoke drifted across the hedge.

He didn't like these deep cuts. The sharp ones were easier, you could find them and heal them. These diffused inside you and got lost there.

"Why the glum face, Henderson? Owens won another medal." Taylor had found him and sat down at the table, bringing an entourage of reporters with him.

"Missed you at the stadium," said the southerner, trailing in their wake. "We cleaned up on Jesse. Mind if I join you for a quick one?"

"Suit yourself, Jennings," muttered Tom.

"Up for another showdown, Henderson? Remember St. Louis, the bar on ninth? They broke out the bourbon and you tried to take on me and the boys from Atlanta."

"Not my drink," said Tom. "Not my bar."

"Admit it, you can't keep up with the good ole' boys. Lucky I was there to cart you to your room. Otherwise, you'd still be in the bowels of the Missouri justice system, up to your ass in Mississippi mud."

"Mnhh," said Taylor. "How clever of Mr. Henderson."

"Clever my ass!"

"Your shots, Mr. Henderson," a soft voice purred, and Tom looked up into the fluid green eyes of Renate, his favourite waitress. A week of lessons had not succeeded in twisting her tongue around the word "scotch". She bore down on him, tray in hand, and slid a fresh glass into his hand. The conversation stopped as the reporters eyed the full breasts that shifted about in her bodice. As she turned to leave, the edge of her dirndl skirt caught Jennings squarely in the face and he erupted into chuckles.

"How do you like that? A peekaboo for Henderson and a swat in the face for me! What's he got that I ain't got?" No answer was forthcoming, as the Englishmen were busy trying to placate a nervous French sportswriter.

"Keep your cafés stocked, Paris is safe."

"Let the Germans have their fun. They've been through a lot, economic disaster and all that. Look at them now, ants and bees, happy as larks."

The words caught in the haze of smoke and hung there. Three oversized portraits of Hitler, Goebbels and Goering glared down at them from the wall. Tom looked around for Renate, whose name was of no consequence really, who could have been any barmaid in any city in the world. He watched her mopping up a nearby table with her strong white arms, the same arms that would later sprawl across his chest in his room as she slept, while he stared at the first haze of morning at the window, the empty bottle of scotch on his nightstand. It was a still life of his existence, not a masterpiece by any means but bearable, which was more than he could say for his recent interlude with the tango. That interlude had left him with an unease the scotch couldn't soothe. Some part of his spirit was on the move, shooting pulsars of emotion far afield that he couldn't corral into the safety of the saloons where all his Renates held court and the supporting cast told the same jokes over and over again.

Taylor was getting up, muttering about fresh air, and Tom rose to join him. The tables were roaring again, and his head ached. Jennings saluted him on his way out.

"Going already? Got something lined up with the little waitress? Good for you. Join my table again. Next time stay a little longer."

"Hell, there's no one here sober enough to read a clock," said Tom. Still, he had to admire Jennings for being on the money. At midnight Renate would be at his door, champagne glasses in hand. On his second night at the Andalusia he'd already pulled apart the layers of dirndl and unfastened the lace garters underneath, which held up nothing but white cotton stockings, her contribution to German ethnicity. For now, he hurried to catch up with Taylor, who was striding across the lobby toward the doors.

They walked up the Wilhelmstrasse toward the British Embassy. Near the Pariser Platz there was a flickering of light and the sound of singing, and they saw marchers coming toward them like fireflies. Tom had seen these torchlight parades before and they didn't move him, but these particular marchers sang beautifully. He could see their faces, adolescent faces solemn with the guilelessness of youth, and felt a sudden anger. What did these children know about the world? The vanguard had already moved far ahead when a pair of marchers cut too sharply to the curb, and one of them stumbled. The boy regained his balance quickly but not before the flame of his torch had brushed Tom's sleeve.

"Damn!" he yelled. "Watch it!" He flapped his arm in the air, though the flame had merely singed the cloth and not touched his skin.

The boys gaped at the scorched sleeve, their faces ashen in the torchlight. "Mein Herr! Mein Herr!" they murmured, and Tom looked down into mortally frightened fifteen-year old eyes.

"It's nothing," he said. "OK! Wiedersehn!" His scanty German deserted him and the boys dashed off like startled deer.

"Let's have a look, old chap," said Taylor. "Why, it's nothing. You'll survive."

"Clumsy, these Hitler Youth. Ruined one of my best shirts. Poor bastard—probably a nice kid without that torch in his hand."

Taylor stopped and leaned against a lamppost. "You do see what's going on here, don't you? Wait until the Games are over and Hitler really goes into action."

"By then I'll be far away. You and your countrymen can handle it."

"Stay here. Why would you want to be elsewhere?"

"What the hell are you talking about, Taylor? I can't speak German and the scotch is terrible."

"No, no, not here. Come to London. I can easily get you on with a paper there. In something other than sports. We Englishmen are very interested in how America interprets this brewing fracas. You don't have a wife, do you? No urchins, no apron strings, no strings of any sort?"

"Forget it. I couldn't live on cucumber sandwiches."

"Do you really want to spend the rest of your life covering baseball games and getting hung over on cheap bourbon?"

"Of course not. I want to get hung over on cognac with you at the Paris Ritz."

"I see. In other words, you don't give a damn about any of this."

He didn't like being pushed into corners. "Sure I do. As much as I've ever given a damn about anything." There. Let Taylor figure it out for himself.

The Englishman stopped at a kiosk to buy a newspaper. It was drizzling steadily now, and the Brandenburg Gate loomed massive in the dusk, its pillars wine-dark with rain, draped with swastika flags as incongruous with their stately surroundings as the scrawls of children among Rembrandts. Night was rising out of the east. The breeze had picked up and clouds were rolling in. Rolling in, he thought, from the plains of Westphalia toward the Pripet marshes, where Frederick the Great's junkers and Napoleon's fusiliers still cleaned their guns. Carrying the stench of Flanders on the evening breeze. The blood of Europe's warriors had barely dried from their most recent battles, and here were new warriors lighting their torches.

He scoffed at his own romanticism. But Taylor's words nagged at him. The prospect of ending up like Jennings was one he'd accepted long ago. If he died in a bar drinking bad whiskey, so be it. What did it matter where you died? Still, he couldn't deny that Europe had caught his interest, and there was more to it than that. It was the previous evening, the remarkable girl, the fallen runner, the way the old man reminded him of his own father. He didn't usually indulge in fancies, but if life was a voyage, he knew he had forfeited his berth. If he wanted it back, he would have to change something.

Helsinki

1

The summer of 1939 was the most idyllic in living memory, as if nature were administering its own antidote to the poison seeping through Europe. The papers were full of stories about the crises on the continent as Hitler and the Allies edged closer to a war that everyone knew was coming. Stalin tried to bolster his frontiers by pressuring his neighbours for territorial concessions or mutual defense pacts. Finland was one of his chief targets and the situation kept Björnström busy attending meetings and negotiations with his colleagues in Helsinki.

Tina privately thought the danger was too outlandish to contemplate. Especially on hot, still afternoons when the sun warmed the pine needles and on evenings that never darkened and night was a dream you dreamed last winter. At midsummer, the festival of Juhannus in June, her family celebrated at their summer cottage. The flag was raised at six and they sang a few songs. Then they adjourned to the sauna where new birch whisks lay fragrant and green on the benches. Afterwards they sat in the lawn chairs eating crepes with strawberries and drinking homemade mead. The evening bubbled with laughter from other picnic tables down the stream, the splash of fish jumping, and bees searching for nectar in the daylight that refused to die. Huge bonfires gave the white night a mad orange glow. The next day she and Paul sailed out to the islands. The breeze was right and they were soon at Aspen Island, where the dance pavilion was; tucked behind it was Spruce Island, which had the best coves for sunbathing. They pulled up there and climbed up the rocks, slabs of granite polished by the waves and bleached by the sun.

She spread the blanket on a smooth ledge of rock and they stretched out side by side. Seagulls circled the spruce trees and she let the summer day seduce her, one sense at a time, until she felt at one with the sea and the sky. Paul began to fondle her carefully as he always did, starting at the edge of her breasts, slowly circling the nipples, waiting for her signal that she was ready. They didn't have sex very often and when they did, he always waited for her signal. Sometimes this pleased her, sometimes it didn't. Once she had actually told him, "Pretend I'm one of the barmaids at the pub!" After all, it was 1939, not the Victorian Age.

She knew very little about sex. Her only female relative at hand was Aunt Gunilla, her father's icy unmarried sister, not the sort to give advice on intimate issues. Selma, their housekeeper, might have, but the gospel of what nice girls did and did not do was one Tina could chant in her sleep. Now, she gave no signal, because she had other things on her mind. Every now and then he turned away abruptly, as if something was too difficult to bear. Finally he kissed her almost in anger and clutched her waist so hard she twisted free.

"What are you so afraid of?" He lifted himself up on his elbow and gazed into her face.

"Nothing. Look at those spruce boughs," she said, pointing to a clump of branches someone had stockpiled for a bonfire. "See how they're pointing at you and me. That's an omen. Spruce boughs pointing at a couple at Juhannus means they're meant for each other." In truth she'd just invented this omen herself, but it was close enough to the ones she'd heard in the sauna from her girlfriends to be convincing. "We'll be together like this forever, won't we?"

He lay back down on the blanket, and took so long in answering that at first she thought he was asleep. Then panic crept into her throat as she saw that his eyes were wide open, and that he hadn't answered 'Yes'.

"If that's what you want," he said. She picked up a twig and pounded it on the rock, harder and harder, as if it might shake the words she wanted to hear out of him. Why can't you just ask? she thought. Through her anger a lifetime of questions and answers flashed through her mind. She knew what he needed to hear. He needed to hear that the daughter of a prominent family would be happy marrying a man whose father worked in a sawmill. That it didn't matter if he hadn't mastered the rituals of schnapps or the settings at a five-course dinner. That she would be content living in a one-room flat in a mediocre neighbourhood and that her Helsinki friends would no longer whisper about him, calling him a Red rug rat, a child of the proletariat, a peon's pup.

But she couldn't say these things to him. To say them would be to throw them in his face. His eyes would harden and he would refuse to look at her, the way he did when he gave the sails to her, because it was her father's boat. And as usual, instead of trying to sort out his feelings, she got angry.

"What kind of answer is that?" she snapped.

He sat up and began to throw pebbles into the sea. "It's not an answer," he said, "because it's not an answer for me to give."

"Don't talk in circles."

"I need to get a decent job."

"You have a decent job. And Papa has you on his short list for the junior aide—"

"I'm not cut out for deskwork. And you know I'm no diplomat and never will be. Besides, I don't want to wander all over the world. This is where I belong." He swept his sunburned arm across the expanse of ocean sparkling in the sun. "I want to work with boats, something like that. I need to get a job. On my own."

"Don't be provincial. Contacts are everything."

"No. Self-respect is everything."

She understood his need to succeed through his own efforts, but what if he failed? Would he give up on her then, as he almost had on his Olympic dream? No, it was better to keep prodding him. She couldn't wait for his life to catch up to hers, for him to walk to her the long way round, his way. He might not make it and she would lose him.

Her heart pounded as she gathered up the blankets and bundled their things together. She started to walk toward the boat but he pulled her close to him. His skin smelled of sun and salt, his lean hips dug into hers. She broke free of him, gripped by a fear she couldn't name. She could name marriage; it evoked trousseaus and family portraits with children and dogs. She couldn't name sex. It evoked something she couldn't control.

"Tina—" he stopped and looked at her with a long stare that was unmistakably a question. But she didn't know how to answer a look. So she stepped into the boat and fiddled with the jib. She knew that would annoy him, because he was keen on being the sailor. After a while she relinquished the sails to him, and they stayed out on the water until the sun sank into the sea.

2

She left the question of her future with Paul unanswered for the time being, but it was brought up the next morning by the Björnströms' house-keeper, Selma, who had always been much more than a housekeeper. When Tina's mother died, Selma took the reins of the household firmly in hand, leaving the grieving widower to deal with his loss and stepping in as guardian to the motherless girl. It had been that way ever since. She also tried to instill homemaking skills in her young charge, with mixed results. During the summer, Tina willingly picked wild strawberries for Selma to use in her desserts. She'd found a basketful on Spruce Island.

"You should have gone further up the island," said Selma, tasting a handful of the berries. "These aren't very juicy." She pushed back her thin, somewhat frizzy dark hair into its white cap and adjusted the apron that pinched her stocky waist into an hourglass. Her grey eyes sparkled but the curve of her mouth was severe. "I suppose Paul didn't say any-thing about marriage this Juhannus, either. You have to light a fire under that young man. If you leave herring in the marinade too long, it will fall apart."

"Paul and I are not dead fish," said Tina. "We're living, breathing human beings trying to work things out so they're just right."

"Still, if he doesn't propose this summer, you should enroll at the University of Helsinki. That would give him something to think about. And your father would certainly be pleased."

Yes, he would, thought Tina. He'd sometimes mentioned it would be nice to have two historians in the family. As for Selma, she had come to them a decade ago, a brokenhearted young maid jilted by a landowner's son, and no other suitors had ever materialized. In her eyes, waiting for a man to marry you was foolishness. She'd worked from the age of fourteen, first on her father's farm and then in a manor house where she'd learned how to fold linens correctly, how to set a table for a nine-course meal, the difference between sherry and port, and many other things that were a source of great pride to her.

"I know him. He's waiting for the next Olympics," said Tina. "He wants to make up for the medal he lost in Berlin."

"Well, next year he'll get the chance to try, and at home, too."

"Berlin was a lifetime ago," said Tina. After Hitler's Games had ended and he'd rolled out his true agenda, the world began to scramble—either for cover or for position, her father said. The Western allies, Russia, Japan, America were all in flux. The 1940 Olympics had been slated for Tokyo, but in 1938 the International Olympic Committee abruptly shifted them to Helsinki, unhappy with Japan's militarism.

She got up and walked over to the wall, so she could see the poster hanging there more clearly. She studied the Olympic rings in the upper right hand corner, the perfectly proportioned runner wearing nothing but a pale shade of green. *The Olympic Games, Helsinki, July 20 to August 4, 1940.* The Helsinki Games would succeed, she was sure of it. No one would be crazy enough to start another war.

"Yesterday I walked to the new stadium with Papa," she said. "There were some foreign sportswriters there, ranting about the trouble in Europe. Papa said it's not our affair because we're neutral and we've told the world so. They said, 'What makes you think the world is listening?'"

"Never mind. Silly foreigners."

"At least I have my old Paul back. He's out training right now."

It hadn't been like that when they'd returned from Berlin. Paul had gone straight home and she hadn't seen him for months. When he came back to Helsinki, she tried to comfort him, helped with his therapy, took him to dances. Still he seemed more distant than before.

"If you don't want to see me any more, I'll understand," he'd said one night.

"See you? I don't want to just see you. I want to be with you. Forever. Don't fret about the medal."

"I'm not fretting. It's nothing." But she could see in his eyes it was everything. Shortly after that he entered the army to complete his mandatory year of military service. When he came back, he continued running half-heartedly for a while and then gave it up altogether. Once the 1940 Games were transferred to Helsinki and the new stadium went up, he went to see his former coach and began to run again in earnest.

3

The summer of 1939 was so hot that geraniums wilted in the window-boxes, the hospitals overflowed with victims of heat stroke, and even the market vendors folded their tents and joined the exodus to the cottages. It was easy to forget the crisis gripping Europe during languid afternoons in the birch groves. Nevertheless, the Finns could not ignore the dangers of the international situation. In August large numbers of young people volunteered their efforts to build up fortifications in Karelia, at the eastern border. Paul enlisted for two weeks and while he was gone Tina stayed at the family summer house near the city of Kotka on the south coast.

Late in August Björnström invited some weekend guests for a crayfish fest. This was a three-day affair that had its own rituals and protocols. Tina hovered on the edges. She had no interest in the schnapps, and the dinner conversations frightened her, with story after story of the hydra of war entangling Europe.

In any case, she preferred dancing to eating, so she set up a gramophone on the outdoor patio. She stacked the records by genre, the latest American swing tunes, classic Viennese waltzes, and of course her beloved tangos. One young man, pink-cheeked and a few kilograms overweight, danced with her a lot. He was surprisingly agile and he didn't speak about Czechoslovakia or Poland, but about sailboats and Shakespeare. His name was Gustaf and he came from a wealthy Helsinki family, and she had to admit she was flattered by his attention.

After the guests left, her father took her aside for lemonade on the patio. He cleared his throat a few times and finally said, "Gustaf asked me about you."

"Oh?"

"He asked if you were free."

"Free? Don't they all know about Paul? They've seen him often enough."

"Mmm, yes. But that situation is not entirely clear to them." He opened a bottle of cognac and spiked his lemonade with it. "Nor to me."

She patted his hand. "It will be."

"I like Paul," said her father. "Should I talk to him?"

"No, don't worry, Papa. It will be clear soon." She spoke with confidence, because despite their enigmatic conversation on the island, there was no real doubt in her mind about her and Paul. A look of relief crossed her father's face and he smiled.

"Good, good," he said, and bit into a square of crispbread garnished with crayfish.

She knew the reason for his relief. He'd never nudged her toward any of the scions of Helsinki's patrician families, most of whom he dismissed as dilettantes or worse. Paul had always been the son he never had, and as long as Tina was with him there was no danger of losing her. It was a double blessing for an aging widower.

Paul came back, tanned and with a muscular swagger, and they spent more afternoons sailing in the islands. The question of marriage didn't come up. She wasn't sure it ever had, but it didn't matter during those long summer days when it seemed that the sun would never set and night was gone for good.

In late August came news of the Molotov-Ribbentrop Pact between Russia and Germany. Björnström attended hasty meetings with his colleagues and seemed perceptibly older after each of them. The pact was a deal to carve up Europe, he said. A free hand for Hitler in the west and Stalin in the east. Rumours were already circulating about a Secret Protocol that placed Finland in the Russian sphere.

On the last evening of August, Tina sat with Paul by the ocean, watching as the reflection of the pines turned from blue to violet and a pair of trumpeter swans flew overhead. For centuries her people had struggled to stay outside the quarrels of their neighbours. Now their voices drifted across the noisy European sky like the faint cries of the swans heading south.

The next morning Hitler invaded Poland from the west, and two weeks later Russia took the eastern half. Tina still clung to her hopes as the white nights gave way to dark evenings and the heat of the sun left the land. Then in October came the summons from Russian Foreign Minister Molotov for a Finnish delegation to travel to Moscow. The three Baltic countries had just paid their visits and signed their sovereignty away, and now it was Finland's turn.

4

"Take this scarf or your lungs will freeze. If you must go out there at least take precautions against hypothermia."

"What would I do without you, Taylor?" asked Tom, pulling the plaid woollen scarf around his neck.

"Drown, freeze, starve, any number of possibilities come to mind."

Tom stepped out on the wind-lashed deck. With all her lights blazing, in solitary flotilla cadence, the *Sylvia* crawled eastward through the arctic night. They had left Stockholm at nightfall. Thank God the sleek steamer knew her way through this archipelago, he thought. It was a place that offered no comfort to a traveller. The Baltic Sea was not as frigid as he'd expected it to be in October, but the chill cut through his coat immediately. He could see dark islands outlined against steely water, with flashes of crags when the moon burst through the cloud. Spruce and pine stood a melancholy guard in the night. Somewhere at the end of the archipelago lay Finland, the latest hot spot in the path of the fireball that was scorching Europe.

This was the last place he'd expected to be but the autumn of 1939 had been full of surprises. He remembered the August day when news broke of the Molotov-Ribbentrop pact. He was on a fishing holiday in Scotland when the telegram came from his editors, calling him back to make sense of the deal between dictators. Now, it seemed inconceivable they hadn't understood its meaning. After the dissection of Poland, Moscow turned its sights north.

The wind stung his eyes with icy spray and he headed back into the dining room. Philip Taylor sat at a window table surveying a platter before him heaped with smoked salmon and caviar, while a polite steward refilled his wine goblet.

"It is the Gulf Stream, you see," said the steward. "It crosses the Atlantic, reaches up into the North Sea and the Baltic, and brings warm water from the Gulf of Mexico."

"Jolly amazing," Taylor nodded and turned to Tom. "Amazing, old boy. We're riding on waters warmed by the sunny shores of Mexico. Very likely if you reached in, you might pull out a stray long black hair left behind by a sun-loving senorita."

"Nobody's sunbathing out there, Taylor."

"So. What did the American eye see out on the deck?"

"Same thing an English eye would see. Islands. Lined up like stepping stones."

"To where? Hardly civilization."

"To the edge of the world."

"And the edge of the world becomes its centre, for a moment." Taylor sighed, and scooped caviar on a slice of thin bread.

"Afraid you'll fall off the edge, Taylor?"

Tom immediately regretted his sharp words. Although he rarely struck up friendships with colleagues, he'd made an exception for Taylor. After Berlin, they had both moved into political journalism and their paths often converged as they dogged the Nazis every step of the way from the Anschluss of Austria to the blitzkrieg of Poland in September. Lately Taylor's voice had acquired an acidic sting when he called him the American eye, in reference to his column, "An American Eye on Europe". It ran in one of London's top dailies and was a major success, evidently cause enough for the Englishman to suspect that his American protégé was outshining him. When Tom left for Helsinki to cover the crisis with Moscow, Taylor booked passage on the same ship. There was little action elsewhere at the moment, the Western Front having bogged down into a staring match between Germany and the Allies.

"Help me out," said Tom. "You know every quotation in the world. That line about being called one by one. Is that the Bible or is it Shakespeare?" He pulled a notebook out of his vest pocket. "One by one they were called—Latvia, Lithuania and Estonia signed away their existence to Moscow. Now Finland has been called but stubbornly continues to resist." He looked up and leaned forward, pencil in hand.

"Yes, the Finns have their *sisu*," said Taylor. "I learned the word from Björnström years ago. An intransigence which translates into valour or pigheadedness, depending on the context. Alas, this time their resistance is futile. Stalin will not allow them to control their own destiny. Meanwhile, help yourself at the splendid table of food over there. Whatever happens, this trip has already paid off handsomely from the culinary aspect. One of our better crises, wouldn't you agree?" Taylor dabbed at his moustache, mopping up a renegade cluster of caviar.

Yes, he would. They had ridden a real roller coaster in Europe since the glamour of the Reich turned to thunder. He couldn't deny it had been entertaining. But the war that finally started in September seemed anti-climactic, just one more ruckus.

"I'm thinking of going home for awhile, Taylor."

"Home? You have no home. Why go anywhere now, when it's just beginning?"

"It's all over."

"Piffle. Don't lose interest now. Your column is going strong. Even I must admit it's very good. Now really, three years ago did you imagine you'd be covering the conflagration of the century?"

"Just running from one brushfire to another. Damn firefighters, that's all we are."

Tom took a bite of smoked salmon but the boat was rocking harder now and his stomach rebelled. He was weary of crises. Their cachet had grown stale for him long before Poland, long before Munich, and now it reeked. Worse, the inanity of it all had chipped away at his fragile enthusiasm and reduced it to a feeling that what he really needed was an afternoon at the ball game to set the world right.

He looked out at the desolate ocean. Taylor was right, of course. It was hopeless for the Finns, it was hopeless for everyone. Then suddenly the moon emerged out of a wreath of clouds and the water dazzled white and brilliant, as if a million subterranean candles had been lit. He could see the islands clearly now, misty blue, the spruce feathering their crests, the feckless moon dancing above, the sky a maze of shifting blue shadow and pure white light. The North had turned on its loveliness and he understood why those who lived here would be loath to give up an inch of it.

5

Tom awoke with a start, still dressed in the clothes he had worn the night before. There were voices in the corridor, the clank of baggage against the walls. He groomed himself as best he could, peering into the tiny mirror, then climbed up to the main deck.

Passengers queued up to disembark, shuffling in the early chill. To the right, the sun rose in a pale azure sky. He could see the skyline of the city basking in the morning light, the green dome of a white cathedral looming high. It was a watercolour landscape lightly brushed. Fishing boats dodged each other in the choppy water and old men dragged in their catch. Women in woollen coats scurried from the boats to their stalls in a marketplace at the shore.

"Rather lovely," said a voice at his shoulder. As usual, Taylor had found him first. "They call Helsinki the white queen of the Baltic, you know."

On shore, they walked past crates of herring that shimmered like quicksilver, bins of mushrooms and crimson lingonberries. Further down, there were reindeer pelts and birch bark shoes, felt boots and colourful Lapp leggings, and dagger-like knives in embellished leather sheaths.

"Stop for a minute," said Tom. He lowered his bags to the ground and stretched his arms. "I smell fresh coffee."

"Yes, yes, but wouldn't you rather have a civilized tea at the hotel?"

Tom was already at the nearest kiosk. The girl behind the counter handed him two steaming mugs and selected the right coins from his palms. They sat down and drank the brew, strong with a mild aftertaste, watching housewives and businessmen queue up for coffee, buns, and fish rolled up in newspaper.

Two young men in army grey pushed through the crowd. One had ensign's stripes on his shoulder. They sat down on the bench beside Tom.

"Good morning," he said to the ensign. "Do you speak English?"

"A little."

"What's going on with the military here?" Taylor's voice ratcheted up a notch, sensing an easy prey. "One hears rumours of mobilization."

"Oh no, just Extraordinary Maneuvers."

"You must be expecting something."

"No," the ensign winked at the girl in the kiosk. "We'll just camp in the bush for a while. Until the negotiations are settled. The call-up began October tenth and most of the men are already out in the field. We've been waiting for days now."

"Where exactly are you going?" asked Taylor.

"To Karelia. The eastern border. Probably the Isthmus."

Tom was still fumbling for his notepad when the soldiers stood up and prepared to leave. "We have a train to catch," said the ensign. Over his shoulder he said, "By the way, if you're looking for the Hotel Kämp, it's just over there." He pointed to a Victorian-style building a short two blocks up the Esplanade.

"How did you know that?" asked Taylor.

"Foreigners always stay there."

They picked up their bags and walked to the hotel. In contrast to its neo-gothic exterior, the lobby of the Kämp breathed modern elegance. The marble pillars and rosewood tables gave a sense of order and light, and impressionist murals lined the walls.

"Lovely," said Taylor. "A jolly good change from the clutter of London. The elite of the nation gather here. They say Sibelius himself is a frequent visitor."

"Is there anything in the world you don't know, Taylor?"

"I knew enough to book us into the Kämp," said the Englishman with an aggrieved air. "This is the hub of everything. We won't have to stick our noses out if the weather gets nasty."

Later they set out on foot. First along the Esplanade, which followed the harbour and then diverged into two roads separated by trees and park benches. From there they branched into side streets, noting the places a reporter might need to know. The post office, telegraph office, a department store, a liquor store, a bus station. Tom called this the Sniff and Piddle tour, the sort of thing curs do when marking out new territory. Taylor, of course, saw it differently.

"Heed the architecture, old chap," he harrumphed as they emerged into a large square ringed with empire-style buildings. The white cathedral they'd seen from the steamer loomed above them. "God knows I've tried to instruct you. This Senate Square, for instance. The picture of neoclassical order."

"Well, Taylor, I go by statues and so far I've only seen a bare-breasted woman and a poet. No guys with swords."

"Look, there's your swordsman." Taylor pointed to the statue of a Russian tsar in the square.

"A foreigner with a sword."

"In front of a massive white Lutheran cathedral. This is a pious people."

Their souls couldn't be resting easily, thought Tom. Everywhere he saw sandbags and taped windows, fortified building entrances, steps leading down into bomb shelters. Ordinary people hurried by, placid women in tailored coats, men in bowler hats, but the streets were unusually empty, and there was something odd about the emptiness he couldn't quite put his finger on.

They crossed a park where the lawn was rent by a jagged trench that workmen were extending, throwing up mounds of dirt with their shovels. Another bomb shelter, Taylor said. In a shop window Tom noticed a poster advertising the Games of the Twelfth Olympiad in Helsinki in 1940, and suddenly he realized what was odd about the streets. Their emptiness was a selective one. They were devoid of young males.

It was dusk when he and Taylor arrived back at the Kämp. A waiter came to take their order, and Taylor pulled a map of Finland out of his top pocket.

"Help out a tourist, my good man," he said to the waiter. "Where is the Isthmus?"

In the southeastern corner of the map, the waiter circled a narrow bridge of land between the Gulf of Finland on the south and a lake called Ladoga on the north.

"The Karelian Isthmus," he presented his drawing with as much panache as a poached salmon. "The eastern gateway into Finland. Our main defense line runs across it." At the eastern end he drew a star and labelled it Leningrad.

"Your border is that close to Leningrad?"

"Yes. They say you can hear the church bells of Leningrad in the border towns. The border is too close for the Russians but that's where they built their city. What can we do? Move Karelia?"

Taylor asked about the empty streets. Yes, said the waiter, some people had left the city for the safety of the countryside during this crisis with Moscow. Schools had closed. These were merely standard precautions during dangerous times. Blackout rules were in effect and the waiter drew black velvet drapes across the windows. The drapes shut out the cold Helsinki night as they basked in the glow of the Kämp's amber globes, and sipped Beaujolais under the laughing Parisian eyes looking out from the murals. Taylor was engrossed in his after-dinner cognac when he suddenly remembered that he had meant to call his old friend Björnström. When he returned from the telephones he was smiling as broadly as his moustache would allow.

"Reached Björnström on the first try."

"He's still in town?" Images in quick succession of a blond girl, a fallen runner, a violet patch.

"Yes. And he invited us to dinner."

6

The news that Tom Henderson and Philip Taylor were in Helsinki stunned Tina, and a sliver of guilt chafed in her heart. She had searched for Tom's face in the knots of foreign newsmen that gathered at the Kämp and on the train platform in the throng sending off the Finnish negotiators to Moscow. She and her father stayed in town through the crisis, though many of their acquaintances left for the countryside. She continued to work typing and translating documents at the Defense Ministry office near the Senate Square. It was a short walk from their flat on Elisabeth Street. Paul escaped the first call-up to Extraordinary Maneuvers in October because he'd re-injured the Berlin ankle during a training run. That was why he was still in Helsinki on the night of the dinner.

Berlin was a faded memory but as the dinner neared, she became more and more curious about what three years had done to Tom Henderson. She bought a new dress and planned the menu with Selma; she borrowed American swing records from a colleague at work—Goodman, Ellington, Shaw. To impress the American guest.

The evening of the dinner, Paul arrived an hour early. This was not unusual in itself, for his flat was one spartan room sub-let from an octogenarian who was deaf to requests to turn up the heat. Paul escaped whenever he could. What was unusual was that this evening he had elected to wear a tie, a formality he disliked.

While the men fussed with the wines, Tina set the table and then rushed to the kitchen to help the beleaguered Selma. They had decided to treat the guests to an English feast. Selma had no difficulty with the roast of beef, but the Yorkshire pudding mystified her. "They call this food?" she railed. "Puffed dough to accompany an unsuspecting roast? Idiocy!" Tina mollified her by promising not to compromise on the basics: home-made rye bread, and herring in Glassmeister sauce, a concoction of carrots, red onions and spices in vinegar that was venerated at their table. The guests could take it or leave it, but its place was unassailable.

The doorbell rang promptly at six.

"A good sign," nodded Björnström. "Foreigners are so often tardy."

As Selma let the guests in and took their coats and hats, Tina hung back a little. Berlin was a long time ago, and they were strangers from a cosmopolitan world she hadn't visited since then. The American was just as handsome as she remembered, and better dressed. Taylor extended a bouquet of winter roses and she stammered that someone must have been schooling them in Finnish customs, whispering to Selma to put them in the white vase, the largest one.

"Come in, come in," said Björnström, and they strolled into the sitting room.

"A lot of books. You must do some serious reading," said Tom, walking over to the bookshelf.

"Yes, I suppose we do." Tina ran her fingers across the spines of her favourite volumes. Her mother's Jane Austen, her father's Shakespeare. Melville and Tolstoy, and of course the *Kalevala*, Finland's folk epic.

Tom looked around the room. "Beautiful place you've got here," he said, his eyes searching her face as if looking for something he'd lost and wasn't sure still existed.

"Thank you," she said, "but I'm sure you've seen much finer ones in London."

"No. Grander, maybe, but not finer. There's a difference."

His words pleased her because she loved their apartment. It was spacious and high-ceilinged and her mother had decorated it with a mixture of traditional Finnish and eclectic European. Behind the sofa she had hung a homemade *ryijy* rug, hand-woven with folk designs, and next to it a small Renoir she had picked up in Paris.

"What are these?" asked Tom, looking into the shelves of an étagère.

"Dresden china dolls."

"And what's that? The red wineglass."

"That's our Russian goblet," she said. She took it out carefully. It was gold-rimmed and inlaid with jewels. "It belonged to Alexander III, the tsar of Russia. He had a fishing lodge fifty miles east of here, a beautiful spot on the rapids. They came there every summer, sometimes with friends. One year, one of the children of these friends wandered away and got lost. The tsar's people were desperate. People have drowned in the rapids. The child was found safe and sound a day later by my grandmother. We have a summer house nearby and the child had wandered on to our land. In gratitude the tsar gave her this goblet."

"May I?" Tom extended his hand. She glanced at her father, who did not like anyone handling the goblet. He was busy pouring sherry. She placed the goblet in Tom's hands.

"Heavy little toy," he said. "Must have had strong arms, those tsars, to lift this baby. Especially full of Beaujolais."

Selma rang the dinner bell, and he put the goblet back in the shelf.

"You're looking well," she said as she walked to the table at Tom's side. "Europe seems to agree with you."

"Some parts of it do."

"I hope you enjoy your stay in Helsinki," she said, smiling as brightly as a travel agent.

Over dinner, they talked about the Olympics, the new stadium, the weather. Taylor extolled the Yorkshire puddings, and the roast beef was done rare as Tina had instructed. She kept an eye on Paul and the American and noticed that they both dithered over which fork to use during which course. They'd just finished dessert when the buzzer to the apartment rang. Someone asked for Paul. He excused himself and went out the door to the vestibule.

"Let's adjourn to the softer chairs," said Björnström. He was in a good mood. "Ah, I remember London in the autumn. The fog merely made it more intriguing. A city of famous ghosts and great memories." He began pouring cognacs for the men.

"In school," said Tina, "we read about the history of Europe. It was full of the names of other countries. Never ours."

"You certainly have the world's attention now," said Taylor. His eyes were bright with the ruthlessness of a circling hawk. "Why don't you just give Stalin what he wants? He's only asking for a small piece of your land. Is that too great a price to pay for peace?"

"Why, Philip! He's asking for our sovereignty," said Björnström, lighting a cigar. "You can't barter away sovereignty piece by piece. It is indivisible. You either are or you are not."

"Like being pregnant." As soon as she said it hot blood rushed to her face and she prayed she would flame out into a pile of ashes. There was no excuse for such inanity except that she'd had a sherry and two glasses of wine, and was anxious because Tom was sitting there drifting off into a world of his own. Her father's frown hit her squarely in the eyes. Not only had she offended his old-school sensibilities but had also made light of a topic very close to his heart.

"Or like existence," said Tom unexpectedly. "Some things are indivisible. Absolute. To be or not to be, eh, Taylor?" The words slid off his tongue along the same flat trajectory as his earlier remarks about hotel rates and the quality of whiskey, but his eyes had a knavish flicker. She realized that he was bailing her out, diving in to rescue her from the murky pond into which she'd thrown her silly pebble. Both her father and Taylor were looking at him with a mystified expression, diverted by the prospect of a serious discussion on the issue.

"One could argue that there are degrees of being alive," said Björnström.

"If you make a distinction between life and existence, which we do," said Tom. "Otherwise, most things are relative. Take being tall. You may think you're medium height, but to a child, you're tall. To a giant, you're short. Or obesity. Or being drunk. Same principle, isn't it?" He glanced at her and she caught a marginal wink.

"I suppose it is," she muttered, wilting under her father's glare.

Taylor had had enough. "So existence and pregnancy and sovereignty are absolute, but height and obesity are relative. Well, now that we've fit the theory of relativity to everyday life, please go on, Dr. Björnström." Tina's father continued to watch her, but he went on.

"Simply put, dictators are like sharks. If a shark gets hold of your leg will it just take the foot? No. Did appeasement stop Hitler? No."

"The security of Leningrad is a legitimate concern to the Soviet Union," snapped Taylor.

"Really," Björnström sounded hurt. "That's the oldest line in the world to justify aggression. Hitler used it in Czechoslovakia and Poland." He stalked to the bookshelf, lifted out the Russian goblet and threw it down on the marble hearth. Tina gasped. Shattered glass lay strewn on the hearth. Selma rushed in with a broom to sweep up the shards, muttering in Finnish.

"Thank you, Selma," said Björnström. He turned to Taylor, perfectly composed. "You see, the trinkets of the East mean nothing to us now. We're in a struggle to preserve our existence as a western democracy. No more nor less."

There was a tense silence. Then Selma brought in the coffee and jam cakes and the mood turned affable again. She had baked them especially for the occasion, the favoured cakes of the national poet, Runeberg, as they explained to the visitors.

"Did he write the story about the birch tree and the North Star?" asked Tom.

"No," said Tina. She could feel his eyes on her, and the memory of the Berlin night flickered in her heart. That reminded her of something else.

"Look at this," she said. She went to the bookshelf and drew out an envelope. "Tickets to the opening ceremonies of next July's Olympics in Helsinki, at our beautiful new stadium!" They warmed the room like sunshine as she waved them in the air, and they all crowded around her to admire them.

She stood holding the Olympic tickets when Paul returned from the vestibule, his eyes flashing. He had a piece of paper in his hand, too. White and rectangular. Suddenly she realized what it was and her knees nearly gave way.

"My order to report," he said. A deep silence, a sense of planets realigning. Selma, watching from the kitchen entrance, hid her face in her apron.

"But you're not ready," cried Tina. "Your ankle—"

"I saw my doctor this morning. He gave me a clean bill of health. The army doesn't waste any time, does it?"

"Surely they don't expect you to go tonight?"

"I'm supposed to leave immediately. I could take the midnight train east. It's just that I want to see my father in Kotka. And I have some things there to pick up."

"Where's Kotka?" asked Tom.

"About fifty miles east of here," said Björnström. "That's where Paul grew up. Our summer house is near there." He stepped forward, clasping Paul's shoulders. "You shall not leave like a thief in the night. That's preposterous. You're already late in reporting, one more day won't matter. Go home in the morning, see your father, and take the evening train from there. You're not going anywhere tonight."

This brought slight comfort to Tina, only a twenty-four hour delay of this unthinkable thing, which she knew had happened to thousands of young men across the nation already. She half-listened as Paul explained that he had registered with the military district of his birth parish in Central Finland. His father had come from there years ago to work in the sawmill in Kotka. It only became clear to her later why he'd done so. If there was trouble, his widowed father would seek safety with his relatives in the country and if something happened to Paul, she would not have to deal with it. Of course, he didn't say that now, merely joking that there were cousins in that regiment he wanted to see who owed him money from long-ago poker games. Björnström said it doesn't matter, he will find the right regimental officer to make the arrangements with in the morning.

Tina stared mutely at Paul, clutching her Olympic tickets. Then the room whirled and she dashed for the kitchen, half-hearing Henderson say he'd like to see Kotka, and Paul telling him to come along for the day and return to Helsinki in the evening.

For Tina, the rest of the evening dissolved into a blur. All she could see was the white card in Paul's hand.

Broken Wings

1

"Let me show you *my* ocean," said Paul with tour guide élan. Tom had noticed the change in him as soon as they had arrived in Kotka, shortly before noon. His feet landed on the rough cobblestones with proprietary affection, and he inhaled confidence with the wind, a salty wind that carried a sulfurous bouquet. Smokestacks pierced the sky like needles, turrets of the sawmills that had brought the city prosperity and lured families like Paul's from the countryside. From the central market square they turned east to the harbour. Ships of assorted sizes bobbed in the docks, taking on plywood and lumber. Beyond the harbour, planks stood bundled upright like spears, and russet-red tenement buildings perched on the rocks. Paul pointed to a window on the second story of one of the buildings.

"That's where I lived as a child. We had one room. But it wasn't bad. There were larger families, with eight or nine people to a room."

"Couldn't have been much fun."

"Sure it was. Like at Christmas. Kids running from door to door for a cookie, and in every room there was a tree. Not much on it, maybe an apple and a few straw angels, and always white candles." He walked to

the gate of the tenement yard and leaned over, calling "Moppe! Moppe!"
A grey cur crawled out from under the porch and limped toward the gate.
"He's still here. He must be fifteen years old, a junkyard dog Methuselah.
Hey, remember me?" Paul rubbed the dog tenderly and its chinked ears
perked up. "No time to visit the old house today. Here, let's cut through
Big Park."

He led the way between hedges of rustgreen rose bushes and groves
of silver fir and then down a hill leading straight to the sea. The wind
scudded up, stinging their faces, whipping up eddies of dry brown leaves.
At the bottom was a nondescript marina, its sailboats pulled up for the
winter, and a causeway leading out to a wooded peninsula.

"We go out there to smoke herring," said Paul. "Our small Baltic
herring, you know. That's my Riviera right there. A summer day,
stretched out on those rocks in the hot sun—life doesn't get any better."

He gazed at the shore, the wind ruffling his straight blond hair. The
clouds grew dark although it was still mid-afternoon. Sea and sky merged
into a wall of grey.

"I love the sea," he said. "I love it in the sunlight and I love it when it's
grey and angry. It's always there and it's always mine."

They headed back up the hill, the icy wind biting their ears.

They had left Tina at the home of her Aunt Gunilla, where she was
scheduled to have a short luncheon. Gunilla lived in a large yellow plaster
house not far from the red-brick Lutheran cathedral whose spire soared
into the sky as a counterpoint to the smokestacks across town. But when
Tina marched across the lawn, Paul hung back at the street. The door
opened and Tom caught a glimpse of a maid in starched white.

"Come and say hello, Paul," Tina said. "Then you can take Tom for a
tour of the city while we have lunch."

A tall woman appeared in the doorway just as they reached the
portico. She had the same blue eyes and watercolour features as her niece,
blond hair whitened by the years. She greeted Tina with kisses on both
cheeks, nodded to Paul, and shook Tom's hand with polite indifference.
Then the women disappeared inside. Paul turned on his heel and started
back toward the city centre.

"Do you know Tina's aunt?" asked Tom.

"Oh, yes. We have a very simple relationship. She pretends she doesn't speak Finnish and I pretend I don't speak Swedish, and we just nod to each other. This street was always sort of a dividing line. When I was a boy I had no business in this area. These weren't my people."

It's a complicated world out here, too, thought Tom. He hadn't thought so on the bus rumbling eastward from Helsinki along a highway that snaked through solid rock, with stands of spruce and pine growing straight out of the top, and now and then a glimpse of the sea. The road led to the Russian border, the inscrutable east, the Siberian taiga unchanged by the millennia. Grey clouds drifted like ghosts across the sky and he remembered that it was Halloween. It was the first time in years he'd thought of it.

They passed an apartment building with shops on the main floor. A door flew open and a young woman dashed out, dark-haired with movements like a sparrow. She rolled her hands in her apron and smiled brightly at Paul.

"Marita!" He stopped and turned to Henderson. "Tom, this is Marita. I've known her since we were children. She works here in Lind's store. We can go in and warm up."

They ducked inside the store, cozy and cinnamon-scented, with tables by the window. Marita brought them coffee and pulled up a chair beside Paul.

"How've you been?" he asked.

"Fine. Just the usual. Keeping busy. What are you doing in town?"

"On my way to the frontier. Tonight, on the late train east."

"You too. Damn!"

"It's OK. This will all come to nothing."

"My father and brother are already out there. What worries me is my grandmother. She lives alone on a farm in Karelia. Too stubborn to leave."

"Don't worry. The danger will be over soon."

"Can you stay for dinner? My flat is just upstairs," she stopped, glancing at Tom, whose presence she had apparently forgotten.

"I—have an appointment." Paul flushed. She nodded and touched his sleeve.

"Go then," she whispered, "but don't forget who you are. She never will."

Paul frowned, but he patted her on the shoulder and said, "Take care of yourself. See you next summer."

He and Tom continued walking. It had begun to snow, light flakes that circled the corners, clung to their upturned coat collars, followed them down the winding street toward the centre of the city. Paul's home was in a cluster of oblong wooden houses around a courtyard. Inside the courtyard he stopped, digging in his pocket for the key.

"You know, I like Marita," he said.

"Pretty girl."

"Our parents are good friends. Or used to be. Her mother died the same year my mother died. Three years ago. A bad winter for pneumonia."

"I'm sorry."

"Marita—" Paul leaned against the landing. "Marita doesn't really approve of me any more. She doesn't like that I associate with the upper classes and their daughters. Says they'll never accept me. Maybe she's right. But why can't a working man listen to Viennese operetta? Or be a patriot?" He leaned toward Tom. "Why should I have to follow some Marxist manual? Being an individual isn't an upper class luxury, is it?"

"Absolutely not. The individual is the spine of the nation."

"Exactly." Paul seemed relieved to hear his views confirmed, having flung them into the cold air like white runes.

2

They entered the flat and shook the snow from their coats. A grey cat sidled by and retreated to a corner. The floor was covered with woven rugs, and the furnishings were sparse. A rocking chair, a sofa, a pine table. A bevelled wooden shelf on the wall with a medal on it.

"My father's," said Paul, pointing to the medal. "For thirty years in the factory. Now that he's retired he usually goes downtown in the afternoon for coffee with his friends. He has no telephone so I couldn't let him know I was coming. Look, we have a little time on our hands.

We meet Tina in an hour, and I need to see my father. You don't mind waiting here?"

"Not at all."

"I have whiskey—that's your drink, isn't it? Also I must pack some clothes—woollens, socks, sweaters. Excuse me for a moment." He started toward a bedroom door, then turned back. "No, let's have a drink first. The packing can wait. "

He took two glasses and a bottle from a cupboard and poured. The whiskey was strong and smooth and they settled in with their drinks, a small lamp burning on the table.

"You know," said Tom, "I would never have guessed that old dame was related to Tina. What a cold fish. And that's some house she lives in." He felt uncommonly at ease, almost too much so, and he noted that Paul seemed relaxed as well. Maybe there was something to the notion that it was easier to open up to strangers. The whiskey didn't hurt, either.

"I've been inside it once," said Paul. "She invited me and some other athletes for dinner just before we left for Berlin." He ran his fingers through his hair and grinned. "My friend Jaakko and I pulled off a good one."

"What did you do?"

"You know how the upper crust drinks their coffee out of those tiny cups, with cognac on the side. You're supposed to alternate coffee and cognac. Well, the waiter knew Jaakko and instead of pouring coffee in our cups he poured cognac. So we were alternating cognac with cognac."

They chortled like teenagers.

"Gunilla noticed after the third round and the cognac stopped." Paul leaned back in the chair, his eyes growing hard. "She's never invited me back, thank God. Those people—when they put out their silver and china and start with the toasts, and talk about who saw Sibelius and who went to Paris—I feel like I'm at the cottage the time Gunilla called me a tenement rat, and I know I am a tenement rat and I'll never be anything else. And I don't feel sad about it or happy about it, I just feel like there it is."

They sat in silence for a few minutes.

"Tina and her father seem to be decent," Tom finally said.

"Yes."

"You know, I thought you two would be married by now." The words came out almost before he thought them. Under normal circumstances, he kept his tongue firmly in check no matter how many whiskeys he drank, but he told himself that these were not normal circumstances and for some reason he felt like a boy skating on a frozen prairie river, nearer and nearer the soft ice.

Paul stiffened and said nothing.

"You're leaving tonight to play war games," Tom went on, riding the rush of liquor. "You don't know when you'll be back. Are you going to propose? "

"I was going to do that at Christmas," Paul mumbled, as if he had indeed just reached that decision. "That's the customary time."

"Customary? What's customary about a time like this? There's a war on, and your country is staring into the abyss. Don't leave things to custom."

The waning light closed in at the windows, and Paul poured more whiskey.

"If I'd won a medal in Berlin," he said, "everything would be different."

"Berlin?" Tom remembered what had happened in Berlin, but the connection escaped him. "I know how you feel. We all handle those things in our own way. God knows I didn't handle mine very well—" he paused, deciding to steer clear of his own convoluted attitudes for the moment, "—but you have to let it go. Otherwise, that one bitter mouthful will spoil the whole apple." He stopped, not sure of what he was trying to say, certain only that he sounded like a second-rate newspaper hack and disconcerted by the suspicion that he was really talking about himself.

Paul slumped in the rocking chair, and said, "If I'd won the medal I would have been—acceptable."

"Hey, pal!" said Tom. The cat, which had tentatively crept out of the corner, jumped back to safety. "That's just the whiskey talking. Booze makes you say crazy things, and that was a damn crazy thing you just said."

"You're right," Paul said. "It was nonsense." He looked at the clock and jumped up, stammering about packing. As much as he truly liked Tom, there was no one in the world with whom he could share this particular line of thought. He finished his whiskey in a loud gulp, as if to confirm that it was to blame. Seeing that Tom was busy writing at the table, he packed his knapsack and leaned against the window watching for his father. Snowflakes drifted through the murk of the dying day. The lights of Market Street flickered over the old wooden houses. The street led to the square. His father would be coming from there, having lingered at the café. He would cross the square, then enter the indoor market with its curved brick archway to buy sausage and a loaf of bread. He would pass the apothecary and, further down, the Police Station.

What was it the American had said, about knowing how he felt? No. No one could now how he felt unless they had lived his life. He stared at the street that led to the Police Station. Even though he couldn't see it, it was as familiar to him as a recurring nightmare. He knew the place from the inside. How many thirteen-year olds could say that? Almost twelve years had passed but if he closed his eyes he knew he would be there again, and the fear and the cold would crack open the skin that had grown over the raw bones where the fractured heart of his childhood lay. He closed his eyes.

3

It had turned cold in October that year, too, the year he was thrown in jail. The damp clung to the bars of the window, then trickled down and sat in miniature lagoons on the windowsill. From there it seeped into the walls and floor, and into the lungs. There was little heat in the drafty cell. Paul shivered and Markus began coughing again. His coughing was worse every day now, deep rasps that Paul could hardly believe could come from a nine-year-old's chest. He shouted for the guard to bring more blankets, but he knew it was futile. If you shouted for too long the guard got angry and came and shook you by the shoulders. Worse yet, he would forget to bring you gruel in the morning or the bowl of potato soup they called supper. This was their fifth night in the cell and they had already gone without meals twice. So, he gave up the yelling and bound the horsehair blankets as tightly as he could around his little brother's limbs. He had relinquished his own blanket to Markus on the very first night but it was not enough, he still coughed and tossed and turned on the hard cot. There must be a law about throwing nine-year olds in jail. Himself, he was thirteen. He could take it.

Their parents hadn't been allowed to see them, though Paul knew they came to the police station every day. He could hear his father's voice, pleading and shouting in turn, and the weeping of his mother. They hadn't been allowed to see the others, either. Joonas, Jaakko, Lasse, Anders. The boys who had been thrown in jail with them. A gang, the police called them. Paul thought of them more as a book club. They had all read *The Last of the Mohicans,* and modelled their adventures on their perceptions of the American frontier. Markus came along because he could fit into places where the larger boys could not. They all lived in the tenement houses and attended the public school, a long wood-frame building complete with potbellied stove. Outside school, life was a scramble. They trolled the streets for booty, looking for shiny candy wrappers to use as currency in their games, occasionally finding odd jobs that earned real money. Their activities brought them under frequent scrutiny by the police, who tended to see incipient anarchy in the tenement children.

The guard walked by and hissed "Shh!" at them. In the dim corridor light Paul saw a flash of his uniform, a sight he loathed to the point of nausea. His anger kept him warm. If Markus could get angry he might warm up too, but he could only cough and cry for his mother.

"Why did they do this to us?" asked Markus. This had become a ritual, this litany of questions and replies.

"Somebody made a mistake."

"Who?" Paul had no answer, though he had mulled this over many times. The police? Maybe, but on the other hand it was true he had stolen something. Justice? God? How could God do this to children?

"When can we go home?"

"Don't worry," whispered Paul. "I got you into this, I'll get you out. That's a promise." The words came out by rote but in reality he had no idea what to do. All this over a few apples. He stretched out beside Markus on the cot, trying to warm him and warm himself and ignore the beast that clawed at his empty stomach. When he thought of food he half fainted and the scent of apples seemed to fill the cell. He remembered how warm and smooth they felt in his hands and the dry grass in his shoes as he ran for the orchard fence. And Tina's blue gaze when he presented her with the finest apple of all.

Tina. The pretty blonde from the private girls' school on Church Street. This street had always been one of the book club's favourite venues. Going one way from the red-brick cathedral it led to the market square. Going the other way it led to the city's genteel neighbourhoods and the school attended by Tina and her friends. Although Paul and his club members would never have been invited to the homes of these girls, they were not strangers. Friendships sprang up in parks and shops and at the market around the strawberry bins. That was where he'd met Tina one Saturday in August. The following week Paul insisted on diverting all the club's expeditions to the sidewalk across from the girls' school. If they were fast enough they got there just as the girls spilled out, giggling and chattering. Most of them ignored the band of urchins lounging against the fence that encircled Ahlstrom's apple orchard, but Tina did not. She remembered Paul from the marketplace and threw him a scathing glance. Within a week they were exchanging insults across the street and one day she crossed over to his side. The next day, some of her friends also crossed the street and spoke with the boys, blending insult and flirtation. For them it was a joke, this mock courtship with boys who wore threadbare jackets and shoes with no socks. But for Tina it was more. Paul knew it was. She told him things, sweet things. One day she told him that his eyes were colour of drifting woodsmoke. That wasn't something a tenement boy heard every day.

One September day, Paul was recounting the story of a rescue the gang had performed at sea, based loosely on a real event, when one of the girls suddenly shouted, "If you're so brave, prove it! We want apples." She pointed to Ahlstrom's orchard, where the autumn sun caught the glint of ripe red apples on the tree.

Paul hesitated. It was true that he and the boys had, on occasion, made off with an apple or two, but always after dusk. It was another thing to try it on a busy street in broad daylight. Still, Tina was eyeing him with intense curiosity.

He scaled the fence, ignoring the slivers of wood that pierced his hands, and ran into the orchard. Seeing no one, he shinnied up a stout tree and picked half a dozen apples, then descended with bulging pockets. At the fence he yelled "Catch!" and threw the apples over one by one; then he saw Old Man Ahlstrom trotting toward him on creaky legs. Paul vaulted over the top and presented the best apple, tucked inside his shirt, to Tina, before they all scattered.

Halfway through mathematics class the next morning, a constable knocked on the door and read a list of names to the headmaster. The list contained the name of every member of Paul's clique, including Markus. With no further explanation the boys were pulled out of class and marched to the Police Station. They were placed in separate cells, although Markus was allowed to stay with his brother. A white-gloved detective came in the evening and questioned them about assorted recent thefts in the city. None of the boys knew anything about these crimes, but they were kept in jail nevertheless. Their parents lacked the funds to hire a lawyer.

Markus broke out in another fit of coughing and began to wail loudly.

"Shut up in there!" the guard shouted. "Go to sleep."

Paul knew they couldn't jail them forever, but he didn't know how long Markus could endure. He sat up, cramped and cold, trying to think of a way to escape. He hadn't been sitting long when the clink of the cell key made him jump. The guard opened the door and told them to get lost. They were free. Paul bundled Markus into his arms, fearful the guard would change his mind, and carried him out into the office area. His parents rushed toward them and as they embraced, through his tears he saw another couple, a tall man with grey-streaked hair and bushy gold eyebrows and a woman in a fashionable dress and cloche hat. Beside them stood Tina, dabbing at her eyes with a white muff.

"It's just to scare 'em, Dr. Björnström," the sergeant said, with an affable shrug. "Otherwise they rob good folks like yourselves blind."

Tina's father glared at the sergeant.

"Nine years old," he snapped. "The other, thirteen. I'll report this to the commissioner."

"Come now sir, can't we just overlook it?" the sergeant smiled. "Just an overzealous officer. Still bitter about that Commie trouble a few years ago."

"Our family has never been Red," said Paul's father. "Not every worker was Red. And not every Red was a criminal. For that matter there were criminals on both sides."

"Anton!" Paul's mother looked at him in panic. "It's not our place to say—"

"On the contrary, Mrs. Salmi, it is your place to say," said Tina's mother. "This is a democracy."

"It is indeed, Ma'am," the sergeant was jovial now. "And these kids are going home this very minute." For the first time in five days, Paul saw his brother smile. The adults exchanged a few words and handshakes at the door, and when Paul's mother broke down in sobs the woman in the cloche hat drew her close and embraced her. Then a black automobile drew up and the Björnströms drove away. Paul's family walked home through the dark streets. He'd never thought of the smokestacks as beautiful, but now they looked majestic, soaring toward the moon and encircled by the stars. Halfway through Big Park he began to run, stumbling over the rocks and up the hill toward the tenements with their tiny lighted windows, toward the warmth and light of home.

A few weeks before Christmas Markus came down with bronchitis, and was sickly until he died of pneumonia the next year. Paul never forgot or forgave, convinced that the experience in the cell had weakened his small brother to a point where he could not survive ordinary illnesses.

That was the beginning of his relationship with Tina. Her parents came to visit the tenement, bringing fruit and chocolate for all the boys. Tina's father took a personal interest in Paul, encouraging him with his schooling, helping financially on occasion. This was assistance that Paul's father did not turn down, realizing its significance. Instead of starting work at the sawmill when he was fourteen, Paul graduated from high school and enrolled in reserve officers' training school, where he learned to run.

The Olympic medal would have been his passport into their world. He would have been a hero, with guaranteed access to anyone's world.

There was a shuffle at the door. His father had returned and he rushed to greet him. This would be a difficult good-bye. The old man was alone now, and he missed his dead wife. Paul made him promise that at the first sign of trouble he would leave Kotka and stay with his kinfolk in the country. After the talking was done, he gripped his father's hand tightly, and then he and Tom gathered up their belongings. Near the market square they passed a café. Tom said that he would eat dinner there and work on his notes, and meet them at the train station. Paul did not object.

4

The most painful goodbyes are the ones that are unsaid, Tina told herself later. They never leave your dreams alone. For years she replayed that October evening when Paul left for the border like a scene from a movie. As if it was an unsatisfactory take and she would get a chance to do it over again. What did they talk about during those hours together? They met at a restaurant and had a bottle of wine with dinner. He gave her the address of his relatives, if she should need to get in touch with his father. If his father left for the country. If the situation got serious. If the mail didn't get through. There were so many ifs. Did she tell him she loved him? Yes, she must have. All along she sensed there was something he was trying to say, but the words got sidetracked in the maze of details.

Later at the station they held each other as they waited for the train. The familiar old station now stood transformed into an alien ground, swept by a cold wind and blowing snow. Paul shielded her with his coat and whispered, "When I come back—". Just then Tom Henderson appeared on the platform and joined them. He would take the train back to Helsinki with Tina. It was too late then to talk of private things.

Young men stood in twos or threes, or leaned against the wall, often with a girl's head buried in their shoulder.

"What are these civilian guys doing here at this time of night?" asked Tom.

"They aren't civilians, they're soldiers. Soldiers of a nation short of money for uniforms. See that pin on their hats? That's the only uniform they got. We call it the Prime Minister's Model."

"Why?"

"He gave a speech not long ago that we can be proud we don't have warehouses of rusting guns," said Tina. "That we spent the money on butter instead."

"Butter is fine but it won't kill Russians," said Paul. "For artillery we have museum pieces, we have no antitank guns. . ." His voice trailed off. "A poor country has to choose. Guns or bread. We chose bread."

An announcement crackled over the loudspeaker. "Ten minutes, Paul," said Tina, fighting back tears. "Ten minutes until your train leaves."

A rippling movement in the station, final hugs exchanged.

"There's an apparition for you," said Paul rather unkindly.

A tall, white-haired woman in furs rushed toward them. With a shock Tina saw that it was her Aunt Gunilla. She thrust a pair of thick mittens into Paul's hands, the kind with a movable index finger for shooting in the cold, and wished him luck in perfect Finnish. Tina barely recognized her voice, which she usually held far back in her throat, as if unwilling to expend it on her listener; now it was clear and affectionate. Then with a sweep of the fur coat, she was gone.

The train arrived, and Tina began to sob. Paul gave her a long, hard embrace and then lifted her off the ground like a child.

"Tom," he said with a grin, "if things go bad, get her to a safe place. Her father, too. To the countryside or Sweden. Or America. She's stubborn but she'll go."

"Oh!" Tina wriggled free. "Don't be ridiculous! Things won't go bad and you'll be back before you know it."

And then Paul was gone, and the train puffed eastward into the night.

Tina and Tom boarded the next train back to Helsinki. The drapes were drawn shut, which suited her well, as there was no need for him to see her tears. She sat beside him and blessed the darkness.

"Cheer up. He'll be home soon," he said.

"Oh, I know. It's just that—it's wrong that he has to go out there to God knows where, for God knows what reason. Wrong that any of them have to."

"He's crazy about you, you know."

"What?" This was the last thing she expected to hear. "What on earth did you two talk about this afternoon?"

"Women."

"Oh, really? And where are yours, then? You speak in plural."

"Just women in general. He didn't share any secrets with me. And I didn't share any with him." He leaned back and put his feet on the empty seat across from him. She closed her eyes and pretended to doze although what she really wanted was to grill him with questions. Meanwhile, the train stopped in a small village and a solitary man rushed into the car. He immediately began to chatter nervously to no one in particular. Tina sat up in surprise. This was uncharacteristic of her countrymen, who generally paid as little attention to each other as possible.

"What's he so worked up about?" asked Tom.

"Molotov made a speech. He broadcast all the Russian demands for the whole world to hear," she said. Suddenly she was drenched with sweat. "They can't back down now."

"Relax. It's Halloween. They're trying to spook you."

"Halloween?"

"A night when the witches and goblins come out. Kids go from door to door begging for treats. We went out dressed in white sheets, when I was a boy."

"In Chicago?"

"No, a small town. On the Canadian prairie."

"I've seen pictures of the prairies. So wide. You can probably see forever."

"Pretty far. Never as far as you'd like."

"Don't you get homesick?"

"Not everybody needs a home."

She would have asked him what he meant but suddenly she remembered Paul, riding in the opposite direction to an unknown place, while she sat here chattering about autumn rituals and geography. She decided to sit out the rest of the journey in silence but Tom was in a talkative mood.

"So tell me about you and Paul," he said. "What kinds of things do you do together?"

"Ordinary things," she said.

"Like what?"

"Go to the movies, in the summer sailing and picking berries, in the winter skiing. We go to the Fennia for coffee and cake. To the Fazer when Dallape is playing. That's the best band in the country. We do a lot of dancing." That will suffice, she thought. He'll say something like, "that's swell", and fall asleep. But he did not. In the darkness she could hear him breathing, so quiet was the car and so intently was he listening.

"Go on," he said. His tone was insistent, almost pleading, and so she steered her mind toward its memories of the mundane as she would have coaxed a nag from the meadow to the road.

"Sometimes we go to the country. Last spring we took the train to a little village north of here, to look for Paul's ancestral home. His parents moved away from the farm when it became too difficult to make a living. Before that the farm had been in his family for three hundred years. We found the turnoff to the farm and a new house was there, a modern house with electricity. Paul would have left but I went to the door and knocked. An old woman was living there. She made us coffee and told us stories about Paul's family. Then she showed us the foundations of the original house. They're still there, huge stones overgrown with moss. We walked up the steps and around the perimeter. And then—then something came over me, a vision or déjà vu. I could see things that happened there, as if I was actually there. A child being born in the sauna, a son in a dragoon uniform, the women spinning and knitting, then a wedding with bowls of stew and potatoes. The quarrels, the dancing, the dreams dreamed." She stopped, because she could not go on. In truth the experience had moved her deeply and she couldn't convey it properly to him or to anyone. Paul had laughed at her. "And the strangest thing was the birch tree. There was one right beside the old house whose trunk was bent almost exactly the way as the birch by our flat on Elisabeth Street. You can't imagine— it's impossible to explain."

He said nothing. The train slowed down and ground to a halt, and someone jumped off the car. They were passing through a town on the outskirts of Helsinki. The brief opening of the door let in a few moonbeams and in their light Tina saw his face the way she had seen it in the moonlight by the violet patch in Berlin. His eyes had the same mild cast, as if looking at something that brought him great pleasure.

"All this must be very dull compared to your life," she said. "What do you do with your lady friends?"

He laughed so loudly that voices in the train car began muttering in Finnish, "idiot", "keep it down", and other complaints.

"What's so funny?" whispered Tina.

"Nothing really. Just that very few of them are ladies and none of them are my friends."

She didn't laugh. Had he just been teasing her after all, feigning an interest in her inconsequential life? The train was slowing now, sliding into the station yards. She wrapped her scarf around her head and prepared to leave. On the siding she said a perfunctory good-bye to him and, declining his offer to get her a cab or accompany her on foot, she walked back to Elisabeth Street alone. It seemed wrong to be escorted home by a stranger when she'd just said goodbye to Paul, and sent him off to the borderlands in the cold autumn night.

Selma was in the kitchen waiting.

"The professor is still out," she said. "They're all at the Kämp listening to the radio."

"It's just the latest Molotov bluff. He's trying to make us lose our nerve." She was surprised to hear herself echoing Tom's assessment of the situation.

"Did you take a cab home from the station?"

"No, I walked."

"Walked! With this blackout, you walked?"

"It's more dangerous in a cab driving through the black streets. I know my way home. Don't worry about me."

While Selma chattered about the dangers of the darkness, Tina turned on the radio. The program was over for the night and she heard only static. She knew her father would be a long time coming home, and so she had a cup of coffee from the thermos and went to bed. Her mind was still on her parting from Paul, as inadequate as it seemed now, with everything left unfinished between them.

The darkness bothered her more than she confessed. That autumn was the darkest of her life. Autumn in the north is always gloomy, with daylight fading in mid-afternoon. Now it was a festering darkness. She walked home from her office through blacked out streets, losing her way on familiar paths, wet leaves dropping on her face. The few lights that still burned in public places were shrouded and dimmed. Tram bells tinkled on cars with draped windows, and the outbound trains were packed with people fleeing to the countryside, mothers holding children tightly, old folks clutching suitcases. Buildings and trees she had known since childhood became unrecognizable shapes.

5

October turned to November and the Moscow negotiations dragged on, keeping Tom in Finland. The darkness bothered him, too, far more than he'd expected. The northern night struck hard, depressing in any circumstances and exacerbated by the overhanging crisis. *La mélancolie*, Taylor called it. It seeped into the soul, made you want to weep, made you want to die. Besides the darkness, he noticed the silence, punctuated only by the tapping of knitting needles. Everywhere he went—department stores, banks, offices—he saw women knitting furiously. If he asked the reason, the answer was always the same: "For the boys." The women sat engrossed in knitting and engrossed in listening. It was the hush of a nation straining to hear what was being said hundreds of miles to the east in Moscow. A hush where the click of a knitting needle was deafening. He took to going on long walks around the city, usually alone, sometimes with Taylor. The Englishman often refused, claiming that the click of knitting needles reminded him of the French revolution, of bloody-minded crones. For Tom it was simple. Helsinki is a small town at its core, and he was hoping to bump into Tina on some street corner. He hadn't seen her since Halloween night. He walked up to Elisabeth Street on dark evenings when mist clung to the lampposts, remembering the pleasant apartment there, thinking about his own memories, thinking of things that had nothing to do with the Moscow crisis.

6

It had something to do with the snow. There had been snow in Chicago, of course, and before that in Toronto, but not this kind. The kind that drifted over the highways and piled up in roadside dunes. That was the snow he remembered from his home town on the Alberta prairie. The cold was the same, too. He remembered the prairie cold. You'll never be a runner, his friends told him. You can't train out here. But he ran every day, even during the winter except on the most frigid days.

When he was seventeen, he graduated from high school, his room filled with medals and trophies, owner of the Western Canadian junior record for the mile. He stayed in town over the following winter working at his father's store, saving money for his first year at the University of Toronto. That winter was mild and he ran every day, five miles down the country roads outside town. One February afternoon he was halfway through his run when the wind picked up and blew drifting snow across the road, whiting out the landscape in a second. He lost his path and stumbled into a barbed wire fence. Trailing blood from a badly cut chin, he plowed through the field to a farmhouse. The farmer's wife let him in and bandaged his chin. She gave him hot soup while her husband hitched up the horses, and they bundled him into the wagon and took him home.

In the late spring, he took his father's new car for a spin, saw the farm-house, and drove up to offer his belated thanks. The farmer's daughter was there this time. How corny could you get, he thought, a farmer's daughter! But if you grew up on the prairie, what were the odds that your first sex would be with anyone else? And some farmer's daughter. A pretty blonde, her family came from one of the northern countries, he'd forgotten which one.

"Please sit down," she said, her voice with a trace of northern lilt. "You look very hot. Would you like some iced tea and pie?"

While she was gone he looked around the tidy room. Crocheted doilies, colonial chairs and needlepoint florals, and against the wall a black upright piano. He walked over to the piano, because it was very similar to the one in his own parlour at home.

"Do you play?" he asked her when she returned.

"No," she said. "My sister did. Since she got married and moved away, no one does. It's likely out of tune." She walked over to the piano, flicked off some dust with the corner of her apron and drew back the dustboard. She picked out a few chords with two fingers. The tone was hard-edged and thin.

"It is out of tune," he said, and sat down on the bench.

"Ah, so it's you who are the pianist," she wagged her finger at him.

"My mother taught me a few songs," he said.

"I'm sorry about your mother," she said. His mother had died two springs ago, and in a small community everyone knew about the passages of life. Even this stranger knew about Fiona Henderson's death. He tried a few arpeggios. The keys were sticky but slowly he fumbled his way through the first few bars of *Nola*, and then it all came back to him. He finished the piece, and swung into *The Glowworm* for good measure. She sat on the edge of an embroidered chair cushion, leaning forward and watching him. When he was finished, she clapped.

"I've heard a lot about your athletic prowess," she said. "I had no idea you were so multi-talented."

It pleased him that she knew about his running. He was going to ask her what she'd heard about his prowess, but she motioned him toward the pie. When they'd eaten, he got up, muttering about leaving.

"First let me help you with the dishes," he said. This was something he did quite often at home, and what he really wanted was an excuse to stay.

"Oh, I'll do them later. I must hitch up the horse and go to the apothecary."

He offered her a lift. The car overheated just outside town, and he turned off the engine. He helped her down from the running board and they strolled into the field, a meadow where the clover grew high, and a caragana hedge gave shade all afternoon. He pulled her into the grass, and she laughed. It was so hot there was not much in the way of clothing to remove, so it happened too quickly to remember much, except his unbearable urgency and the sunlight warm on her long, sleek thighs as he pushed between them. Afterward as they lay sprawled in the grass she reached up and plucked a handful of yellow caragana blossoms and scattered them in his hair, calling him her golden boy.

He met her there almost every day for the rest of the summer. As they lay under the caraganas, he ran his hands over her body, studied it from every angle, found its secret places. She collected purple thistles, ladyslippers, and daisies from the field, and plucked the petals chanting, "He loves me, he loves me not."

"I love you," he said and at that moment he was sure he did.

She wrapped the daisy chain around his waist.

"What else do you want to do besides be a runner?" she asked.

"All kinds of things. First I want to win an Olympic medal. Then I want a college degree. Maybe in medicine." He was thinking of his mother, who had wasted away from a tumour before his helpless eyes. "I'd like to see the Seven Wonders of the World. And the kangaroos in Australia. The bridges of Venice. The onion domes of Russia."

"That will take a whole lifetime. You might need help."

"I have you."

In September he started university and they wrote every week. But around Halloween he received a letter from her with the news that she was pregnant. He wrote one more letter, a short note that ended, "I love you." Then he stopped writing. He hated himself, but he didn't know what to say. Neither did he have the courage to go home at Christmas. The next time he went back, in June, she was gone. When the Sewing Circle convened in his Aunt Lee's parlour, he heard the vicious whispers about the farmer's daughter. Not a word about him. She had conducted herself with a noblewoman's discretion.

Love, he decided, was too fragile a word for his clumsy tongue. He resolved never to use it again.

Molotov's Breadbaskets

1

The Moscow negotiations broke off on November 13th and the negotiators came home. Stalin saw the Finns off with handshakes all around and spirits rose cautiously. Some were convinced this was the end of it.

Tom's editors urged him to move on to greener pastures, as the eyes of the world turned away from this improbable land where for a brief moment it had seemed something dramatic would happen. Yet he couldn't bring himself to leave. The situation was not stable, he wrote; there were still huge numbers of men in the field and an eerie silence from Moscow. Move on, came the answer. To Poland, where there were corpses to be counted. To the Baltics, to see how many Russian advisors had arrived.

By late November he was running out of excuses. Then, one evening as he sat in the Kämp lounge, it occurred to him: Taylor was still here. Suddenly this fact intrigued him. Taylor did no research and had rarely stepped outdoors after the first snowfall. All he seemed to be doing, in fact, was waiting.

The next day he made a point of lunching with Taylor.

"Listen to my report from last night," he said and pulled out his notebook. *"The Home Guards have collected thousands of items to send to the boys for entertainment. I counted 62 gramophones, 22 accordions, 59 mandolins, and 81 other musical instruments."* That's the kind of scoop I'm sending to London. My editor is pressuring me to move. What do you think? Are we wasting our time hanging around here? Did Uncle Joe sweep the whole thing under the rug?"

"I shall miss these vodka martinis," said Taylor, showing no sign of having heard, then hissing, "Dashed good luck, old chap! There's someone who can answer your question."

In a far corner of the dining room, Tom saw the unmistakable silver head of Björnström in a small circle of Finns, several of them in military dress.

"Björnström?"

"No, the one beside him. Surely you recognize Marshal Mannerheim. Aristocrat, father of Finnish independence, tiger hunter, head of the defense council."

"Yes, I know who you mean. Didn't know he was that tall."

Before they could move closer, the group dispersed and the Marshal disappeared into the hallway. Björnström ambled toward the door, but Tom caught his eye and the old man changed course toward their table, slowly, like a listing schooner.

"Do you have time to join us for luncheon?" asked Taylor.

Björnström glanced at his watch. "Really, what use is a pocket watch to an old man? They only remind us of the days when we had schedules to keep." His eyes sparkled, the watering of old eyes under stress. "It is fortunate that you flagged me down or I might have forgotten lunch altogether. Well, imagine this. How fine to see you both!"

"Was that the Marshall you were speaking to just now?"

"Yes. It's no secret that he is unhappy. He thinks that to continue to resist Moscow is to risk war, and our tiny army is short of everything."

"But surely—" said Tom, unprepared for such gloomy news, "it won't come to that. Your army won't need to fight."

"Isn't it time your countrymen took off the blinkers?" Taylor's eyes bored into the old man with hawklike precision. "They walk by the bomb shelters as if they aren't there. They look at the dirt piles beside them as if they're flower beds."

"Finns can be very obstinate, I'm afraid," said Björnström. "We will continue to believe they are flower beds until someone proves otherwise." He lit a cigarette. "Bad habit. If you see my daughter, please don't mention the cigarette. She is as strict with me as with a child. I don't mind. It makes an old man happy to know his children care about him."

Lunch was served, but no one moved to unfold the geometrically positioned linen napkins. Finally Björnström lifted his glass and proposed a toast to peace. At this, Taylor turned his head away. Tom saw his eyes, stripped of polite veneer, stricken with anguish.

He wired his editor that evening: "Rumours of impending developments. Intend to stay another week."

2

Björnström spent more and more time away from home, meeting with his friends in the military and in politics. One evening when he called to tell them not to wait up for him, Selma hung up the receiver and sat down at the table, elbows squared, eyes blazing.

"I don't believe the professor is eating proper meals," she said. "What they serve at that hotel is anyone's guess, assuming these men take time to eat at all. That isn't doing the professor's ulcer any good."

"Come to think of it, he's been looking thinner lately," said Tina, suddenly angry at herself for not having noticed it sooner.

"Exactly." Selma marched into the kitchen. After some banging and clattering, she emerged carrying a box filled with towel-wrapped plates.

"What are you doing?" asked Tina.

"If Mohamed won't come to the mountain, the mountain shall go to Mohamed."

"You're taking food to him? You haven't been to the Kämp in years." Tina's voice rose as she imagined Selma wandering through the pitch-black streets, stumbling and lying in the snow with a broken ankle, freezing to death.

"I know this city like the back of my hand. Don't you worry about me, sweetie."

"No. If anyone goes, I will. I'm used to walking out there under the blackout rules. Give the box to me."

"I can't let you, a young girl—"

"Selma, I am not a young girl! I'm a grown woman, and I walk this route every day. I know the staff at the Kämp. I know where to find Papa. Come now, you know very well I'm right."

Selma shook her head but obeyed. Tina pulled on her coat and hood, tied a scarf tightly around her neck, and took her warmest mittens from the closet. When she was bundled up, Selma extended the food box to her the way she used to hand over schoolbooks in the mornings.

"Be careful," she said, wiping a tear from her eye.

"I'm not going to the North Pole. I'm only going to the Kämp."

"Not much difference in this weather."

At the Kämp Tina hurried through the entrance, then hesitated. Despite her brave words, she was a little nervous. During the Moscow crisis the old hotel had taken on a new persona. It was full of strangers wearing sheepskin coats and ski sweaters, loud reporters and attachés who had sprouted out of nowhere and according to rumours, half of whom were spies. As she walked past tables draped with raucous guests it was clear the stories about Bacchanalian goings-on were true, and she cringed at what had become of the elegant hostelry she had known since childhood.

She knew where to look for her father. He would be on the second floor, far from the throng, in one of the private conference rooms. At the elevator she ran into a party of drunken reporters, who leered at her and peppered her with questions. What's your name? What do you have in the box? Can you stay a while, chérie?

She'd told Selma she was a grown woman, but at that moment it was not entirely true. She bolted like a frightened child and decided to walk up the staircase instead of waiting for the elevator. Besides, it was a walk she always enjoyed. The wide arching staircase leading up from the lobby was so beautiful she'd spent many hours when she was young sitting in an armchair downstairs and admiring it. She walked up slowly, running her hands along the wrought-iron railings, stopping at the landing to gaze at the painting on the wall, the portrait of a woman who could have climbed straight out of fin-de-siècle Paris. When she got to the second floor, she sat down at a table overlooking the staircase and the massive chandelier below. For several minutes she sat there, admiring the symmetry of the railings and the marble pillars, imagining she was having afternoon tea. The reverie ended when she heard noises in the corridor that led to the private guestrooms. A door opening and closing, laughter, footsteps. She got up and walked to the corner and peered down the hallway.

An American female reporter, a noted beauty whose arrival had been publicized in the papers, was playfully chasing a man who was clad only in a white towel. From the back it looked like Tom, but Tina couldn't be sure. She stood at the corner, trying to hide yet unable to look away.

"Stealing towels! I'll report you," giggled the woman.

"It's from the hotel sauna," he said. "They loan them to you. Honest." The voice was not Tom's and Tina sighed with relief.

The woman laughed and tugged at the towel. It came off and she swung him around and embraced his naked buttocks. She fell to her knees and fondled his hips and then his genitals. He pushed his groin into her face.

Tina turned and walked back to the rotunda though her legs could hardly move. Her breasts tightened and swelled, and her body ached with acutely sweet pain. As she sat down and tried to calm her shaking hands, she heard more laughter from the hallway and the click of a door closing. Slowly the ache in her began to subside. She knew what it was, and its force frightened her. When her romance with Paul began she'd felt the same stirrings but she pushed them away. And pushed him away. The spectre of a child out of wedlock haunted every girl's dreams. She couldn't find the words to explain to him that her reluctance came from her own fears, not his unworthiness.

She sat immobile, angry at her body for its disloyalty, angry that the lust she felt was sparked by thoughts of Tom Henderson, not Paul. She was still sitting there when she heard her father's voice. He was coming from the conference room in the far corridor, chatting with a friend. When he saw her he hurried in her direction. She linked her arm through his and they walked home. Only at the gate of their apartment did she realize that Selma's food box was still at the Kämp.

3

The blister on his palm burst again, and the shovel fell from Paul's hands. He removed his glove and dried the fluid oozing over his fingers. His back ached, and he straightened up and leaned against the rampart. The Karelian soil was stony and unforgiving, a mixture of bog and granite not suited for trench or dugout. The shovels struggled with it, clinking their displeasure.

He'd only been in Karelia once before, during the fortification work the previous summer. Then it had been hot, the sun beaming out of a perfect sky, the woods full of cuckoo's cries and the scent of the pines mingling with the dust kicked up by the excavation and moving of boulders for tank barriers. The fast-talking, lively Karelian girls came out of the surrounding farmhouses and set up long tables in the meadow, covered them with white tablecloths and heaped them with all the food, milk and juice their larders could provide. They invited the workers to lunch. The Karelians had struck him as being too light-hearted to be Finns. Even now he could see few signs of anxiety here in the border towns. Some people had left their homes in October and then returned, believing the argument was over for the winter. The local menfolk were stationed elsewhere, leaving the women, children and old men to finish the autumn chores. Sometimes he and his fellow soldiers went to the farms in the evenings and helped bring in the last of the hay and mulch the fields.

The fields. Never had fields been as fascinating to him as these. The November afternoon withdrew its light from the flat expanse of land they called Cape Hook, a looping peninsula carved out by the river Taipale as it descended into Lake Ladoga. The Taipale was the eastern end of the main defense line on the Isthmus. For weeks now he'd studied the landscape out there, trying to memorize all of it—fields, woods, schoolhouse, roads, and the river beyond, flowing under a steep escarpment. That was where the Russians would come, if they came. He would have to remember the location of every tree and hillock, every hayloft and outhouse.

A stinging wind kicked up snow into his face, cooling the beads of sweat on his forehead. He watched the men around him pack up and drift away, talking of the pea soup waiting at the mess hall, and fell into step beside Markus, his sergeant, a farmer's son from a parish in central Finland. They'd become good friends, being billeted in the same farmhouse.

"Where the hell is your shovel?" asked Markus in sudden panic, looking at Paul's empty hands.

In horror he realized he'd left his shovel where it had fallen, at the bottom of the half-dug trench. This was no minor offense. When he'd arrived, the company had no shovels at all. Men were picking at the rocky ground with sticks and makeshift wooden implements, even their rifle butts. The army had run short of everything, tools included. It took a week of pleas and curses to get the shovels and they were not to be treated lightly. Still, he was too tired to trudge back in the dark to get it.

"I know where it is," he muttered. "It won't walk away in the night."

"You'll be in deep shit if the Lieutenant sees you."

"Nah. He'd write a poem about it."

The Lieutenant, their company commander, was a writer in civilian life. This had initially caused some hilarity among the men and grumbling about being led into battle by a poet. The pen is mightier than the sword, someone quipped, but can it also stop a tank? Luckily the Lieutenant proved to be both fair and competent, and soon the company began to respect and even boast about its literary leader. Still, there was no need for him to know about the missing shovel, so Paul wolfed down his pea soup, cooled his mouth with milk, and dashed into the sauna.

Steam billowed out of the sauna door. Inside, rows of naked male thighs glistened with sweat in the glow of the fiery rocks, and the hiss of water punctuated the drone of voices. Sweat rolled off backs and foreheads and birch whisks flailed, thawing frozen capillaries, softening callouses, loosening numb joints. He found a spot beside Jokinen, his frequent chess partner and the resident accordionist of the company. On the highest bench where the heat burned with brimstone intensity, he saw the broad features of Markus, cheeks ablaze. After a few minutes the three of them burst out headlong into the night, cooling down their bodies with handfuls of snow. Suddenly out of the darkness came the thud of hooves, and two officers on horseback appeared. One was the Lieutenant, the other was an older man, a Captain from battalion headquarters. Paul and his companions snapped to attention, covered their genitals with one hand and saluted with the other.

"Never mind, boys," said the Captain. Paul knew him by reputation as a flamboyant veteran of several wars, foreign and domestic. "There's nothing under there I haven't seen before. Probably seen a lot bigger, for that matter. So, are you devils behaving yourselves? Don't forget, we have the little woman system here. If you don't work hard and fight hard, the little woman will find out. I have the addresses. You'll have no business going home!" The officers chuckled, and rode on.

"It's like bloody school all over again," muttered Jokinen. "You mess up, and you get it from the teacher and then you get it from the old man when you get home."

"Except with the little woman, you won't get it at all," said Paul, and they doubled over with laughter.

"Why do you care? You don't have a little woman," said Markus, as they ran for the sauna, bare feet sliding across snow-covered rocks. He was a newlywed and had already written to his bride about close encounters with Russians. Many of the men had done the same, some even citing imaginary skirmishes.

"I have a little woman," said Paul, "and she has ways of finding out."

Later, in the farmhouse that had been his home for weeks now, he sat with pen and paper before him, and tried to compose a letter to Tina by the dim oil lamp swinging above the table. The lamp swung like a pendulum, moving with the currents of cold wind seeping through the window. He was the only one still up. Even Jokinen had put his accordion away after coaxing out his wistful melodies for hours. He read over his letter once more, trying to hone his words so they expressed his feelings precisely, something he was not used to doing.

"Dear Tina, You asked about life in the army. There's not much to tell. Food and cigarettes, cold and boredom, digging fortifications, the hot sauna and the crowded farmhouse, the oil lamps and the campfires. The feeling of being wrenched from all your moorings into a peculiar existence where there is no future. I've fit in with the men better than I expected. They're a placid lot for the most part, going about their business with taciturn doggedness. Most of them are from the same parishes. Here we all have the same point of reference, the army camp. Home is a precious, receding memory. In normal times we'd all be fiercely independent and even loners, but an unfamiliar new bond is forming here."

It was surprising how easily it formed, he thought. For instance, his friendship with Markus, who was the son of a large landowner, the kind that had driven his father to seek work in the sawmill rather than eke out a living as a crofter. Markus also belonged to the Civil Guard, a patriotic semi-military organization, and he looked much too serious at evening vespers. He had a fine tenor voice and a habit of singing in foreign languages. And as the final straw, he had the same name as his long-dead little brother. But as the long nights lingered he began to look forward to Markus singing his arias, and the drone of his modest chatter. When they went to the farms, Markus showed him how to mulch. And one Sunday how to catch a pig, kill it and roast it over a spit. We'll make a farmer of you yet, laughed Markus over roast pork by the fire that evening.

He'd tried to convey all this to Tina, but felt that his words seemed clumsy. Even worse were the passages where he tried to express his love for her, and the regret he felt over their parting, over the proposal he'd failed to make. "I love you," he wrote again. "When this is over, everything between us will be settled."

4

Paul often played chess in the canteen in the evenings. Someone had salvaged the chess set from a local family of evacuees whose chess players were away in some other bivouac. The canteen was run by the Lottas, a women's auxiliary named after a nineteenth-century army nurse named Lotta Svärd. The Lottas had arrived in November and set up the canteen in an abandoned schoolhouse. Now it filled to the rafters every night and cups of coffee lined the counter along with the sweet bread called *pulla*, cigarettes and matches. Jokinen brought his accordion and his melodies drifted over the smoky haze like a guardian angel's harp over her charges.

Markus often asked Jokinen to play something Italian on his accordion, perhaps *O Sole Mio*. Then he would sing along in his beautiful tenor. "My father once heard Benjamino Gigli in person," he announced, ignoring the snickers that went around because the word "Gigli" sounded vaguely like a colloquial Finnish term for male genitalia. "He won a prize at a choral contest to attend a concert in London—or was it

Stockholm? Of course, I myself haven't heard any of the great tenors." Markus had never been away from the farm. He had never seen Karelia before, let alone Italy, but he spoke about Italy all the time. His ideas came exclusively from the songs he knew, especially a popular Christmas carol about a small migratory bird named Sylvia singing of the northland from her winter home.

"Yes, I'd like to spend the winter in Tuscany with Sylvia," Markus said one snowy evening. "I'd like to see those cypresses and olive trees, and sit on a hill looking upon Etna, drinking the finest wine of the land."

"You can't see Etna from Tuscany," said Jokinen.

"How would you know?"

"I just know. Etna is on an island somewhere."

"Find a map," said Paul.

They rummaged through every backpack and corner of the farmhouse.

"Damn. Only maps of Karelia."

"Ask the Lieutenant."

They phoned company headquarters.

"He's checking with the Captain," said Paul, hanging on to the receiver.

"And how would the Captain know?"

"All his Foreign Legion experience. Algeria, Morocco. They called him the Desert Scourge."

"What'd he do there, spread the clap?"

"Can't see Etna from North Africa, either," said Jokinen, picking an Oriental tune on his accordion. Markus' cousin, a pale soft-featured pig farmer, stood up and fished a cowbell from his pocket. He'd confiscated it from a barn and intended to send it home to his wife. Now he clicked the bell like a castanet, and undulated around the room in belly dancer style, shirttails tied high on his waist.

The door opened and the Lieutenant walked in. Every hand flew up in salute, and the cowbell rolled across the floor. For an instant he glared at them, having worked hard to establish a reputation for discipline, but then his eyes softened and he grinned.

"Glad to see my men are so passionate about geography. No, you can't see Etna from Tuscany." He winked at the belly dancer. "Nor from Cairo."

They poured him the last of their coffee and he fished a map of the Mediterranean from his inside pocket, and pointed out the location of Sicily. He also had a package that had arrived from the ladies of their home parish. As sergeant, Markus drew the honour of opening it. The men crowded around him, eyeing the cakes and cookies neatly wrapped inside. A card lay on top of the contents.

"Read the card," said the Lieutenant. "Everyone wants to hear news from home."

Markus hesitated, frowning at the words.

"What's wrong with you? Read the damn card," said Jokinen. "God, it's been a long time since I've looked a doughnut in the face."

The Lieutenant took the card. He read it to himself and looked up, his eyes a darker grey than usual. "The card says these confections are to be distributed to members of the Civil Guard only." He scanned the room. The men looked puzzled, some ashamed. At home, everyone knew who was a Guardsman and who was not, but here the distinction had been forgotten.

"That's bullshit," muttered Jokinen, himself a Guardsman.

"I agree," said the Lieutenant. "If all of you feel the same way, we'll hand these out to everyone." No one argued, and the package was divided equally among them.

"Thank you for your patriotism," said the Lieutenant. "I expected you'd react this way, and you did."

"Never thought of it that way, sir. It's nothing fancy. Just that we're all in this together," said Jokinen.

"Who said there was anything fancy about patriotism?" asked the Lieutenant.

There was no comment, and none was expected. He knew his men. Each of them sat upright, alone with his thoughts. The Lieutenant folded up his map and the letter, and put them back in his pocket.

"Good night, boys," he said, and walked out in his unobtrusive way.

Paul thought about it as he bit into his spice cake, a privilege not intended for him by the hands that had baked it. He remembered Berlin, the exhilaration of following his blue and white flag in the parade of athletes, hearing the anthem of his country. What he felt here was different. It flared up every time his shovel pierced the stony Karelian soil. It seeped up from the land, it blew in from the pines and birches. It stung in the wind from the river and carried the scents of the cities and towns. It kept them warm between the thin blankets, and burned in the baleful looks eastward and the glances at photos of those left behind in the places they remembered as home. You heard it in words muttered around the campfire that if camping out here in the bush could ensure the safety of the nation, then here they would stay, for as long as it took.

The canteen had a radio. The men crowded around it in the evenings, humming along to their favorite tunes. Its music was proof that the world they had left behind still existed, that orchestras still played somewhere.

"I found my little darling in Karelia,

So tiny, so dainty and so fair."

The radio also kept them in touch with the latest news. Cautious whispers arose that the Russians had backed down. Then fresh charges erupted from Moscow that the Finnish vermin were provoking war. Rumours sprang up daily, hourly. The most devoutly believed rumour was that America had given its word to Finland that it would not allow the Soviet Union to trample on the rights of a small democracy. It snowed again, and on the evening of November 25th a car drove up to company headquarters in a flurry of screeching tires. Paul saw the Captain he'd encountered outside the sauna emerge from the car and leap up the stairs, fur hat askew, shirttails flying. Evening vespers were cancelled and instead the company commander spoke to his men about an alleged incident at a border town called Mainila. The Russians accused the Finns of firing into their garrison and killing seven soldiers. The Finns produced evidence that the Russian claims were impossible. None of it had any effect on Moscow.

Then came the news that the Soviet Union had broken off diplomatic relations with Finland. All leaves were cancelled. Jokinen put down his accordion and glared at the radio. "Damn! When am I supposed to do my Christmas shopping?" His complaint evoked little reaction except for a few curled lips that would have passed for smiles any other evening. By now it was clear that this would be a highly irregular Christmas. All the promises muttered round the campfire, all the vows in the letters they had written, all of them would have to be kept.

5

During the last week of November, Tom had no difficulty punching out headlines that satisfied his editors. Privately he believed the border incident was just another squall in a long-simmering samovar, but it gave him an excuse to prolong his stay in Helsinki. The city was familiar to him now, and its modesty and silence pleased him. Also, he had found oases from the hotheads at the Kämp.

One of these was the Fennia, on a side street off the Esplanade, an establishment that by day was a busy café, by night a restaurant with a dance floor upstairs. Behind a façade of Art Deco posters, traces of nineteenth-century ambience lingered, particularly in the wide staircase that led upstairs, stopped halfway there at a landing with an ornate iron balustrade, then diverged in two directions, the left side leading to the tables, the right to the dance floor. Tom saw in the Fennia a microcosm of the life of the nation. It was all business as usual with a full menu, but on closer inspection he could see it was in a state of flux. Waiters and busboys seemed to vanish into the ceilings like the Cheshire cat from Alice in Wonderland. But this cat always reconstituted itself, as replacements stepped in for the missing staff. The music never stopped although the membership of the orchestra changed every night. In the middle of a set, the bassist received his card to report; the next evening the drummer was gone. The saxophone player left for the countryside.

Finally there came an evening when all that remained was a lone trumpet player. The sight of his gutted bandstand was too much for the proprietor, who sent in his headwaiter to improvise a foxtrot on the saxophone. Two patrons rose up from the tables and took up positions on percussion and bass. A melody emerged from the sax. Black and brooding, the grand piano sat in silence, its keyboard glowing under an indigo spotlight, its cushioned seat empty. Afterwards Tom could not remember getting up and sitting down at the piano, only the blue light shimmering over the keys. By then he was on his fifth or sixth scotch. He remembered the applause when he finished the piece, a gypsy melody that he picked up from the others and morphed into a jitterbug in E-minor. His fingers skittered over the keys with an ease that astounded him. This is one hell of a fine instrument, he thought. He was about to stumble back to his table when he noticed the patrons were standing and clapping and his impromptu fellow musicians were waiting for him to strike up the next number. He raised his hand. When he brought it down on the keyboard, he rolled off a series of arpeggios and segued straight into *I Get a Kick out of You*. The waitresses came up to him and wiped his brow with linen napkins, and set out tumblers of scotch for him along with plates of lox and devilled eggs.

When he returned to the Kämp, the lobby was deserted. A small group in the press room was hunched over a radio. He heard the date, November 29th, and something about a diplomatic breakdown. He made straight for the elevator, not about to let another tirade from Molotov spoil his mood.

In his room, he relived his adventure on the piano, running the tunes through his head, improvising codas and intermezzos. Then he spent a long time thinking about the jazz combo he'd belonged to in college. They called themselves the Glitterbugs and wore sequins on their lapels that fell off during the performance and littered the floor. There was a time when he thought they might be good enough to play the clubs in Toronto or Chicago, but that dream had died an early death along with many of his other dreams.

6

On November 30th, Tom woke up later than usual, groggy from a night of short naps interspersed with gulps of scotch. He looked out and saw the sun shining over Helsinki, promising a fine day. In no mood for breakfast, he bought a cigar at the stand in the hotel entrance and bounded outside. Only one dark puffball cloud marred the sky, moving in from the south. The city had largely returned to business as usual and the Esplanade bustled with people on their way to work. Tom turned toward the market square, where hot coffee was always on tap.

He heard the exploding bombs at about the same time as he heard the air raid sirens. Columns of smoke rose in the distance, and he could make out the rumble of engines. His first thought was that the Finnish air force was conducting drills over Helsinki and some lunatic had loaded real bombs. Squinting at the sky, he could now discern the dark outlines of planes inside the harmless looking cloud rolling in from the south. From Soviet air bases in Estonia, he thought, a sudden pain in his gut. This was no drill.

The drone of the planes grew louder and he looked for a bomb shelter. Fortunately, the Esplanade was dotted with them. At the nearest one he joined a queue of pedestrians converging at the entrance, moving with almost unnatural calm, some pausing to scan the sky as if inspecting a downpour. The planes, clearly visible now, trailed minuscule falling objects like chocolate drops. A policeman rushed up, haranguing the crowd in staccato Finnish to get inside the shelter. Tom descended the rickety stairs and leaned into the cold underground wall, pinned on both sides by women in woollen coats, their handbags clutched to chests. The thud of detonations continued as the bombers seemed to pass almost directly overhead. His armpits drenched with sweat, he cursed. Damned Russians! Sneaking bastards, attacking with no warning.

The sirens still wailed but the noise of the planes receded and vanished, and he climbed outside. He could learn nothing here, and his nerves would not allow him to stay. He ran across the Esplanade and back into the Kämp. Reporters, guests and staff darted about the main floor of the hotel with no apparent purpose, and for a mad instant he laughed, remembering the guppies he kept in a bowl in his bedroom as a child. Then he spotted Taylor in the hallway, pipe in hand, eyeing the telephones.

"Where have you been, old chap?" asked the Englishman.

"In a bomb shelter. What the hell is going on?"

"Stalin has apparently reopened negotiations."

"Another war of nerves, or something stronger?"

"Word has it that the Red Army invaded Finland at numerous points across the land borders this morning. And now these bombers. You really should have stayed in the shelter. They may be back."

"No declaration of war, no ultimatum, no notice of any kind?"

"All quaint echoes of a civilization that no longer exists."

There was a commotion at the cigar booth. A small girl ran in, crying and screaming "Mama! Mama!" The cigar vendor scooped up the girl and stroked her hair, but the child would not be comforted. She slid down to the floor, leaning against the wall and sobbing. "Dreadful mistake, letting the women and children return to the cities," said Taylor. He lunged for a vacant telephone, shouting back at Tom, "Press conference at the Foreign Office at noon. Meanwhile stay sharp. Watch the sky."

At the Foreign Office they squeezed into a crowd of reporters swarming a pair of attachés. The basic facts were cobbled together: the Soviet Union had that morning attacked Finland by land, sea and air. Further details were scarce. Tom stood helplessly, notebook in hand, pencil shaking, recording the names of cities and preliminary damage estimates. In Helsinki, the bombs had fallen mainly on the outskirts. Another press conference would be held later in the afternoon, said the nervous attachés, when more would be known.

Taylor suggested they walk toward the railroad station, which had been a target judging from the direction of the planes. The all-clear had sounded, and people in the streets resumed their activities, moving with the same calm Tom had noted earlier, with a determination bordering on ferocity, as if the slightest touch of panic would bring everything crashing down. Seeing nothing remarkable at the railroad station except queues of people with suitcases, bags, and children waiting for the first train out of town, they headed back to the Kämp. On the street they saw a newspaper boy on a bicycle, and motioned to him to bring a paper. The boy parked his bike and ran across to their side of the street. Suddenly the sirens screeched again, anti-aircraft guns opened fire somewhere above them, and the earth erupted with flying glass and dirt. Sprays of flame went up on all sides and a bus on the corner ignited, its screaming passengers trapped inside. "Incendiaries!" cried Taylor as they scrambled for cover. Tom buried himself in a recessed doorway and pulled the paperboy in beside him, diving for shelter from splinters, knowing they were doomed if the building took a direct hit.

The attack seemed interminable, beyond reckoning in seconds or minutes. His ears rang with the sirens and explosions and the distant cries of the injured. He could not bring himself to venture out and offer assistance to anyone. All he could do was recite the prayers of his childhood. He smelled urine and wondered if it was his or the boy's. At first he didn't notice that the explosions had faded away. When he did, he and the boy gingerly crawled out. Miraculously, the building still stood above them, but the air was thick with smoke and the stench of something worse, much worse. Through the haze he saw the bus, still aflame, with charred forms of human beings inside. His stomach churned and he vomited, the dregs of his coffee running green across the snow. He saw the boy inspecting a tangle of metal across the street, the remains of his bicycle. So small is the margin between life and death, he thought. A passing stranger's need for a newspaper.

Late in the evening he sat in the restaurant at the Kämp, trying to piece together what had happened. The planes had not come back; he had run from Foreign Office to the hotel to various other offices, and tramped through the smoking rubble out on the streets, until out of sheer exhaustion he decided to stay put at the hotel. The Kämp was in full siege regalia. Newspapermen sprang up from nowhere, some fitted out in ski suits, leggings, and flamboyant fur hats. They expropriated the smoking room for their typewriters and kept up a steady stream to the telephones. The few guests that remained were jostled as the correspondents ran from one conclave to the next in high excitement.

"Sure beats the Western front. Barely a thousand casualties there in all this time."

"A pox on the Phony War. This is more like it!"

"Passengers burned alive? Where?"

Their high spirits offended Tom. A Scandinavian reporter who had passed the burning bus chortled about it for hours. He couldn't believe his luck, a burning bus with people still in it—this would be the best scoop of his career, he swore.

Near midnight, the reporters started thinning out. "Most of them have hired cars to take them to a country villa for the night," said Taylor. "Rumour has it that the Russians are going to knock the hell out of Helsinki tonight. Your own legation has already left town. I'm sure you could get on board if you hurry."

"I'm not going anywhere. If the Russians can't aim straight in daylight, they won't do much damage in the dark." The Soviets had hit a Lutheran church and a Technical Institute, killing several professors and students. They'd also hit the Russian Legation. Bombing your own legation! he'd laughed to Taylor. Whose five-year plan dreamed that up? They had also demolished apartment buildings and the bus station. Women and children trying to leave the city had been killed by shrapnel. After dropping their bombs, the planes had come back and strafed civilians in the streets.

Several shadowy figures appeared in the deserted hallway. Tom recognized the silvery head of Björnström and behind him, a tall man in uniform striding toward a back exit. Taylor jumped out of his seat. "Mannerheim!" he cried.

"Forget it," said Tom. "The commander-in-chief wouldn't be hanging around here on the first night of his nation's war."

Björnström had seen them and meandered toward their table, across a floor littered with crumbs, linens, dishes, papers, and other remains that the harried hotel staff had been unable to clear away. He leaned into his cane and collapsed heavily into the leather chair beside Tom.

"You're still here," he whispered. "I thought all the correspondents had left town."

"So they've started bombing your flower beds," said the Englishman archly.

"Yes. I've been out walking, seeing what they have done to my city. There are many fires still burning. I was on my way home, but I had to rest."

"I wish I could tell you—" Tom began, fighting an impulse to hug the old man.

"So many dead. Here, and all over the country. And our boys at the front, are they holding tonight? Look at these—the Russians dropped them along with their bombs." Björnström fished a crumpled ball of leaflets from him pocket and tried to smooth them with unsteady fingers. "Listen to this: 'We come not as your conquerors but as your liberators.' And this: 'Don't starve. We have bread.' Bread! They offer us bread when we have mountains of surplus butter in our dairies!"

The old man gasped for breath and Tom offered him his scotch.

"Was that Marshal Mannerheim leaving just now?" asked Taylor.

"No. But the Marshal has been in town all day."

"What was he promised?"

"Promised?"

"From whom—" Taylor's voice was so brittle the old man flinched, "—do you have a commitment? England? France? Germany?"

"Your English friends would know that better than I," murmured Björnström, his eyes watering slightly, old eyes needing rest. "Germany? That's outlandish. It was Germany's deal with Stalin that created this situation. Always the same struggle for us. What can we do?" He paused rhetorically. "It reminds me of an English folk tale."

"If you're referring to Humpty Dumpty, remember that he couldn't be put back together again."

"No, it was about a man who was sentenced to death, but made a bargain with the king that if he could make the king's horse talk he would be spared. The king gave him a year to do it. The man's friends thought he'd gone mad. 'Horses can't talk,' they said. 'You'll die anyway.' The man said, 'Perhaps. But within a year, the king might die, or the horse might die—or the horse might talk.'"

Björnström pushed away the scotch. "That's all my country can do right now. Hope that the horse will talk."

In the ensuing silence, it seemed that the three of them had the hotel to themselves. Presently the old man rose, and bowed to them courteously. "I must continue my journey home. My daughter will be worried about me."

Tom kept his voice steady as he dragged on his Camel. "She's still here?"

"Yes, working at the Defense Ministry on Government Street. Not far from here, actually. A dangerous place to be. How can I argue? I can't bear to leave, either."

Though the old man protested that he feared neither darkness nor Russian bombers, they walked him home. The fires still burned, orange fountains in the night, fireworks of a macabre carnival. A strange shuffling noise scratched the silence, the sound of hundreds of pairs of feet, unseen walkers on their way out of the city. Some were lost children walking together, unaccompanied by adults. Once again Tom thought of the story about the birch tree and the North Star.

The next day, President Roosevelt of the United States of America issued a protest to the Soviet Union regarding the bombing of Finland. Molotov answered that there had been no bombing and there was no war. The Red Air Force, he said, had merely dropped loaves of bread to feed the starving Finnish proletariat. The Finns, desperate for a laugh, began referring to the Russian bombs as Molotov's breadbaskets.

A Winter War

1

Sleep was out of the question for the Björnströms on the first night of the war. "No Russian is going to chase me out of my home," said the professor, his Finnish obstinacy intact. Selma barricaded the doors and lined up anything in the apartment that could serve as a weapon. Then they did what they always did under duress—brewed strong coffee. And waited.

That first evening, Björnström went to the bookshelf and pulled out the Olympic tickets they had bought a few short weeks earlier. "In ancient Greece where the Olympics began," he said, "they suspended wars so the Games could go on. In our world, the Games are suspended so wars can go on."

She poured a cognac for him and tried to hide her tears.

"Thank you," he said, lifting the glass slowly, as if taking communion. "We need all the fortification we can get at a time like this. The Russians are raining incendiaries on our cities, invading our country all along the border. Thousands of Karelians are packing up in the middle of the night and setting out on foot. Put the tickets away, my dear. Never show them to me again." She wept for him, an old man adrift in memories of a civilization that was deserting him.

It would be several months before the Olympic Committee officially cancelled the Games of 1940, but they knew it that evening. And in the bleak candlelight they saw their nation plucked clean of the feathery nest of words—neutrality, League of Nations, world order—that had kept it warm. Out of the rubble the stark reality emerged that they were alone at war with the Soviet Union. Once having faced this, however, their collective will snapped to the task at hand. Shock turned to anger, and all the old Finnish divisions—working class and upper class, Swedish-speaker and Finnish-speaker, rural and urban—vanished overnight. For the first time in the history of the young republic, every heart beat as one heart. Keeping an eye out for help from the west, they looked for strength where they always looked, to themselves. For Tina the first days of the war fused into colours—the blackness of their solitude, the ice-white certainty that they would never give in, and the searing red rage that made warriors of them all.

2

Tina yearned to join the Lottas and work in the field, but her skills in English translation were more useful where she was, in her job on Government Street, typing and translating documents. It tormented her that there was nothing more she could do.

The Fennia was around the corner from her building, overlooking a courtyard off the Senate Square. She often took her coffee breaks there. With Paul she'd been a frequent visitor, enjoying its coffee and pink-iced French pastries, and then going upstairs to dance on its fine parquet floor. Now she sat at a corner table, staring at the courtyard where a few gaunt trees swayed in the wind from the harbour. A gust of wind blew her napkin off the table and she glared at the open doorway. A tall man stood halfway inside, trying to hold his hat on his head. It was Tom.

As he stood there the tension began in her chest. She was not prepared for this. She lifted the napkin up to her lips and turned away from him. Perhaps he wouldn't see her and would continue up the stairs. Perhaps she could just pull on her red hood, bend her head low and edge past him to the door. He took off his hat and as he stood by the window the slanting rays of the sun crossed his brow, outlining his mild blue eyes, and before she knew it she was standing, as straight and tall as a sunflower on a July morning.

He saw her and turned toward her table. She reeled in her brain and told herself calmly that this was stroke of luck; here was an American whom she knew personally, who could perhaps be helpful.

"What are you doing here?" she blurted.

"More to the point, what are you doing here? Why aren't you in the country?"

"Papa won't go and I won't leave him. And my work keeps me here. Anyway, the countryside isn't safe either. They bomb the railroads and the villages. Strafe passengers when they try to get off the trains. Is there no international law against that? Especially the incendiary bombs?"

"They forgot to send the International Law book to Moscow."

He rubbed his hands together and took a sip of the coffee the waiter set down for him. Despite the heavy topcoat he wore, he was shivering. As he took off the coat she noticed it had a yellow armband.

"What's that for?" she asked.

"Target practice for the Red bombers. Kill the reporters first." He offered her a cigarette and as he extended his arm she saw that his grey sweater hung loosely on his wide, angular shoulders. "Just trying to make you smile. It's press identification during air raids. Permission to stay above ground if we choose. To risk our necks for a story."

"It's not funny. You shouldn't be on the streets on clear days like this. The bombers could come back any time." Her voice broke and tears filled her eyes. "Mowing down civilians! What kind of state is capable of such atrocities?"

"A tyrannical state run by a madman. One of several kicking around the world today."

"So," she said, watching his face for the slightest hint of glee. "You got the story you were waiting for."

"Surely to God you don't believe this is what I was waiting for."

In truth she did not. His eyes didn't burn with excitement at the mention of the war like the eyes of other reporters she'd seen as they inspected the rubble. But she needed to hear him say it or she could not have said another word to him.

"How are things with you?" she asked. "I've heard that all the press services have been consolidated at your hotel."

"Yes, they put everything under one roof. We never have to leave if we don't want to."

"Which is why I'm surprised to see you here." Is it for me you came? she thought, and then felt ashamed for thinking it. She noticed that his dark hair had a few grey strands at the temples, fine-boned straight temples that framed his brow.

"I get fed up with the bedlam there. Reporters aren't known for their manners. Of course your military command isn't helping much. All we get is a brief communiqué in the evening. So the reporters drown their sorrows in the usual way."

"Yes, I remember the scotch." She kept her voice steady although the mention of the communiqués set heart pounding. She typed out military communiqués every day.

"Come and see the Kämp for yourself," he said. "Have dinner with me tonight. The food is still decent." He tapped his cigarette on the ashtray and his long fingers kept up a minute march on the tablecloth as he gazed at her.

She paused, her red angora hood in hand. "I've seen the Kämp. Many times."

"Never as it is today. It's something you can tell your grandchildren about."

She hesitated for a moment, then went to a telephone and put through a call to Selma saying she would be late. In fact, she had no intention of going home until she had seen his communiqués for herself.

The Kämp was a battlefield all its own. Correspondents jostled each other looking for Press Bureau representatives to corner for information, bellhops wove in and out calling out names of journalists. Telephone bells tinkled constantly and newspapermen streamed through the swinging doors, toting typewriters like gunslingers, shouting greetings to colleagues last seen in Spain or Poland. The hotel staff were taxed to the limit but somehow succeeded in meeting everyone's needs, although the telephones were in constant turmoil. Meal service had slowed to a crawl, but few complained. Tom found an alcove near a window where the black velvet drapes gave off the odour of perfume and stale cigars. He ordered up a schnitzel and a Riesling and before Tina had removed her hood, her glass was full. The Riesling took her back to the Andalusia, to the champagne bubbles bursting as they rose to the rim of the crystal goblets, just as the world had drifted and shattered in the years since that day in Berlin.

"The West cannot let us down," she said. Wine always made her emotional and she was emotional to begin with that evening. She wanted to steady her fingers on his arm, to weep on his shoulder. "We're the last outpost of Western culture in this corner of the world."

"That's the feeling I had on the ferry coming here. Nearing the edge."

"We've created a perfectly good democracy. We won't allow anyone to take that away from us. I can quote Shakespeare and Stendhal, I know the lyrics to *Tosca,* I know Beethoven's symphonies. I've read the Gettysburg Address and I know what Ahab said to Starbuck." She buried her face in her hands and sobbed for a moment.

"That's the Cause, then," he said.

"Cause?"

"Just a line from our own history. A way of life worth dying for."

Dinner arrived and as they ate she noticed that he shifted his fork from his right hand to his left in the European manner, and knew his way around a place setting with the best of them.

Later they squeezed into the Press Room, formerly the Kämp smoking room and favoured haunt of Sibelius and other luminaries, now the scene of a nightly fiasco over telephones. Tom confided that his agency regularly lost out in the race to the phones, due to others having been quicker off the mark to make arrangements with the Kämp operators and with colleagues in other cities.

"If your military command was a little more outgoing we wouldn't have this fire drill every evening. This communiqué is the only information we get and it's short on details and long on secrecy. That's why you have this frenzy, like buzzards converging on a dead rabbit." Her eyes widened. "Sorry. Didn't mean to sound so crude."

"It's all right," she said. It wasn't his language that unnerved her, but her growing certainty that the documents he was talking about were the same ones she translated and typed every day. In the afternoon they arrived from General Headquarters, a summary of the previous day's military events. They were then translated into several foreign languages and distributed to the foreign press at nine o'clock at the Kämp. Her mind raced as she tried to think of a way to link these documents and Tom Henderson to herself and the advantage of her country. She barely noticed the melée around her when the clock struck nine. Captain Zilliacus, chief liaison officer with the foreign press, walked into the room, wearing his affable smile. The noise stopped and he began to read out the words she had typed out six hours earlier at her office. As she listened, her plan was taking shape. The communiqués were not secret documents, after all. They were meant precisely for press distribution. She would just distribute them a little early to Tom Henderson. He would have them on the wires hours before his competitors did. He was an American and getting help from America was one of her nation's top priorities. It made perfect sense.

He jotted down his notes and then offered to walk her home, saying he wouldn't get to the phones for at least an hour. She laughed at his protestations that she should not be on the streets alone.

"The only danger in Helsinki now is from bombs, and they never come at night. All the derelicts and drunks are in the army. Don't worry about me."

"But I insist. I really do."

"Well, come for the walk if you like, but not for the sake of protecting me."

"I want to hear what Ahab said to Starbuck."

"You must know all that."

"I've forgotten."

He helped her with her coat and walked with her to Elisabeth Street. At the doorstep she whispered good-bye and told him to be at the Fennia at three o'clock the next afternoon. She was trembling from the cold and also because she knew she had crossed a personal little Rubicon. All her father's old lessons about the paving stones of destiny came back to her.

You lay them down one by one and make up your destiny as you go along. You can change direction but you can't see the end.

They worked out a simple system. Tina took a coffee break at the Fennia every afternoon. After she typed the communiqué, she folded an extra carbon copy into her handbag and dashed to the café, where Tom was waiting at the corner table. As she drank her coffee she wrote out a translation for him by hand. It wasn't difficult, because the communiqués were brief during the early days of the war. She helped him locate the places on his map, names that would soon be very familiar: Taipale, Summa, Kollaa.

She never felt guilty about what she was doing. The communiqués were meant to be broadcast to the world and she was simply giving an advantage to someone she wanted to assist. She dismissed the rush of pleasure when she caught sight of Tom in the café as girlish silliness. After all, her fiancé—though Paul had not proposed, she thought of them as being engaged—was out there somewhere in the battle zone where the nation's fate was being decided. The communiqués made her relationship with Tom professional, not personal, she told herself, even as in her mind she could hear Selma's voice saying, "Just whom do you think you're fooling, young lady? And why?" She could have answered Selma's first question: Probably no one, least of all herself. The second puzzled her. She hadn't stopped loving Paul. Then why couldn't she get Tom out of her mind?

Tom understood the significance of her offer, too, and along with elation it brought him unease. This was emotional territory where he rarely ventured. He shared his bounty with a colleague from a major American daily, who at first was dubious about sending out a translation done by some typist that Henderson had befriended. But when the translations proved accurate, he gladly took them and they got their stories out to London and New York a good five hours ahead of everyone else. It worked beautifully, and no one could deduce how they were doing it. In different circumstances, he would have been overjoyed to scoop the competition every day, but in the present situation he felt little joy about anything professional. It had become too personal.

3

On December 6th, a reception for foreign correspondents was held at the Kämp, officially to mark Finnish Independence Day but also to show the world that the government was still in place. On the second day of the war, Stalin had installed a puppet government headed by a Finnish Communist exile in a border town, and declared it to be the only legitimate Finnish government. During the first chaotic days, some foreign reporters accepted this and even reported that the "old" Finnish government had fled the country. In truth, it had convened in emergency session in Helsinki on the first evening and then moved to a secret location. Several key members were on hand to meet the press at the Kämp.

Tom didn't look forward to the reception. His scooping of the communiqués had kicked up a duststorm of resentment among his colleagues and he disliked confrontations. He strode into the room, and instantly drew a small crowd.

"Well, well, here's Hot Shot Henderson," snapped Cranston, one of his American rivals. "So what's the latest from your crack sources?"

"Lay off, Cranston. Whoever told you this business was a cricket match was wrong."

"You won't get away with it for long, you bastard."

"It doesn't matter in any case," said a British reporter. "The hammer and sickle will be flying over Helsinki any day now."

"What exactly is happening?" This was an American reporter whom Tom had met in Spain, known for her provocative dresses and affairs with celebrities.

"There are two wars going on," said Cranston. He placed a slice of rye bread on his palm and covered its bottom half with mustard. "This is the Karelian Isthmus. That's one war. Conventional trench warfare along what they call the Mannerheim Line. Up here, north of Lake Ladoga," he plunked down an olive to represent the lake, and stretched a vertical line of mustard to the top of the slice, "is the second war. Wilderness, bogs, forest. That's where the mobile Finnish ski troops have the edge. The Russians will be tied down to the roads and there aren't many. I have my sources, too, Henderson."

"They're hitting the Isthmus hard, naturally," said the Brit.

"Yes. The Finns expected that, but not the scale of the attack in the north. So they've already had to commit nearly all their reserves. The bull pen is empty."

"Looks like lights out for Finland, then."

"Have you seen any sign of a blitzkrieg?" asked Tom. "I haven't. The Finns have a plan, too. Delay, retreat, delay, then take their stand at the Mannerheim Line."

"The Mannerheim Line? Does it exist? Wasn't it invented by a French reporter dreaming of the Maginot Line?" Laughter rippled through the group.

"How can you write the obituary while the patient is alive? Maybe the Finns can hold out until help arrives."

"Help? The Scandinavian neutrals are paralyzed, the Germans have a deal with Stalin, the Allies are too far away, and Uncle Sam is staying out of it. So who's going to help them, Henderson?"

He couldn't think of an answer.

"It had the makings of a good David and Goliath story," drawled Cranston, stuffing another rye sandwich into his mouth. A speck of mustard from his earlier artistry dotted his lapel. "But this David is done for. The Russians are driving across the Isthmus as we speak."

Tom stalked away. He hated their arrogance. Even worse was the fear that they might be right.

4

Aunt Gunilla was missing. Björnström had rung the yellow mansion repeatedly and received no answer. Aware that the Russians had bombed Kotka heavily, they feared the worst. Only Tina's intransigence prevented him from catching the first train east. I will go, she told him, and Selma hid his spectacles and wallet for insurance.

After handing Tom the communiqué in the afternoon, Tina informed him he'd have to manage the next day or two without her help. She would be out of town.

"May I go with you?" he asked. "You shouldn't travel alone."

"Alone? Right now, no one is ever alone in this country. And why would you want to come? Your news is here."

"A new angle never hurts. And you need someone to watch over you. They bomb and strafe the trains and roads. You told me so yourself."

She studied him for a moment. She could hardly argue about the danger. "Come if you like. We won't be in the war zone itself. Make sure you bring warm clothes—I mean really warm. Do you know what it's like to be outdoors at twenty below?"

"As a matter of fact I do," he said. "I've cleared a path through a prairie field in January. Someday I'll tell you about it."

The next morning they boarded a drafty bus going east. The highway was a snake of a road between overhanging pine and spruce stands, now icy and treacherous. Somehow the bus arrived at its destination nearly on schedule, in the early afternoon. It snowed most of the way, lessening the danger of bombers overhead. In Kotka they found the yellow house locked, but showing no damage. However, as they walked toward the city centre, the streetscape deteriorated into piles of debris, with random gaps among the intact buildings.

"The millinery! The café, the hardware store!" Tina stopped in her tracks in front of a row of freestanding chimneys surrounded by charred rubble and black snow. She picked up a hat with feather still in place, a kettle, a child's knit cap. "Barbarians! And they say they aim only at military targets."

They wandered through the pockmarked streets and near the market square they encountered a maid who did cleaning for Gunilla. "Madam has left the city," said the maid. "She's working at the evacuee centre east of here. They're so overloaded, all those poor Karelians still walking out of the war zone, it's a disaster. You can find her there."

They arrived at the evacuee centre a few hours later. During peacetime, the little town was known for its lindens and for a patrician veneer bestowed by the cavalry regiment stationed there. Here, as everywhere, all veneers had been peeled away by raw danger and the evacuees from the Karelian borderlands who spilled into the town and wandered about like pilgrims in search of a shrine.

The Lotta Svärd women's auxiliary had converted several buildings into indoor campgrounds. They manned the doors, doling out bread and cheese, coffee and milk, coaxing smiles from tired eyes. Gunilla was in the kitchen beside a cauldron of soup, stirring and mixing. The grande dame Tina knew was gone and in her place was a woman she had never dreamed existed, wiping sweat from a face bare of cosmetics, wisps of white hair dangling out of a hairnet.

"Tina! So glad you're here," she said. "Would you help me with the soup?"

"Why, of course," said Tina, picking up a ladle. Tom stood and watched until a passing Lotta nearly knocked him over with a platter of bread.

He wandered outside. When the regular soup Lotta returned Tina went in search of him and saw him at the train platform, where evacuees and their possessions were being unloaded from boxcars. He carried an armful of boxes, and in his wool hat and boots he looked like any other helper.

"Sorry," she said, catching up to him. "Things were just so hectic in there I couldn't leave. Are you cold?"

"Cold? I'm sweating. These belong to a woman whose belongings got soaked on the train. But now I've lost her. I wish I could understand what they're telling me. They must think I'm the village idiot."

"It doesn't matter, as long as the train is unloaded in a hurry. They say the situation is worse on the road. Things are completely jammed up."

They cut across the railyards toward the highway. The road was at a standstill and yet it moved, as if the earth itself were shifting westward. The refugees willed themselves forward, leading cattle and horses, pulling or pushing wagons and carts. They came dragging sleds and carrying hens and dogs and infants. They spoke quietly as they waited to file into the shelters, leaving wagons at the roadside. Cows wandered aimlessly, separated from their owners. They tried to keep the panicky animals on the road, but they slid into the ditches and writhed and bellowed in pain as their udders and hooves froze and stuck fast to the snow. Many of them died there.

"We have to get these people to leave their wagons for the night and go into the school," said Tina. "They'll freeze out here. It's going down to minus twenty-five."

She approached an old man who was leaning on his cart. A table covered the floor of the cart, its four wooden legs pointing upwards, making the cart look like a four-poster bed on wheels. Guarding it sat a small, grim-faced boy, feet dangling over the edge. The old man began to speak, his voice deferential but insistent.

"He's looking for his wife and daughter," said Tina. "They got separated on the road. His belongings are here on the cart. His family has eaten at this table for fifty years. He wants me to promise it will get to where they're going—." She choked up.

Tom reached up to help the boy down from the cart. Reluctantly, defiantly, the boy swung down. Tina bent to steady him and took his wrist in her hand.

"Oh!" She cried in sudden pain. Blood spurted from her finger and she sucked at it and inspected the boy's threadbare sleeve. There was a sharp object inside. The boy muttered something and put it in his pocket, but would not surrender it. Grandfather and grandson slowly walked toward the schoolhouse door.

"What did the kid have in his hand?" asked Tom.

"A gramophone needle. They'd just bought a new gramophone and they couldn't bring it along. So he broke off the needle. So the Russians couldn't play records on it. So the Russians couldn't—"

She tried to stop her hands from shaking. Night was falling. From a cart drifted the strains of an accordion. A box of black bread materialized that they broke in pieces like chocolate and passed from hand to hand. She lost track of Tom and when she found him again, he was staring at a small girl in felt boots and red tailored coat. She could have been no more than three years old, and she was sitting half covered by the snow in the roadside ditch, weeping. Tina watched him for a moment. He took one step toward the child, another step back. He crouched down, studying her from different angles, and slowly began to creep toward her.

"Carry her to the school," she said, pushing her way to his side. "Someone's probably frantic with worry about her."

He still held back. "What if I drop her?" he whispered. "Or hurt her arms or legs?" She understood then. He had never held a child in his arms before. "You won't."

He picked her up gently and she screamed in terror. He tucked her inside his jacket and tightened his grip, gave her bread, and crooned an improvised lullaby. He was so intent on shielding her from the jostling carts that he didn't notice when her crying stopped and she clutched his neck. By the time he reached the school she was sound asleep and they had to pry her from his grip, finger by finger. He paced back and forth and debated aloud whether he should keep her and take her with him to Helsinki, maybe to Chicago, but Gunilla wrapped her in a blanket and he calmed down.

They walked out of the school and he lit up a cigarette. A sickly moon appeared, tangled in a web of white clouds. Good, she thought, the planes won't come tonight. He stared at the southeast horizon, which glowed intermittently orange in the black night.

"Don't worry," she said. "It's not the Russian artillery. They're nowhere near here."

"Then what is it?"

"People's homes and farms. They burn them. So the enemy will have no comfort. Listen, a train leaves for Helsinki in a few minutes. You go. I'll stay here a while longer."

"No, you're coming with me. You need sleep."

He steered her toward the station and she had no energy to argue. The train was full, puffing its imminent departure. Refugees and their luggage crammed the seats and aisles, and here and there a wounded soldier in uniform. Someone made room for Tina on a seat and she dozed.

She awoke when the train lurched to a halt. Thin rays of light filtered through the curtained windows and she could hear the drone of oncoming planes. The passengers rushed for the doors and scrambled out. They waded through ankle-deep snow toward the shelter of the trees. Tina could not see where the bombs were landing but explosions shook the earth and then the chatter of machine guns strafing the tracks and the woods. Tom dragged her to a large boulder under sturdy pines and pushed her down into the snow. He buried her head inside his jacket and tried to cover her body with his own.

Eventually soldiers came and herded them out of the woods. The track had been damaged but would soon be repaired, they said. The train was serviceable. They stood up, every joint numb, and walked around, trying to keep warm. Snow was falling. As the benign white sky enclosed them Tom held her close and she did not resist.

5

When Tom arrived at the Kämp, Taylor was waiting for him with the news that while he'd been out of town, Mitch Webster had arrived.

"The famous war reporter."

"Head of the European Bureau of UP. Anyway, old chap, your wings have been clipped. Webster organized a petition, and now the authorities have decreed that the communiqués may not leave the country before nine o'clock in any form or under any circumstances."

"Fucking arrogant bastard." Tom was furious, although he knew the scheme could not have gone on much longer in any case. The other reporters were getting too steamed about it. And it was not so much the loss of his scoops that infuriated him, he realized; it was the prospect of not seeing Tina any more.

"Never mind. It was a fine ride while it lasted. I tip my hat to you."

"That monstrous raccoon job? Don't bother, Taylor. But it's nice that you're talking to me again." The old banter between them still amused him. He'd missed it. "I'd still be scooping all of you if Webster hadn't shown up. Some clout he has."

"He led the charge, but we all supported him. He just has the knack of getting things done. Quite a decent chap, really, one of the finest of our kind. Ever met him?"

"No. I expect he'll come around to crow over his victory."

"No, that's not like him. He's all business. Not like some of the other toffs here."

They had just checked their messages when Taylor stopped to talk to a balding man with a thin moustache and joyless brown eyes.

"Do come here, Henderson. Meet your nemesis, Mitch Webster."

After an awkward moment, Webster extended his hand. Tom, for his part, was more interested in meeting the legendary newsman than in harbouring grudges. Webster had covered every war and conflagration on the globe for the last twenty years.

"Will you be staying at the Kämp?" Taylor was asking.

"Not for long," answered Webster. "I'm going to the front. The communiqués say next to nothing."

"Marshal Mannerheim is not a fan of the press," said Taylor.

"Nor should he be. His tiny army couldn't withstand leaks of classified information. But I have to get out of this madhouse. You can't cover a war from behind black velvet curtains." Webster went on his way, a man on a mission.

6

There was a birch tree in the small park just off Elisabeth Street that Tina had loved since she was old enough to walk there. When she was small she would run to its shade on summer afternoons and lean against its scrollpaper white bark. Its slender sweet leaves knew all her secrets. She watched it grow and bend, watched the trunk turn spindly, then strong again, watched the branches make their way upwards. The winter her mother died, the tree seemed to wither, though that was likely her imagination. Then it grew sturdy again.

Daylight was fading fast as she walked home from work the day after the trip to the evacuee centre, and dark clouds promised more snow. Tom was waiting for her at the corner of Elisabeth Street to tell her that the arrangement with the communiqués was over. By then he was quite philosophical about it. They walked to the park and sat on the bench by the birch tree. Her feet were set in ice and she couldn't feel her toes but she wanted to rest by the tree. "Trees have lives like humans do," she said. "One bad year, a dry spring or a season of trouble can twist a tree permanently as it can twist a life. See that linden? I'd like to ask it what happened to make its branches lean eastward? Or that oak—what left it with that crook in its trunk? Or that poor spruce with the ragged branches—so many gaps, yet it did the best it could, do you see how high it grew despite the bare patches?"

She walked over to the birch and inspected its white bark. "Trees all look fine and leafy in the summer. You only see the real tree in winter. Then you can see when the hard years were, when the wind was too cold or the soil poor. Or the rain failed."

She didn't think her words were particularly enchanting, but he stood beside her and gazed at the tree as if it were the first one he'd ever seen, the first ever created in Eden, even in this unlikely Eden of ruins and blackened snow. There was an ugly cavity where a bomb shelter cut across the park, right beside her tree, and as she looked at it the panic returned, the panic of their mad dash for cover from the train. She leaned into his shoulder.

"There are no violet patches here," she said. "But we know our trees."

She could feel him shivering, which was not unusual for that winter, but his eyes glowed as though he had a fever, and they were fixed on her. There was a suspended moment, the kind when you can't bear to close the door at the end of a visit.

"Would you mind if I still came to the Fennia now and then?" he finally asked.

"Not at all. There'll be things I can still help you with. Deciphering maps, that sort of thing."

He leaned to kiss her cheek and she turned her face toward him. His lips brushed hers softly, and they whispered good-night. There goes another Rubicon, she thought.

After that, every day she watched for him to appear in the doorway at the Fennia. When he did, she felt a bliss that erased her sorrows, a tide of endorphins she felt in every cell of her body. He's here. He's here, and nothing else matters. As he walked toward her, the tableau around her sprang to life in colours, scents and sounds she'd failed to notice before, all wonderful. The gloom she'd felt seconds earlier; the casualty lists, her fears for Paul, the bandaged heads of soldiers at the station, Selma's prayers, all dissipated in a happiness that moved her straight toward him so she could hear his voice, look into his eyes, touch his hand. She felt a bliss so powerful she was ashamed of it, for this was no time to be happy. But every time she saw him or thought of him it seized her again, and after she left him she went dancing home on the icy streets, dancing around the dim flat, slow dancing under the quilt in her bed.

7

December 16, 1939

Taipale

Dear Tina,

I am in the dugout, tending the fire. It's two o'clock in the morning, the others are asleep. It's warm in here, almost too warm, except when someone opens the door. The men snore and grunt; the air is not what you would call fragrant. Take the 'normal' odours of men in close quarters, and add piles of sweaty clothing, snow-soaked boots and socks and foot-rags, and leftover food stuck here and there. On the upper wooden planks it's so hot they sleep in their undershirts; down below they freeze their feet. In their sleep they shift arms and legs and roll over each other. They scratch their heads and private parts, even in their dreams battling the lice and fleas that appeared soon after we moved into the line. Nobody knows where they came from because we were all clean when we got here, but that's life in the dugout. You sleep, eat and breathe as one, and if the roof takes a hit you die the same way. Shadows from the swinging oil lamp float over the men's bodies. It's almost cozy. Always coffee on the stove.

You have to learn fast out here. Things like the noises of shells and grenades. Which ones will go left or right, when to duck and when to keep going. Otherwise you're shipped out quick on one of the sleds they use to transport supplies forward and bodies to the rear. Or in a wooden box marked "Do not open." I bumped against one of those once, and it clattered inside. Everything freezes quickly here. During our first week the weather turned frigid and the temperature just keeps diving— minus twenty, minus thirty degrees.

So much has happened. My baptism of fire, for one thing. It was the night the Russians crossed the river, December 6, Independence Day. We'd been holding them off all day, but in the evening they got a foothold on Cape Hook. At four a.m. we began to stumble forward across a pitch-black field. All I remember is burning haylofts, machine guns blazing, being pinned under a stone fence. The Russians are still on Cape Hook, digging toward our positions. Even when they don't attack, the artillery fire gets you splinter by splinter, arm by arm, shattered gut by shattered gut. Every day someone catches it. We had a few "quiet" days watching the Russian fires in the woods; they don't give a damn about camouflage because they know we don't have the guns or shells to harass them. They live over there like in a boy scout camp. But let them see a feather of smoke on our side and we get a blast faster than you can say Molotov.

Then yesterday morning they really came at us. Guns, infantry, and for the first time, tanks. That's when I saw it clearly—that they were aiming at ME. That shook the cobwebs out of my brain about the Fifth Commandment, or whichever one it is that says Thou Shalt Not Kill. Try telling that to yourself at the bottom of a trench under artillery fire. I burrowed into the frozen wall, the earth jumping, grenades and shells flying along with clumps of earth, tree shards; my sense of balance gone and the ground swaying. The barrage lasted for three hours, and our own guns were absolutely silent. We knew that due to shortages our artillery had orders to shoot only at the juiciest, most efficient targets. But we couldn't understand their not replying at all. We understood soon enough. They waited until the Russian barrage lifted and their infantry massed in Cape Hook field. We saw them coming, following their tanks, plodding straight on. When the core of their formation reached a certain point, our guns opened up. They went down like stick men, milling around, stumbling over their dead, while our guns methodically cut them down. Some made it back to their woods, a few kept coming behind the tanks. We shot every browncoat that made it into shooting range, but their tanks rolled right through our positions. That scared the hell out of us. None of us had ever seen a tank before. After dark our tank killers crept out with their explosive bottles. They're devilishly effective. Some wag christened them "Molotov cocktails" in honour of the guy producing this show, together with Uncle Joe.

Today they came at us again. None of their infantry got past our barbed wire. Some lay sprawled on the wire like bugs caught in a mesh. At dusk the fields rippled with dark piles of Russian dead. I have to confess that I felt joy seeing them go down. At the time, that is. Now, away from that hysteria, the memory of those piles never leaves my mind. I often wonder how the Russians get through all this. We at least know why we're here. What does a Russian know? You're shipped to an unknown wilderness, handed a gun, told to plow across a snowy field, and then halfway across the field you die. I hate those brown piles out there.

When we moved up into the line our platoon leader just looked each of us in the eye and said, "The Russians are over there. Keep them out." Every man has taken his own private vow: they will only pass over my dead body.

My best friend here is Markus, the opera nut I told you about. He's not a nut at all, just a little different from most of these farmers. You'd get a big kick out of him. He knows damn near as much about music as you do, and his constant chatter about Italy is music to our ears. When he flops into the dugout and looks around at the dirty snowsuits and boots, he says, "One thing is for sure, fellows, next year I'm spending winter with Sylvia in Tuscany." *Next winter in Italy* is our platoon motto now.

Coming back from patrol one night Markus and I thought we saw a trumpeter swan out near the lakeshore. "There's our ride south!" Markus cried, so loud I had to shush him up. The Russians shoot at any noise. But I think the swan was a mirage. Out here you see all kind of things. What else should I tell you? That you are always in my thoughts? That I love you? But you know all that. Take care of yourself, and your father and Selma, too. And write soon.

Your Paul.

The Swan of Tuonela

1

Tom pushed away his drink and slouched into the green leather chair. "What's happening to me, Taylor? Even the scotch tastes bad, and this is the finest in Europe."

"Don't blame the whiskey. It's you. You're still miffed because of the communiqué clampdown." Taylor cut into a roasted potato and speared a meatball with his fork

"No. I don't give a damn about that any more. Although you'd think those hyenas would be tired of picking at my carcass by now."

Tom now spent the evenings waiting for the communiqués at the Kämp with the other reporters. A small but noisy clique continued to harass him about his defeat at the hands of the press bureaucrats. They were starting again in the next booth, tossing barbs his way.

"I'm going out for some fresh air," he said and stood up.

"Fresh air? What air? It's frozen solid out there. There's a foot of snow and it's minus twenty. But suit yourself."

Tom put on his coat and stepped out into a glacial blast of wind from the harbour. The Esplanade offered some protection from the elements if you didn't mind stumbling into a bomb shelter on every corner.

There was a brittle clear moon and in the semi-darkness the park looked like an elongated graveyard, with plots standing ready to receive their occupants. He turned up the side street toward the Fennia. Tina was already there, at their usual table, staring at a letter she'd just received from Paul. It confirmed her suspicion that he was at Taipale, where the Russians had struck first on the Isthmus. The censors had not deleted the word "Taipale", an understandable oversight by an overloaded army postal service.

"Listen to this," she said, shuddering though the café was warm. "Paul says they saw a trumpeter swan on the river. It's unheard of for a swan to still be here in December."

"A laggard. Or injured. Or both."

"The swan of Tuonela," she whispered.

"Swan of what?"

"In our mythology, Tuonela is the land of the dead. A river separates it from the land of the living and the river is patrolled by a swan."

"Hey," he touched her chin gently. "This is no time for mythologizing. Reality is frightening enough. Besides, maybe it wasn't even a swan. Or maybe they actually saw it in October. Who knows?"

She managed a half-smile and put the letter away. He would have liked to stay and comfort her longer, but he had return to the Kämp for the communiqué. Still, he insisted on walking her back to Elisabeth Street. The moon shed little light and they stumbled on the cobblestones. He took her by the waist to steady her. The walk was a silent one for the most part and that pleased him. A bond was there that required no small talk.

Back at the hotel, he hung up his coat and found Taylor in the lounge. From somewhere at the back came the jingle of a foxtrot and the swish of dancing. Public dancing had been banned when the war began, judged too frivolous an activity in light of the grave circumstances confronting the nation. He'd noticed clandestine dancing before at the Kämp, among the foreign correspondents and their hangers-on, but it had never vexed him as it did now. He ordered a double scotch.

"You know what we are, Taylor? We're leeches. Leeches feeding on the suffering of others."

"Don't get involved too deeply in what's going on here. A newspaper-man can't get caught up in what he's covering. It impedes your ability to observe, and even your credentials as a neutral."

"What makes you think—"

"You never were a good dissembler. I suppose in America that's considered a virtue, you don't like our oblique European ways, you like presidents who cannot tell lies."

"I'm just trying to do my job, Taylor. You know how difficult it is to get a handle on this war."

"You're not yourself. No barmaids, no chorus girls. You've never let a pair of blue eyes throw you off your feed like this before. And isn't it rather bad form, with the fiancé being at the front and all?"

"I don't know what you're talking about. All I know is that around here you have to use every angle you have. We'll see who gets a trip to the front first. Webster's working on it and he has his prestige going for him, but I have a few things going for me too."

That would fend off Taylor for a while, he thought. As for the other thing, he knew it was bad form but he couldn't help it, despite his liking for Paul. The heart wants what it wants, said the poet. He'd forgotten how that felt. Or perhaps he'd never really known.

2

Tom's words proved prophetic when a few days later he was assigned to one of the first tours for correspondents to the Isthmus. Why he'd received the invitation was not clear; he'd certainly never asked Tina or her father to intervene on his behalf. He did know that in the general scheme of things, American correspondents ranked first in Finnish eyes, because of the tide of public sympathy in the United States for Finland and the hopes pinned on that sympathy. This attitude did not sit well with the Brits. Taylor would have to wait for the next bus, literally.

He spent the night in Viipuri, the capital of Karelia, a medieval Hanseatic city whose castle had guarded the borderland for seven hundred years. It was now an icy ghost town, the general headquarters for the Army of the Isthmus. As the bus left Viipuri and a pallid morning rose out of the east, the approaching presence of war began to twist his gut, the amalgam of fear and exhilaration he remembered from Warsaw and Madrid. Only this landscape was pristine white, and he wondered what war in a Christmas card would be like. The charm crumbled when they came over a hill and saw the southeast horizon shrouded in smoke, dotted with cumulus-like black bursts. White-painted trucks and ambulances passed them in either direction, and supply wagons plowed along pulled by horses draped in white sheets. The wagons tottered on the icy road, some laden with explosives, some with wooden coffins.

They disembarked at a small hamlet behind the Summa sector, in rolling wooded hills. The Russians had been pounding Summa heavily for days. New snow lay deep but didn't obliterate the signs of battle— shredded and blackened trees, churned earth where long-range artillery shells had burst. A ruddy-cheeked young officer came forward and introduced himself as Lieutenant Laine, their guide. They were given white hooded capes and someone joked about the Ku Klux Klan, but the value of the capes became clear as soon as they waded into the woods. One blink and the man ahead of you was invisible.

There was a powder burst of snow and something swooped by, leaving only feathery tracks in its wake. It took a moment to realize it was a platoon of soldiers on skis. All you could see of them were the dark rifles slung on their backs. The reporters strained to count them, but they disappeared as silently as white ghosts.

"Just one of our patrols," said Laine. "We're rounding up Russian prisoners. You may interview them for yourselves."

The woods opened to a clearing where a flock of men in brown greatcoats shuffled from foot to foot, guarded by Finnish soldiers. The newsmen were assigned interpreters, and approached groups of prisoners with notepads and pencils in hand. Tom noted the high felt boots, and caps with huge earflaps. Some had gloves, but none wore the mittens with movable trigger fingers the Finns used that allowed you to shoot quickly without freezing your hands.

"This one says he has never eaten such wonderful food in all his life as here," said the interpreter, speaking for a Russian whose collar bore a star. "He is honoured to be taken prisoner by such a great nation."

"Forget him, he's full of shit," said a reporter from New York. "Try the next one. Ask him why they're invading a neighbouring country."

"He says—" the interpreter stopped, blinked, and listened to the prisoner again. "He says they are not in a foreign country. They are somewhere in northern Russia. On a mission to liberate the Finnish people."

After a series of similar conversations, interest in the prisoners flagged. The correspondents began to wander off, scanning the eastern sky where the horizon glowed red and artillery had rumbled all afternoon. A delegation marched up to Laine.

"It's been swell meeting the Red Army," said the New Yorker, "but now show us the damn war."

"It is not possible to go any further today," said Laine. "The artillery fire is too heavy. We cannot guarantee your safety."

The reporters closed in on Laine with barks of indignation. Not an eyebrow moved on his face as he heard them out, then wedged his way out of their circle.

"I am sorry," he said, "but all I can do is invite you to the Lotta canteen to warm up and enjoy some coffee."

"Canteen? You must be hallucinating."

"Oh, it's there all right," said Laine. "Follow me. This might turn into a real blizzard yet!" He inspected the sky and smiled. The snowflakes were thickening.

"We'll put in a complaint," said the New Yorker. "To your superior."

"Take it to Marski himself," said Laine placidly, referring to Marshal Mannerheim by his nickname among the troops. The grumbling continued but the reporters fell in behind Laine. They knew what Mannerheim had said in response to foreign correspondents demanding visits to the front. This is war, he said, not Hollywood. A hot cup of coffee was likely the best deal they were going to get.

Laine led the way through the woods, now a ballroom of whirling snowflakes. Suddenly, the entrance to a shack materialized, camouflaged with boughs and logs. They stamped in and shook themselves like dogs, spreading a good-sized puddle at the entrance.

The room was set with rows of white-clad tables, and coffee steamed in a small kitchen. The correspondents took their seats and all cursing stopped. Two women dressed in the prim brown uniforms of the Lottas emerged and set out coffee and trays of sandwiches. The older of the two glared at the mess on the floor and handed Laine a broom. He swept the slush outside and gave her a good-natured salute. The younger Lotta blushed furiously when anyone looked at her, but performed her tasks with a steady hand.

"What would make a young girl like that come out here into harm's way?" Tom asked Laine. "She could have waited out the war in safety."

"Courage, duty, adventure. Thousands of Lottas and other women work in the war effort; even in the battle zones. They do important work—communications, air defense, medical. And of course, this." He cast a wistful glance around the room and helped himself to a sandwich. "A small taste of the home front is good for morale."

"How would you feel if that was your wife?"

"Well, my wife has an infant, so she's at home. Still, I know what you're saying." Laine leaned forward. "You want them to be strong, but you also want to protect them."

"If they don't need you when there's a war on, when do they need you?"

"Exactly," said Laine. "Women. Always a problem."

Tom sat down and watched the younger Lotta, who looked like an adolescent version of Tina. Women were not a problem, not if you kept it simple. When you started needing them for more than sex, then it became a problem. The word "love" didn't cross his mind, nor was he thinking of anyone in particular. It simply occurred to him that what he had viewed as a problem might in fact be the solution, the answer to the question he saw when he stared into the void where his life should have been. And the longer he thought about it, the more clearly he saw Tina's face. And he saw the face of the evacuee girl and remembered the warmth of her small arms around his neck.

The bus driver stomped in, a pillar of white, and spoke a few quick words to Laine.

"Gentlemen, you must leave immediately," he said, "before the road gets snowed in too badly." They pulled on their coats and scarves and took their leave. The wind had picked up, driving the snow into drifts, piling it in white mounds on the spruce boughs, turning the trees into towering arctic cats with white padded paws. The bus clawed its way along the unlit road, its engine straining as they tunnelled through the drifts; the iced windows yielding only glimpses of trees and the occasional field. The correspondents complained loud and long about travelling so far only to see a herd of prisoners. Gradually the muttering subsided and they slept.

3

The next morning Tom awoke with no memory of pulling into Viipuri and going to his room. He hurried to breakfast and at the back of the room he recognized the solitary figure of Mitch Webster. While he was still considering whether to say hello, Webster waved him over.

"Have you scooped me again, Henderson?" asked Webster, with a rare smile.

"No. We saw nothing of the front. Just prisoners. Hope you had better luck."

"I've just come back from Taipale. Sit down. Help yourself to some coffee."

Tom poured from the white ceramic pot on the table. Damn! How had Webster got that far? That was where Paul was. "Tough spot, Taipale."

"One of the toughest. Of course, they're all tough. Think of the disparity between the two armies. The Finns have cannon dating to the Crimean War. Their ammunition is so low they're not allowed to shoot at anything less than a small village. And yet the Mannerheim Line is tight as a drum."

"So David might have a chance after all?"

"I don't know. But the Finns do the damnedest things. Like the Russian tanks—they blow them up left and right with kerosene bottles they call Molotov cocktails."

"The Russians don't even have snowsuits. What possessed them to fight in the winter?" Tom recalled the ill-equipped prisoners he'd seen.

"They never thought they'd be fighting this long. Stalin figured two weeks at the most. The plan was simple. Hit hard on the Isthmus. Hit hard in the north and cut Finland in half. But their columns got bogged down on the narrow roads, their trucks slid off frozen tracks, their infantry got stuck in the snow. They were stopped cold at the Mannerheim Line. Now, the Line is a just a motley conglomerate of strongpoints, with a few bunkers, tank traps and barbed wire, and miles of foxholes. The Finns knew it would hold for a while. In the north, nobody knew. Then General Winter came along with the coldest winter in a century. Made the Russians pay not just with bullet wounds but also with frozen limbs. And they still come plowing across the snowy fields as conspicuous in their brown coats as crows in a white sky."

Tom thought about Björnström and his horse that might talk. A voice came from the doorway. "Henderson! The bus is leaving."

"You're not going back to Helsinki?" he asked Webster.

"No. I'm going on to General Field Headquarters."

"Got a date with Mannerheim?"

"Hah. Easier to get a date with God."

Tom rose and wished him good luck, then hurried to the courtyard. On the bus he began to write his story and he checked the date. The twentieth of December. Almost Christmas. A good time for a miracle.

4

When a nation is buried as deeply in war as the Finns were, all else falls away. Forgotten were Saturday night dances, ski outings, and unrationed food. But one thing they could never forget was Christmas. The gloomy northern winter made the celebration of light too precious. In peacetime, they made sure there was light everywhere. Candles glowed in every window and strings of electric lights decorated the streets.

The Björnströms prepared for Christmas as they always did. Tina helped Selma scrub the floors, take the rugs into the courtyard, and beat them until not a speck of dust dared lodge in them. They were a nation of rug-beaters and that winter they beat them to shreds, standing in the snow and watching the sky for bombers. Björnström found a small fir tree and they decorated it with blue-and-white Finnish flags and white candles. Behind the blacked out windows the flames burned more fiercely than ever.

The news from the front made them dance with hope. A rally was held in Madison Square Garden to raise money for Finland; Sweden and Denmark sent ambulances and food; volunteer brigades formed in dozens of nations. The faith of the Finns was indomitable. With the whole world behind them, how could they lose? No one knew exactly how they could win either, except that they could not do it alone. They still desperately needed help from the outside.

Thus Tina's personal mission had not changed, only strengthened; and she invited Tom to spend Christmas Eve with them. He arrived promptly at six with a box of chocolates and a bottle of French wine tucked under his arm, both bought at an exorbitant price from the Kämp steward.

They sipped sherry while Selma prepared dinner. Tina put on a record, a song everyone had taken to heart that Christmas:

> "When the candles are lit in the evening,
> in my dreams I'll be back home with you,
> Oh, the candles of home burning brightly
> remind me that I love you so."

Björnström read the Christmas gospel and they sang a hymn before dinner. Instead of the usual Finnish hymn they sang *Silent Night* so that Tom could join in. Selma's ham was succulent and she'd made rice pudding for dessert. Every Christmas she hid an almond in the pudding, and whoever found it was assured of good luck for the coming year. This year they all found several.

They opened the gifts and the room took on a proper Christmas lustre. The Björnströms traditionally exchanged books at Christmas. Tom had gleaned this information somehow and presented Tina with a copy of the recent best-seller, *Gone with the Wind*, and her father with a volume of Emerson. Even a cookbook for Selma. But as Selma cleared the dishes and the three of them sat watching the candles, no matter how they tried to talk about mythology or the American South, the conversation inexorably led to the war.

"Every day, the same words in the communiqués. Attacks at Taipale repulsed," said Björnström. "What sterile words to describe what must be desperate battles." They all knew Paul was at Taipale. The old man knew more about the military situation than he would ever divulge to a reporter. Perhaps even to his daughter.

"I remember the Great War. What a meaningless butchery that was. And now we're right back in it." Tom lit a cigarette. Tina poured cognacs for them and a Benedictine for herself.

"It seems there is always someone ready to have a go. Are you a pacifist, Mr. Henderson?"

Tom looked uncomfortable. He chose his words carefully when speaking to Björnström. "I don't admire war but neither do I admire most things that end in 'ism.'"

"Well, people need their beliefs. Anything that helps them get through this tale told by an idiot." The old man chuckled. "You see how well my London days have served me? I have a quote for every occasion."

"Not if their beliefs blind them to the truth."

"One can live a perfectly happy life in all sorts of wonderlands. Perhaps the happiest of lives. Still, for myself, I would rather face the truth, as we must face the sun, though it can destroy us. If the unexamined life is not worth living, neither is the undefended one."

He had forgotten he had an audience and was speaking softly to himself. His cigar smouldered in the ashtray and he refused Tina's offer of more cognac. He kissed her on the cheek and shook Tom's hand, and shuffled off to his room. Selma called out "God bless everyone!" and then she too disappeared, leaving Tom and Tina alone.

They sat in silence for a long while. Or it seemed like a long while. He looked tired and she expected he would leave soon, which suited her because she felt she should be thinking about Paul. Instead, he began to talk.

"This is my first Christmas dinner in ten years," he said. "I mean a family dinner. And the last one wasn't a happy one. It was right after the stock market crash. The bank was hounding my father and his customers had no money to pay him. We were afraid we'd lose the store. The store had been in our family for sixty years."

"That was when you were in college?"

"Yes. I never did go back to college. That Christmas dinner was like a funeral. But tonight brought back the good ones, the ones before that."

"When you were a boy?"

"Yes. And I believed in Santa Claus, though ours came down the chimney at night while we slept."

"Ours comes on Christmas Eve. Then he has the next day off, like everyone else."

"Sounds sensible to me."

He inspected the slim volume of poetry her father had given her, a collection of the poems of William Butler Yeats. It had a white swan on the cover.

"Does that still bother you?" he asked. "The letter from Paul about the swan."

"The swan of Tuonela? Oh, our pagan nonsense." She spoke casually but in truth it did bother her and she was surprised he remembered it.

"Tell me about it."

"You'll just laugh."

"No. It can't be worse than a fat man falling down a chimney."

"The swan patrols the river of Tuonela that separates the land of the dead from the land of the living. The swan cannot die. One of our heroes—a sort of Don Juan—has to carry out several tasks to win the daughter of North Farm. The last task is to kill the swan. He tries but the gods strike him down."

"And Don Juan dies while the swan lives on?"

"And his body breaks in pieces that drift down the river of the dead. But his mother rakes in the pieces and puts them back together again and revives him—" She stopped, a sudden spasm at her throat. She knew the horror that lurked behind the apathetic words of the communiqués from Taipale. She had seen the coffins in the churchyard, the labels saying Do Not Open, and what oozed and congealed in their cracks. The River of Tuonela now flowed through every city and town and village in the nation, a frozen river that carried the pieces of its fallen heroes back to their mothers.

"She did a damn sight better than all the king's horses and all the king's men," he said. "But tell me something, professor. Why does the most beautiful bird in the world patrol the river of the dead? Shouldn't it be an ugly bird like the crow or the buzzard?"

"I don't know."

"Well, it's your story. Don't leave me hanging." Something in his voice drew her to him, pulled her close and made her want to never stop talking about birds.

"It—" Her body was on fire as her brain raced for an answer. "It must be because the gods want to be sure that before you die you've looked upon the greatest beauty that life has to offer. So you won't want to die. So you'll want to turn back and live."

He said nothing but sat looking at her, his eyes mild the way they had been in the Berlin moonlight, his fingers stroking the wisps of hair on her forehead where the lacquer never held.

"You see how silly it all is," she said, because someone had to speak. "Unless you're a poet, of course." Her tone was erudite now as she tried to elevate the pagan nonsense to poetry, fearing that any minute he would break into the sardonic grin he used to cut down fools at the Kämp. But he did not.

"Some are hawks who kill," he said, "some are doves who make peace, some are vultures who pick the bones of the dead."

"Why, Tom, that's exactly the idea."

"What kind of bird am I?" he asked.

The question was so ludicrous she laughed. But he sat unsmiling, waiting for an answer. Suddenly the war no longer mattered to her, and the world closed in on them.

"I don't know you well enough—"

"Take a guess."

"Maybe an eagle."

"Because I'm brave, free and American?"

"No, though of course you are," she said and drew out one of his cigarettes casually, though her heart was racing. "To me you are an eagle because an eagle lives in inaccessible places."

He turned away and didn't look at her for a while. The scent of the fir tree warm from the candles, almost as sweet as violets.

"Help me."

She could tell from his voice he had never said that before to anyone. The ache inside her grew stronger and in the dim light they drew together. His lips caressed her face, covered her mouth, his tongue met hers; his hand rested on her thigh. A clutching need seized her body, as strong as the life she clung to, stronger even than that. She reached forward, whether to push him away or draw him closer she could not say. As she did, her hand brushed his vest pocket. A glint of gold caught her eye.

"What do you have there?" she blurted, like a teenager close to danger and desperate to pull away. That was when he took out the pocket watch, and she poured him more cognac. He stared at the watch and when he finally turned to her again, his face was old and drawn.

"Tonight is the first time I've worn this watch in ten years," he said. "It belonged to my father."

"Why haven't you worn it? It's beautiful." She turned it over in her hand, and their fingers touched again.

"No more stories. Play that song again. The one about the candles of home."

There was no more talk that evening. He sat with his arm lightly touching her shoulder, and she leaned her head on his. About midnight he got up and she saw him to the door. His lips brushed her forehead.

"No mistletoe," he said. "It should be hanging right here."

"What is it?"

"Our pagan nonsense."

She sat up nearly the whole night while the candles burned low. It was one of those times when life rains down like a shower of shooting stars. The flame of Christmas, the darkness over the land, the coffins lodged in the hospital yard on their way home, her fear over Paul, and now this business with Tom. She sat in the dark and saw the swan rising from the water, soaring into the high clouds with one burst of power. That was it, the click that turned on all the lights of life. There are those who can feel it and those who cannot. She had known from the first that the American could. Paul could, too. It had kept them together all these years, but with Paul there had always been a divide she could not cross. Especially since Berlin, he'd been drifting further and further away. And now her life had changed to this, where nothing else mattered except Tom, and the war almost seemed like an intrusion. No one was allowed to put personal happiness first at a time like this, but this happiness erased everything else. I could be on my deathbed, she thought, and it wouldn't matter.

Only this. As hard as she tried to focus on other things, her body kept taking her back to his touch on her thigh.

On Boxing Day Tom left on a press trip and she didn't hear from him for several days. In the evenings as she lay alone in bed, or sat in the kitchen listening to her father reading the newspaper aloud or to Selma's chatter, she couldn't concentrate for more than a few moments on anything except one question: what was he doing? was he alone? who was he with? what was he saying, what was he thinking? was he sitting down or standing up? was he typing a story? was he reading? having a drink? These questions squeezed the breath out of her. She wanted to tear down to the Kämp and look for him, but it was the fear of what she might actually find, the fear of the blonde correspondent who'd been in the hallway or some other woman with him, that kept her in the flat. So she began to imagine what he might be doing, saw his head bending over the typewriter, saw his arm reaching for a cigarette, saw him hunched over the small table lamp, and she extended her fingers and imagined she could touch his shoulders, his arms, his face.

She'd felt a similar need to know where Paul was during the early days of the Maneuvers, but never with this kind of urgency, never with this panic of not knowing, of needing to be with him all the time, night and day.

5

December 24, 1939

Taipale

My dearest Tina,

I'd like to wish you a merry Christmas but who can be merry right now? I pray every day that Molotov's breadbaskets don't find you. Thank you from the bottom of my heart for the packages you sent. I was the envy of every man in the tent with my cookies and socks and sweaters. Of course I shared everything with them, I knew that's what you would have done.

We're in combat reserve in a wooded campground behind the front, but we had a decent Christmas Eve. Markus found a chaplain and brought him to our tent. He preached a Christmas sermon about the soldier's psalm that you will never come to harm if you believe in God's protection. You know I'm not much for religion, but I've noticed strange things out here, things you can only explain by guardian angels. Of course that's nonsense, it's all luck. Still, during the service the strangest feeling came over me. The pastor's words, the men singing, the whooshing of enemy shells in the wounded pines, the sky lit up by crisscrossing flares—it was a moment I'll never forget.

We brought a small tree into our tent and set one candle on the tree. Just one candle for all of us. The Captain doled out hams. Our pea soup froze solid and we had to eat it in chunks. Then Jokinen played *Silent Night* on his accordion and Markus sang something in Italian. He said it was Verdi, a requiem. That's the odd thing out here. We all get through this business in our own way. To Markus it's an opera.

A full moon is out tonight and four inches of fresh snow on the firs. We've kept the Russians out all along the line. Tell Tom he'd better write a good story about this.

The international attention we're getting is starting to affect the boys. All the packages, for one thing. The ones from home are the dearest but the ones from far away cause the most amazement. They've even set off travel fever. Jokinen, who's lived on the farm all his life and only seen the ocean once on a school holiday, has decided he's going to be a sailor when this is all over. He cranks out seaman waltzes on his accordion until we beg him to stop. The other day a pile of packages arrived from South America. Jokinen was very impressed with one from Uruguay. He turned it over and over again in his hands. "Damned if I'd have had the wits to send anything to the Urluquaians if they got in a pickle," he said. Last night I was on night patrol with him and Markus. The northern lights were out and Jokinen pointed at the red streaks and said, "Red sky at night, sailor's delight. Going to be a fine day on the Pacific tomorrow, boys, we might get as far as Tahiti." A few snowflakes drifted down, more like drops of ice. "What are those, sailor?" I asked. "The tears of the gods," he said. This offended Markus, of course. "What do you mean, gods? You were brought up in the same church I was, and there's only one God," he said. Jokinen just stared at the sky. "Your God turned water into wine, these gods turn water into ice," he said. "Everything turns to ice here, even tears."

Your Paul

6

In his youth, Tom considered himself a bit of an explorer. He knew the back roads and railway trestles around his home town well enough to run them with his eyes half-closed. Running and exploring were corollaries of each other, he thought. They must have been the forces driving humans out of the caves. He ran through the fields on summer nights chasing imaginary mammoths, looking for arrowheads and phantom footprints in the grass.

His successes in running competitions took him further afield and a large part of his enchantment with the sport was the possibility of running in distant places. When he went to college, Toronto became his home base and he explored by foot and rail the small towns and lakeside villages of southern Ontario, with autumn expeditions into Maine and the uplands of New York. He started off in similar fashion as a cub reporter in Chicago, but that was when the curiosity for new experiences left him, gradually and silently, until his rounds dwindled to the radius of the bars and stadiums and racetracks he knew. In Europe his exploring urges resurfaced but it was not until he came here to this unlikely frozen land that they sprang up full force. By now he felt quite comfortable making his way around the city by day. At night, the blackout made walking difficult, but in the moonlight with the snow as a reflector he got around within his fixed parameters. One evening he slipped and landed full bore on his rump. He sat for a moment in the snow, his head spinning. When he started walking he realized that he was heading away from the streets he knew, into a park east of the train station. He saw hollows ahead that looked like a path. If he just followed it, he reasoned, he would eventually circle the park and come back to the railway square.

He walked on, resisting the urge to sit down and rest, knowing that would be his last act on earth. Suddenly a warehouse-shaped building loomed ahead. He fumbled his way to the door and opened it. The main floor was pitch black but candles lit the stairs down to the cellar and music came from below.

At the bottom of the stairs stood a doorman who took his overcoat and directed him inside. As his eyes adjusted to the darkness, he realized he had found a nightclub. Not a genteel one like the Fennia, but a down-to-earth strip joint like those he remembered from back home, with cluttered tables and cigar smoke heavy in the air. The only lights were trained on the stage, where a chorus line was performing. The girls were untalented as dancers and even less as strippers, going through their motions in imitation Moulin Rouge fishnet and satin. He ordered a double scotch. He would stay long enough to warm up, but this place, like so many of its kind that once fit him so well, didn't feel comfortable any more, like a jacket he'd outgrown.

The only part of the club that was visible was the stage. The girls shed their tops in a grand finale and the floodlights burst into full voltage over their breasts. Whistles erupted as the girls jiggled off, but Tom was not watching them. In front of him, two rows removed, he saw a head of silver hair he recognized as Björnström's. He deliberated whether he should say hello, but the problem solved itself when the old man turned around and caught a glimpse of him just before the lights dimmed. No hiding now, thought Tom, and better me breaking an ankle in the dark than him. Scotch in hand, he walked over and sat down beside Björnström.

"Good evening, Mr. Henderson," said the old man with equanimity. "Fancy meeting you here. But then I've noticed that eventually I see almost everyone I know here."

"A man needs a little diversion at a time like this," said Tom.

"Very true, although I'm afraid I can't use the times as my excuse. I've been coming here for years. A habit I picked up abroad. Of course, in London and Paris the shows are real works of art."

"I stumbled in here by accident. Not to say it's the first time I've been in a joint like this."

"Joint? Ah, the American term for it."

"What's this place called?"

"Aladdin's. Years ago it had belly dancers and snake charmers and a harem of sorts in the back. Then the ownership changed hands and all that disappeared, though when the lights go up you can see remnants of the oriental décor. Still Aladdin's lamps on some tables. Presumably the genies have fled. Now the eastern girls are gone and we have our own country maids, doing their best to be exotic. Most of these girls are the daughters of crofters who started out as scullery maids and then came to the city to find better wages. Well, these are the wages they found."

There was a scuffling noise on the floor. A chair pulled up beside them in the dark, and a childlike voice chirped, "Good evening, Skipper!"

Tom squinted at the newcomer. She was from the previous set, a full-chested blonde with broad features.

"Good evening, Leila!" said Björnström. "You were magnificent tonight. Leila spent a year in New York as an au pair girl. She learned English and the latest from the chorus lines on Broadway."

"Oh, Skipper," Leila giggled. "You're much too kind. How are you keeping now that the sailing season is over?"

"Drying out my waterlogged joints and stocking up on rum for next year."

While Leila counted her evening's wages, Björnström winked at Tom. There was a discrepancy in the money, and she excused herself from the table to speak to the manager.

"Skipper?" asked Tom.

"Just a little fantasy of mine. My family pushed me into diplomacy. I always wanted to sail the seven seas. What better place to daydream than at Aladdin's? And who knows when the genies might come back to their lamps?"

Leila returned and studied Tom.

"Let me introduce my friend," said Björnström. "Leila, this is...."

"Amundsen. I'm an explorer," said Tom.

"I thought you died in that dirigible accident," said Leila. "Glad to meet you. See you again, Skipper." She disappeared into the dark aisles and Björnström turned again to Tom.

"You're an interesting fellow, Mr. Henderson. I rather like you, though my first impression was that you were a cold fish. I haven't chatted with a young man for a long time. My friends are old coots like myself. Fine gentlemen but predictable as the planetary orbits. Some of our local Social Democrats are livelier but I can't be seen in their circles. They'd blackball me at the Savoy."

"If you're looking for a young man's point of view, I'm afraid I've passed the expiry date."

Björnström chuckled. "To me you are young. It's always been a source of sadness that I can't talk to Paul comfortably, he's too much in awe of me for some reason. Well, granted I know the reasons, but they're so deeply sewn into our social fabric that I can't change them. That will be up to future generations. In any case, I couldn't imagine inviting Paul to a place like this. I think of him almost as my own son."

"That's natural, given how long you've known him."

"Yes. He and Tina were childhood sweethearts. Tell me, what do you think of my daughter?"

Tom lit up a second cigarette and sat holding one in each hand for a few moments before he noticed. Björnström was a diplomat but his Finnish bluntness was intact.

"I think you've raised a fine young woman. She's kind, intelligent, confident, and I'd be seriously remiss if I didn't mention beautiful."

"The last one would be her mother's contribution. As far as upbringing goes, Tina raised herself to a large extent. It's difficult with daughters. Do you have children?"

His throat constricted and he couldn't speak for a moment. The memory of the farmer's daughter and her child—his child—surged up from the dry gulches of his heart where he had buried it for years.

"I have—had a child. But I've lost track of—I don't know. . ."

"Never mind. Most of us have sown a few wild oats. At least you can still remember yours. I think you need to get out more to places like this. Well, better places than this. You strike me as melancholy, but in the short time I've known you it seems to me you've begun to come out of it. That's good. Life is short. You said once that existence is absolute but life is relative. Aspire to the highest degree of life."

What if I need your daughter to get me there? thought Tom.

"Speaking of my daughter," said Björnström, though they hadn't been speaking of her and Tom had the wild notion the old man might be psychic, "shall we agree that as far as she needs to know, neither of us has ever set foot in this place?"

"Absolutely. Agreed."

"Good. I do try to set an example for her. I've taught her that this sort of thing is demeaning to women, but we all have our little hypocrisies."

They watched the sad little dancing girls for a few more minutes, and then paid for their drinks. Tom walked the old man home to Elisabeth Street, and along the way they sang a medley of English-American ditties that didn't hit the mark either musically or aesthetically.

7

By January the authorities had set up press centres in several cities near battle zones, and foreign correspondents were taken out regularly on trips to the front. One day Tom joined a tour to the town of Porvoo, which had been damaged by Russian bombs. He wanted to see what the Russians had considered worth their attention in the old cultural city, whose only claim to fame was being the home of the national poet, Runeberg. His outrage at the destruction in the village was surpassed only by his outrage at the excited yelp of a female reporter when the bus crossed a bridge and they saw the flames still licking at the boathouses. "Oh, wonderful, it's still burning!" she cried, as she would have cheered the fireworks at a country fair.

The crowd at the Kämp vexed him increasingly. The population of correspondents had swelled to overflowing, and the elixir of covering real combat, albeit from a hotel lounge, was heady, especially when mixed with other elixirs that flowed in abundance.

One evening he found himself alone in the typing room with Mitch Webster, who had just returned from the field.

"Some of those toffs haven't taken off their ski sweaters since they got here," said Webster, fixing his sad brown eyes on the restaurant crowd.

"One must look the part."

"The dance for the telephones is still going strong. What are they bribing the operators with now?"

"Money and chocolates. Charm."

"I'm at a disadvantage there," Webster smiled. "Ever heard of the medieval danse macabre? Dancers whirling faster and faster, to keep out the devil, demons, death. Here they're dancing with their wits."

"To keep out what?"

"The reality out there. The war, the hopelessness of the world in general and this tiny country in particular. The death of illusions."

"Makes you wonder," Tom muttered, "how many of the demons are personal."

"Oh, that—well, who isn't running away from something? In this business you leave baggage at every port of call."

Is that what Tina is? Tom thought. Baggage at a port of call? He knew she was not. This was the end of his voyage, the port where he wanted to drop anchor. And yet how could he, when Paul was out in the field, fighting for his country? He felt like a cad for loving someone else's beloved—as undeclared as the engagement was—but he knew he could not give her up.

Webster stopped typing and peered at Tom around the bright desk lamp.

"So what did you want to be, Henderson? Before you got into this business, I mean."

"Me? A long distance runner," said Tom. "A sports writer. Covered a lot of Major League baseball."

"That's it?"

"Well, officially. Unofficially, there were other dreams. Since I came over to Europe, it's been all about this. The politics, the crises, the war."

"I wanted to write the Great American Novel," said Webster.

"When this war is over you can."

"No. A moment just passes you by and you can't pull it back. Like ducks in a shooting gallery, they just pass you by."

"Well, look what you've accomplished, even if you never write a book. You've got accolades a mile high."

Webster laughed a short, unpleasant laugh. "A mile high and an inch deep. Shallow stuff, shallower than dreams. Get the story, it could be the story of the century. Look at the crowd in the other room right now. All waiting for it."

"Everyone's thinking the same thing. One day there really will be a story of the century."

"But it's always the same story. The quest, the glory, the grave. And how many graves it takes to write it. Sorry. Didn't mean to get pompous on you."

"It's OK," said Tom, feeling uneasy. He'd noticed the downhill slide in Webster's spirits, though it didn't impede his ability to get out into the field. Perhaps what he saw out there was the cause of it.

"Listen, if I were you I'd take that pretty blonde I've seen you with back to America, build a house, run a grocery store, whatever. Get away from here while you can. I have a gut feeling we're in for some ugliness the likes of which the world's never seen. Just having two wackos like Stalin and Hitler in close quarters—here, it's time to go."

It was nearing nine o'clock and correspondents began to file into the press room, along with a Finnish officer bearing a stack of papers. In a back room they cranked up the gramophone.

"A little mood music never hurt a war," said Webster.

In the Forests of the Night

1

In January the Björnströms received a telephone call from Aunt Gunilla's housekeeper. "Madam has been wounded by shrapnel," said the housekeeper. "The bombers strafed a platform at the evacuation centre. She's home now recuperating, but she should be moved out of harm's way." Her rickety voice went on, reluctant to beg for help yet plainly determined to receive it.

Once again Tina set out into the dark streets to catch the next eastbound train. Leaving her father in Selma's hands, his cognac by his side, the diamond-cut crystal catching the candleglow; leaving the Fennia and the Kämp, the demi-glamorous wartime ambience of Helsinki, leaving it behind for the raw theatre of the war.

Kotka in the light of the cold dawn lay shrouded in smoke. With its harbour and sawmills, the city had been a frequent target. The yellow mansion had not been hit, and Tina found her aunt nimbly afoot, her arm in a sling but otherwise healthy.

"We must get you to a safer place, Aunt," she said. "Maybe the summer house."

"Oh, my dear! Can't you see how much work I have here?" she said, and Tina noticed bright eyes peering at her from behind the French doors in the vestibule, where the butler used to stand. Her aunt confided that she had wanted to open her home to the evacuees, but the authorities deemed Kotka too dangerous. So she had gathered a half-dozen orphaned evacuee children, and with her good arm she worked the phone, trying to find guardians for them.

"I'm glad you're here, you can help me set up a schedule of lessons for the children. Let's have lunch and we'll start this afternoon." She caught Tina off guard and so they set about it—writing and reading lessons in the stately library. The children gaped at Gunilla's objects d'art. Patiently she explained, this is a replica of Michelangelo's Pieta, this is a sketch of the Eiffel Tower. Someday you will visit Paris and Rome and see the real thing. Small hands tugged at her sleeves and at the apron of the housekeeper who brought milk and crispbread at two o'clock. Now and then Gunilla drew back, smoothed her hair, pulled her mouth tight and wrapped herself in her shawl, as if afraid that too much of her was showing. But the next tug at her sleeve, and the shawl fell to her waist.

When the housekeeper took the children for their naps, Gunilla brought out a decanter and two brandy goblets. Tina had seen her drink on occasion, but only sherry. This was another change. Gunilla studied the glass for a moment and then moved it slowly toward her lips.

"They say it's good for the constitution," she said, "but it does burn so."

So does life, Tina wanted to tell her. She would have said it, for she'd never been afraid of her, but she was certain she knew it for herself.

"This isn't easy for you, Auntie," she said. "And your own injury— you're neglecting it. You must take better care of that arm."

She seemed not to hear. "And what about Paul? Does he have everything he needs? Does he have money? We must send him money!" She began to open drawers, searching for her pocketbook.

"Money means nothing where he is," said Tina. "Maybe socks and woollens and smokes."

"Yes, that's it. Let's make a package for him. But smokes, my dear, those I do not have. Can we get them somehow?"

And that was how it came about that Tina ventured into the darkening afternoon haze of Kotka, looking for a cigarette vendor. She searched for a long time for a shop, any shop; most of the town merchants had boarded up and shut down. The Siberian wolf coat that Gunilla had loaned her kept her warm as she walked, listening for sirens, farther and farther into the industrial area. The sugar factory still churned on, and near it she finally found a smoke shop.

The cigarettes cost a fortune but she bought as many packs as she could stuff into her bag, and was just paying for them when the sirens wailed. The proprietor grabbed her arm with one hand and his cash-box with the other and they lurched toward a bomb shelter down the street. White-frocked factory girls came running from the other direction heading for the same shelter. They squeezed in and all held their breaths.

Why had she not hurried back to the yellow mansion? Tina scolded herself. Her aunt and the children, alone and helpless, sitting in the dark waiting for the bombs to find them. She was still fretting when the all-clear sounded and the factory girls spilled out. They milled about for an instant, scanning the late afternoon sky.

"Not much to that one," said one of the girls. She looked at Tina and saw the cigarettes in her bag. "Here, honey, give us a smoke."

Tina tore open one of the packages and passed cigarettes all around.

"Damn Molotov!"

The voice was familiar and Tina looked at the dark-haired girl standing near her. With her hair tied back and her eyes tired and drawn, she had not recognized her at first.

"Marita!"

She looked up, small feet dancing on the snow in their heavy work shoes, with the mixture of friendliness and aversion Tina recalled from years past. Marita had never forgiven her incursion into her territory, her abduction of Paul.

"Tina! What on earth?"

There seemed no point in nursing grudges, and they embraced.

"I'm looking after my aunt for a bit. She was wounded."

"I've been working at the factory since the war started. Mr. Lind closed up when the first bombs fell."

"At the factory! How awful!"

"It's not bad. The girls are a jolly lot. We never worry. So far, not a scratch." She waved at her co-workers, who were already on their way back to work. "By the way, I saw Paul on the day he left. How is he?"

"Paul?"

"Relax. He was just passing by. He was with some American."

Tina felt a stab of their old rivalry and there was also something else. It bothered her that Marita looked so useful, so sturdy. She was braving out the war in a danger zone, performing vital work, producing a commodity of substance. Quickly she told her what she could about Paul, and they inquired after each other's families.

"Get your father and Selma to move to the countryside," said Marita. "They're going to bomb Helsinki to bits one of these days."

"I've tried. They're too stubborn to go."

"Try harder!" Marita clutched Tina's forearm. "We have to get our loved ones out of harm's way. God knows I wish I could."

"Do you still have someone in the city?"

"No. It's my grandmother. She lives on a farm in Karelia and she won't leave. The war is still a long way from her but that could change any day. I can't sleep at night for worrying about her."

"But if things get worse I'm sure the army will ensure she's safe."

"Yes, probably." Marita looked unconvinced, but she embraced Tina and started back toward the factory. Tina thought for a moment, then ran after her.

"Listen, Marita. You know my aunt works with the evacuees who come out of Karelia."

"Tina, we haven't been very close and I have no right to ask you anything."

"For God's sake, right now we have the right to ask everything of each other. My aunt knows people there. She can have them look out for your grandmother if the war turns bad."

Tears trickled down Marita's cheeks and mingled with sweat as she tore the corner off a ration booklet and scribbled on it.

"My grandmother's name and address," she said. "Thank you. You have no idea what this means to me."

They embraced again, with real warmth this time. Marita hurried off and Tina dashed inside the smoke shop to warm up before her long walk home.

"Those factory gals are gonna get civilian medals of courage," said the proprietor. "Deserve 'em, too. They stand tall day after day, so the boys can have something sweet to put in their coffee."

Her envy simmered as Tina walked back to the house, perspiring now in the heavy fur. A medal! She was the one who was the patriot, and Marita was going to get the medal. For standing in a factory. Her pique dissolved as the children ran up to greet her, and the housekeeper set the table for evening porridge. Gunilla said grace, and dusted each blue bowl with sugar and a carefully measured pinch of cinnamon. After the children were in bed, Tina joined her aunt for another brandy. There was no use arguing with her about moving to the country. She was as stubborn as her father in her own decorous way.

2

After Christmas Tom began arriving unexpectedly at the flat on Elisabeth Street, sometimes when Tina was home, sometimes earlier when her father and Selma were there, sometimes in the evening. Sometimes he appeared at her office and walked her home. She knew it was her company he sought and this both thrilled and frightened her. But there was more to it than that.

He wasn't content just to sit and chat. He joined them in household chores. Selma regarded this development with severe suspicion at first.

"What's he up to?" she'd ask, after leaving him to stir soup or slice bread.

"I don't know," said Tina, slightly irritated. "Does he have to be up to something?"

"A man doesn't just come into someone's household and volunteer for duty. Something is fishy." She looked at Tina with the same look she had fixed on her when she was fifteen and having trysts with Paul.

"Nothing is fishy," Tina said, staring her down. "Except the soup."

When Selma judged that Tom's interest in her soups and doughs was genuine, she relented. One day Tina came home from work to find him peeling potatoes, cutting out the discolourations with a paring knife.

"You have to get all the brown spots out," he announced. "They could end up on somebody's plate and ruin their appetite."

She could have laughed or could have cried, watching his large hands dig into the skin of the potatoes, leaving their surfaces gleaming white, one of Selma's household dictums that she'd dismissed as trivial but he clearly had taken to heart. Selma began to entrust him with errands to the post office and the market. After he returned he sat on the sofa and spoke about the places he'd visited in the city, the short cuts and side streets he'd discovered.

Björnström took to calling him Amundsen.

"Why does he call you that?" Tina asked Tom. "Amundsen wasn't American."

"No. But he was an explorer."

"Ah, so it's an arctic explorer you are."

"Well, I'm doing some exploring and we are pretty close to the arctic circle."

One Saturday he came over early in the pitch black January gloom to help Selma with her baking. She'd got hold of a good supply of flour and was making the sweet bread they called pulla. Tom took over the kneading.

"All right, Mr. Henderson. Come clean," Tina whispered in his ear, unable to restrain her curiosity any longer. "Why are you doing all this? These household chores."

He turned to look at her, dots of flour on his cheeks and eyebrows. "It's not just the chores," he said. "It's everything. I have a lot of catching up to do. Life is a game of catch up. Trying to get back to where you were before your last mistake."

His voice was as fragile as it had been on Christmas Eve, and she wanted to touch his cheek and brush the flour away. But with Selma nearby she didn't dare.

"There's always new land ahead," she said. "Right, Amundsen?"

"Right, o star of the north."

He continued kneading, punching and pulling, adding flour until Selma rushed over and tapped his wrist, scolding that too much flour would ruin the batch. Just then Björnström came home from his morning walk.

"You have him kneading dough?" asked the old man.

"He's watched us often enough," Tina said. "I think it's very kind of him."

"Yes indeed." Her father removed his coat and sat down in the living room. "Although I can't tell whether he's applying for a position as son-in-law or houseboy."

"Father! The man is only trying to be helpful. Isn't that what we need, help from anyone any way we can get it?"

As she stomped to the kitchen she heard him mumble, "Methinks the lady doth protest too much," another one of his infernal quotations.

3

"Can you believe what they did up here? Two divisions! And these were crack troops, not duds."

The loud voices jolted Tom awake, and at the same time the bus lurched forward and his chin hit the seat in front of him. For a moment he had no idea where he was. He only knew that he had never been so cold in his life and never had a headache like this one, with pincers of cold squeezing his temples and stale cigarette smoke burrowing into his forehead. He reached down for the blanket he had brought with him, which had fallen to his knees. It was a loan from one of the hotels en route and the reason he'd been able to sleep at all.

He was aboard the first busload of foreign correspondents to view the site of the massive Finnish victory at Suomussalmi in the northern wilderness. Sleep was difficult to come by with the January cold whistling around your ears and the impassioned words of the other passengers ricocheting in the dark. They had rambled on about the battle for hours. By now it was well known that two Russian divisions had been decimated, one in the village of Suomussalmi itself and the other on Raate Road, trying to reach the village. This was a knockout blow and a foretaste of more miracles to come.

The bus carved its way through the drifts, headlights on but the road ahead still largely a guess. Outside the icy windows the sky pulsated with streamers of blue and green light. The Aurora Borealis, thought Tom, courtesans of the northern gods. It was a bravura performance that went largely unnoticed by the others.

Someone passed a mickey of vodka around and soon more flasks came out and the toasts began.

"To the greatest victory of this incredible war!"

"Hear, hear! To the heroes of the north!"

Tom took out his own flask and toasted along with them. He was as overjoyed as they were that the Finns had begun knocking the hell out of the Russians as well as holding them off. But he had a bad feeling, a purl of nausea. Probably from the headache, he thought. He decided to go easy on the whiskey.

Dawn struggled over the woods as they climbed down from the bus. They were near the 65th parallel, within reach of the Arctic Circle. Tom looked at his watch. It was ten in the morning. By three in the afternoon, it would be night again. There was no shelter to be seen, although he knew the village of Suomussalmi was nearby and wisps of smoke rose in the distance. Mostly he saw pines, so tall and high-crowned that they would not allow much sunlight even in summer.

"You're lucky," the guide said. "It warmed up today. A few days ago it was minus forty-five." He was a serious young man, polite but not sociable. "Please stay close together. Don't wander off by yourself. There are mines, booby traps, and other things."

"Russian snipers in the woods?" asked Tom.

"No," said the guide with gloomy certitude.

"They say there's nothing left of them," said a New York reporter. "Two Russian divisions, one of them the crack 44th, Ukrainian boys I saw swinging through the fields last summer."

They walked from the bus through the spectral woods, passing a charred house, overturned trucks and tanks. Suddenly they rounded a bend and Raate Road opened before them, the route the desperate 44th had taken in a vain effort to reach its sister division in the village.

Nothing left of them? thought Tom. There was plenty left of them, and all of it was strewn down the narrow road like the droppings of a mad airborne garbage detail, a still life of death.

No one spoke. They struggled to grasp what they were looking at, for everything lay dusted by fresh snow. As their eyes focused on the objects that littered the road, the only sound was the involuntary drawing of breath. Bodies of men, machines, horses, and carts stretched as far as the eye could see. Stiff, uplifted hands, crooked knees, faces frozen solid in terror. The Russians had died as they stood or sat; one corpse leaned on its elbow, others stood like statues, waist-deep in the snow which still drifted over them, whiting out the ugliness, erasing a blemish nature could not bear.

Further on, Finnish soldiers were dragging bodies out of the piles.

"We cannot bury them all," said the guide. "The rest will have to wait until the spring. In the villages around here, the well water is contaminated and can't be used."

He pointed to the dense bush from where the ski brigades had erupted and fallen upon the long column of the 44th as it lay uncoiled on the road, chopped it into sausage links and chewed it up link by link, then let the polar night freeze the remains. From a tangle of frozen bodies and horses, they dug out a large banner with a coloured map of Scandinavia on it. Two soldiers rolled it out for display. A huge red arrow swept across the map, beginning at the border where they presently were and ending at the Atlantic Ocean. If the Finnish army had failed here, thought Tom, all the Russians had to do was cross the country and march up the coast to Sweden and Norway.

Further down, he came upon a circle of reporters and soldiers inspecting a mound of debris. These were not the usual spoils of war, but musical instruments. Trumpets, drums, horns and accordions lay in a jumbled pile, as if a brass band had lost its way and shed ballast.

"What the fuck?" he muttered.

"Propaganda," said the guide. "The Red Army was expecting a hero's welcome here. The Finnish proletariat will rise up in joy to greet them, they were told. I don't know who really believed that. Not Stalin or Molotov. Maybe some of these poor devils, who died with their parade uniforms on."

"Thinking they were part of a bloody glorious liberation," said an English reporter stonily.

On and on they walked, mile after hideous mile. Red stars bloomed on officers' caps in grotesque parody of another killing field where poppies had once blown. Tom had seen such stars being traded at the Kämp. The usual wartime memorabilia....but now he winced at them. His mind reeled before the massive presence of death.

The sickly sunlight waned, and they turned to make the trek back to the bus. There was a sudden swish, and he saw the ski troops, a platoon of them gliding through the trees. They came out of the woods like wraiths, cloaked from head to foot in white, hooded monks. Except, he thought, that monks don't carry rifles under their cloaks.

The walk back to the bus was sombre. Any notions about the romance of war fled before this tableau of frozen perplexed faces, these peasants and workers lured *en masse* to their deaths with stories of a hero's welcome in the bush. No one warned them about the ski warriors who burst out of the silent night and vanished into the woods. The Russians had never seen woods like these before. The overhanging pines meant friendly shelter to the Finns but terror to superstitious peasants from the steppes, and the snow beloved by the fast-moving ski troops was a white death trap for their enemies.

He could hear the growl of the bus as they slogged back in the dark. Blue and green waves of light cascaded in the sky over Raate Road. The northern lights came dancing to the silent trumpets of the parade march that never was, across mahogany faces powdered by snow, above the sentinel pines.

4

"Come with me to the train station tonight. I can get you another scoop," Tina told Tom one afternoon in late January. "Our greatest distance runner is leaving for America. Paavo Nurmi. You can get an exclusive interview."

Nurmi was an Olympic legend, the winner of nine gold medals; he now planned a series of fund-raising events in the United States. Tina watched as Tom spoke to the runner and scribbled notes in the dim light of the hall. Flash bulbs popped and the bursts of light crossed Tom's face, revealing a smile as broad as a teenager's. Tina could hear snippets of their conversation.

"So we both missed the same Olympic Games?" Nurmi was looking at him incredulously. "I also was to have run in Los Angeles in 1932." A technicality over the rules of amateurism had kept him out of the games.

"—for very different reasons," Tom said. And suddenly they jogged off, arms upraised, in a leisurely victory lap to the end of the hall and back. Tina commandeered a photographer and lined up a pose with Tom beside the Olympic hero, both grinning as if they were standing on a podium.

"This was incredible," Tom said as they walked away. "I mean for me, personally. Standing next to the greatest runner of all time—that photo will be buried with me. I owe you a debt again."

"You haven't even repaid the first one. Whatever it was."

"Dinner at the Savoy?"

"Too extravagant."

They passed a movie theatre and she stopped in front of the poster, shining her pocket flashlight on it for a moment. Perfect. Rogers and Astaire's latest.

"Shall we dance?" she said.

After the movie they went to the Fennia. They talked about the dancing of the famous American pair, the pavilions where Tina danced with Paul on summer evenings, and a ballroom in Chicago where you could hear the latest swing tunes every weekend.

"I suppose you were a frequent visitor?" she asked.

"Not really. Mainly I watched."

"You have a lot of catching up to do there as well."

"No, it's too late for that."

"You're being a defeatist again."

"Just the law of diminishing possibilities. You start out when you're young, full of dreams, and then it's a process of elimination. Reality says, here's the deal, chump; live with it." The waiters were clearing off the tables and they got up to leave. Halfway down the stairs he paused on the landing, and stood straight at attention.

"What are you doing?" she asked, already two steps below him.

"Just reliving the moment at the station. Standing next to Nurmi." He stepped down from the landing and took her arm. "You know what's crazy about the whole thing? A few years ago, hell, a few weeks ago I couldn't have done that. I couldn't have stood there with him. I would have been burning up with my old bitterness."

"And now?"

"Now it felt great. Is that a sign of some kind? To be able to accept that some ground is lost forever and go on?"

"I'm sure it's a sign. And for every lost possibility you can find a new one."

"Quite an optimist, aren't you?"

"Cock-eyed, isn't that the American term?"

"Not in your case."

"Tell me about my case."

"Open and shut. You're blue-eyed, not cock-eyed."

She burst into laughter.

"What's so funny?" he asked as they walked out into the dark street, arm in arm.

"In Finland every optimist is blue-eyed. That's their nickname—the blue-eyed ones. It means naïve. Innocent."

"Is that what you are?" He turned and faced her, his hands on her shoulders. His lips touched hers, softly. Her cheeks burned despite the frigid air and she fanned them with her muff.

"Why, Mr. Henderson, what a question to ask a lady."

He laughed.

"I don't think I like you as a southern belle. I like you as a northern star."

"So I can guide you through the night?"

"So I can wish on you."

Halfway home she realized with a shock that they were still walking tightly arm in arm, and that they hadn't talked about the war once during the evening. She was elated and ashamed at the same time.

A lull of sorts set in on the Isthmus, and in the north the Russians dug themselves into burrows. During these January days Tom had little to report aside from the evening communiqués, and he spent most of his spare time with Tina. There was much she wanted to ask him, but he did not respond well to direct queries. They glanced off him and he tossed them back like tennis balls. You couldn't serve straight to him, you had to make him bob sideways and backwards.

"I really envy you," she said one evening.

"Why?"

"So many people respect your opinions."

"Your opinions are just as good as mine."

"No one would believe me. I don't even believe myself half the time. When I think I have something figured out I immediately start wondering what the other side is. It drives me crazy."

He laughed. His laugh came easily now in her company. "I learned a long time ago that most people never know what to think until somebody comes along and tells them. People hate uncertainty."

"It must be wonderful to have everything figured out," she said, and he gave her a dubious look.

"You know I don't have everything figured out."

This was her chance and she took it. "Tell me about the gold watch."

"It's just a reminder. Of someone—something a long time ago. Something I lost a long time ago."

"Why can't you tell me? Did you kill someone?"

"In a way."

His stricken face frightened her and she decided she'd gone too far. "It's late. Go back to the hotel. Think about it. And tomorrow come back and tell me."

He didn't say a word as she saw him to the door and gave him a kiss on the cheek, first checking that Selma was not watching.

He shuffled back to the hotel, kicking up slush along the way. An unexpected thaw had warmed the streets. Water dripped from the eaves, and a chastened harbour wind brushed his face. His footsteps sank easily into the soft snow. It would freeze again at nightfall, but for now it was enough. Enough to take him back to another lifetime when spring came earlier and winter did not kill.

In the hotel entrance fleece coats draped the hallway and discarded fur hats hung on the hooks. He skirted the dining room and took the elevator straight to his room. He looked at the gold watch and rebelled. She had asked him to think about something he had assiduously tried to forget. Why should he dredge up the past because she wanted to hear it? And yet he knew he would. To make it easier, he lay back on his bed and reached for the scotch on the night table.

He turned the watch over and over in his hand. The old pain returned. Time had not healed the wound, just buried it. It didn't take much digging to scrape it bare.

5

A soft wind ruffled the daisies at the edge of the grassy field, and caused a slight trembling in the aspens. The sun, beaming out of a clear July sky, warmed the field amiably. It would have been a pleasant scene, except that this field was dotted with gravestones, and at one gravesite, a coffin lay freshly garnished with flowers. A small group of people in dark clothing stood around it, perspiring in the heat.

"To you, Lord, we commend his spirit," a stocky minister intoned, his forehead covered in beads of sweat. The skirt of his black robe swayed in the breeze.

To the minister's right stood a tall young man in a dark suit, head bowed, apparently lost in thought. The minister turned to him and said, "And now, Tom Henderson has something to read in honour of his father's memory."

The young man fished a piece of paper from his pocket and cleared his throat.

"Sunset and evening star, and one clear call for me,
And may there be no moaning of the bar when I put out to sea."

He read Tennyson's simple words in a voice that often seemed on the verge of breaking, but never did. A sharp-faced woman on his right, in a stern black dress, high-collared and unfashionable, looked up at him in disapproval.

The minister gave the benediction and shook Tom's hand. The crowd drifted away until only Tom and the sharp-faced woman remained.

"You might have read something of a religious nature at your father's funeral," the woman said, sniffing into a lace handkerchief.

"Sorry, Aunt Lee," said Tom, "but that was Dad's favourite poem. I'm pretty sure he would have wanted me to read it today."

"Pretty sure! What would you know about what he wanted? All this time and when do you show up? For his funeral!"

"I'm not going to argue with you at his grave," Tom said. He turned and began to walk away. As he walked, it was apparent that he had a slight limp, that the left knee of his long legs did not hold properly.

She followed him, the heels of her pumps sinking into the grass with every step. "I don't want to argue either," she complained to the back of his head, "but after your mother died, someone should have taken you in hand. It broke my heart to see your father sitting and waiting for a letter from you. You could have written more often."

He wheeled and faced her. "I know that, and I'll regret it to my dying day."

"I suppose you were still miffed about having to give up college. But that wasn't his fault."

"I know that, too."

At hearing these confessions, she fell silent. They stood there in the bright sunlight, and she softened slightly.

"Aunt Lee, I was trying to line up a heart specialist for him in Toronto."

"Did he know that? Did you tell him?" She began to weep again. "Not that it would have mattered. Nothing mattered to him except you. He'd say things like, Tommy's never coming back. Tommy thinks I've ruined his life."

"But that wasn't true."

"No. Why did you let him think so? Your life ruined over a few medals you didn't get? That's all life is to you?" She wiped her eyes with her handkerchief. "I'm sorry, Tommy. I keep forgetting how young you still are. You have a lot of growing up to do. Your father could have helped you with that if you'd stayed here."

He could think of nothing to say.

"You'll be leaving soon, I suppose," she said, "Don't forget the watch. He was deeply hurt because you didn't take it with you, although of course he never said so. But I could tell."

Tom kicked a dandelion and swore to himself. He'd forgotten about the pocket watch.

"Well, I'll be going along," she said, her face suddenly crumpling. "I know you'll be in a hurry to get back to the city, but do try to keep in touch. Even an old spinster aunt deserves a letter now and then."

"Now, Aunt Lee—"

"I'll let you know when the estate matters are cleared up. Mr. Philbert said there shouldn't be a problem."

He bent down and kissed her wrinkled cheek. With a flustered wave she turned to go, and he watched her weave through the tombstones to the dusty road that led from the cemetery to the town, a five-minute walk. Tom stood for awhile and listened to a blue jay squawking in the aspens. He took one last look at his father's grave and then began his solitary walk home.

The old white house was just as it had always been. His father had taken good care of it, even after his mother had died. It was dim and hot in the parlour, the windows draped in muslin curtains. Needlepoint still covered the walls save for one large rectangular space where his mother's piano once stood. His father had sold it to pay off debts, and hadn't filled the spot with anything else. The parlour suited Tom; he had no desire to go out into the sun. It was the darkness he sought now, a darkness he had inhabited since the moment he heard about the death of his father.

He sat on the sofa for a few minutes before he started looking for the watch. There were not many storage places in the small house, and he hit it right the first time. The little box sat on top of the dresser in the main bedroom, beside framed photographs of Tom and his mother and father. He fingered the casing of the watch and stared at the photographs. His memories of his mother were vague, and her serene gaze didn't bother him. But the weary eyes of his father looked out with such sorrow that he began to sob. "Sorry, Dad. I'm so sorry." He remembered the day of his departure. The train station, the platform thick with dust and baggage. He'd been so anxious to leave that he'd barely noticed the gold watch on its heavy chain that his father slipped into his hand.

"Something for you to wear in the big city," the old man said.

Tom had glanced at the watch and pushed it back into his father's hand.

"Keep it. I don't need it." The gift irritated him, although he should have been honoured. It was the only possession of any value his father had left. But at the moment it epitomized his father's failures. What use was a pocket watch in the modern world? He loathed the town, loathed his poverty, loathed the bad luck that had brought him back here from a promising college career, not only academically but in the thing he loved most, running. His dreams had been derailed in October 1929, when the stock market crash wiped out the family savings. He'd come home to help his father run the dry goods store they owned. He found his father's meekness aggravating. It was a dirty world! You had to be tough and cold.

The final straw was the day he fell through a broken step while stock-taking. His knee twisted and fractured. As he lay in pain, he cursed at his father.

"Damn! Couldn't you even fix this step?"

His father telephoned for the doctor and then slumped at the kitchen table, shoulders shaking, clutching at his chest. Tom dragged himself to the bedroom, unable to let his anger go, unable to forgive himself for the ugly words he could never retract. He knew there was no money to fix the step. Just as there was no money for proper care for his knee. The creaky small-town doctor, working for a can of soup or a bag of flour, somehow got a splint around it, but that was all.

"Take care of the knee, son," his father said at the station. "If you're not careful, it may never mend properly."

"And you may never run again," the unspoken words hung in the air. Tom knew his running career was over; their finances would not allow for therapy for the knee or even the chance to enroll in college again. He knew that instead of going back to college as his father believed, he was heading to Toronto to look for a job. All of it seemed particularly bitter that day of his departure, and his bitterness found its target in the pocket watch. How it must have hurt his father. Not only the scorned gift, but the eagerness with which his son fled, and then the long months of not writing, as he made a new career for himself as a sportswriter in Toronto, then Chicago.

Letters came from Aunt Lee about his father's worsening heart. He put them aside, promising himself he would look into the matter of the old man's health as soon as he could. Promising himself he would write a proper apology for his behaviour at the station. Promising himself he would send his father money to fix up the store. Then, the final telegram from his aunt, with the news that time had run out.

His father's tired eyes looked at him from the picture frame. This will never heal, he thought. The next day he found himself again on the same railway station platform where he'd said good-bye three years earlier. Aunt Lee came to the station to see him off. Despite her sharp tongue, he'd always been fond of her. He offered her the deed to his father's house, but she turned it down.

"What would an old lady want with a house?" she said. "Besides, you might want it someday yourself, when you come back here again."

He knew there was no chance of that, but didn't say so. He had no wish to hurt her feelings but there was a chasm between them he couldn't reach across, not to her, not to anyone. The train came in a clamour of smoke and noise. Aunt Lee kissed his cheek and he climbed on board. He found an empty seat by a window, and as the train picked up speed he gazed at the familiar scenes of his childhood with dry, unseeing eyes, until the darkness swallowed the countryside and he slept.

Tina listened as Tom told her all this at the Fennia, and then sat in silence trying to find words to say.

"And you've never gone back?" she asked.

"No."

"Why not?"

More silence. Clinks and small swishing sounds as the waiter refilled the cups and lit the tea candles, the rituals of dusk at the Fennia.

"Cowardice. Denial. Idiocy. All of the above. The fantasy that Dad is still there, that someday I'll go back and make it up to him. You wouldn't think that after all these years it would still hurt so damn much." His eyes were closed and his fingers gripped the white porcelain coffee cup so hard she thought he might crush it.

"You can't change what happened. But you have to let him back into your life." She thought she saw his fingers loosen their grip on the cup. "Your father wouldn't want you to punish yourself. He loved you."

"That only makes it worse. If he'd hated me it would be easier."

"The pain is your cross but people live their lives bearing all sorts of crosses," she said. "You can't turn away from the sun, even a stunted tree reaches for the sun." She flushed. "I'm sorry, that was rude." He raised his eyes and looked into hers.

"What should I do?"

"Always wear the watch," she said, though she really had no idea what he should do. "You can't bury the pain because then you also bury the love."

"I've never talked about this to anyone," he said. And in his eyes she saw amazement that he had talked about it at all.

6

January 1940

Taipale

My dearest Tina,

They call this a lull. No major attacks since Christmas, only small infantry thrusts and the Usual Artillery Fire. And the noise of Russians digging, their sappers tunnelling through the frozen earth, closer and closer to our positions. Stalin makes good shovels. We can't do a damn thing about it. We're so short of ammo we just let them dig. If only we had a few airplanes to rain bombs on their jolly campsites.

Our existence in this bizarre world without night and day is wearing us thin. It's very dim, only two weak oil lamps, not enough for thirty pairs of eyes to see by. The lower bunks are strewn with wounded. Gauze on foreheads, heads wrapped in red-soaked turbans, a hand, a

foot, a leg tied up in dirty swaddling. I take out my flashlight and inspect a fellow bound from head to foot, huge
red stains spreading from his midriff. He won't make it
to the field hospital. Neither will his bunkmate, both legs
blown off, grey from loss of blood. Another sits in fetal
position, knees pressed to chin, trying not to whimper
as he holds his guts. None of them can be moved to the
rear until the daylight fades and it's safe for the medics
to come up. Everything has to be done after dark.
Rations come to the front, the wounded and dead go
back, repairs are made, trenches dug. Worst of all is the
infernal thirst. Every wounded man begs for water but
there's not a drop here in the front line. You can't drink
the filthy snow. There is a well not too far away, but one
day somebody made a dash for it and a Russian sniper
cut him down at the well mouth, and his blood seeped
in, finishing whatever water might have still been there.
I can't bear the murmurs of the poor devils begging for
water. I hate the lies I tell them, that it's coming soon.

Time to rouse the healthy ones for duty. Every guy has to
be shaken awake. As they stumble out, the frozen guards
stumble in, beards dripping with icicles, madmen's
Santas. They croak for food, but all we have is crispbread. Our pockets are full of it and coffee beans mixed
in with shells and rounds and other junk, so you have
to watch what you put in your mouth. The coffee beans
keep you awake. It's the hot food that's the problem.
The Russians have our supply trails in their sights and
getting food up to the line is difficult—the first leg in
horse-drawn wagons, the rest of the way on sleds. They
tried putting the soup and porridge in milk cans but they
spill, leak, get punctured by shrapnel. Now with this
deep freeze, we've taken to bringing soup and milk up in
frozen chunks. Every guy just cuts off his portion with

his knife. That's how the cuisine works around here. Not the Savoy, but we're not starving.

The cold is unbelievable. Minus forty. Yesterday Lampinen dozed off, and woke up with his forehead stuck fast to the rampart. We cut him loose and his loss was limited to a piece of hair and skin. Jokinen the accordion player lost his fingers. Our music is gone now, except for Markus, who still sings his songs. Far from being irritating, he soothes; we lie there half asleep, humming with him. Next winter in Italy! The night Jokinen got hurt Markus changed his tune. Now he only sings one aria, *A Lucivan de Stelle*. He won't sing anything else.

Home is a place I think about in the dugout during the long nights. Or on quiet evenings when I play chess with Lampinen and Markus sings his arias. And when I take out your picture. The Russians are cooking up something. We don't count the artillery fire as activity any more. Yet it bleeds us slowly, chips away our positions and trenches. The landscape at the front is lunar, all craters and black rocks. Stay well, my sweet.

Your Paul

7

Tina knew what was happening between her and Tom was an affair, although she didn't call it that. It was just the road her life had taken. Perhaps she would have called it by its rightful name if they were having sex, but they were not, despite the compulsion to be with each other every moment. He had clearly left the decision up to her and she knew she would have to make it soon. Her body had set off on its own heated tangent and her judgment could not keep up the chase. But the mutterings of the old women in the sauna about hussies buzzed in her mind like houseflies that had to be swatted. Nice girls don't go all the way. Buzz, buzz. Nice girls are wed and bedded in that order. Buzz, buzz.

The change in Tom was anything but discreet. Although no one connected it to Tina, at least not out loud, everyone noticed it.

"He's a different man," said her father. "The war has changed him."

"I always knew there was a fire in him," said Selma. "It must be the almond I put in his Christmas pudding."

And perhaps it was all these things, thought Tina. But it was her company he sought like a man released from prison, and she was the one he took with him into a world it seemed he had forgotten about

They met at the Fennia in the evenings after he filed his report. Despite the ban on public dancing, the bandstand upstairs was set up every night in a commendable show of Finnish obstinacy. Whoever stepped up to play became the orchestra.

"Henderson, play the piano," said Jussi one evening. He was the owner's brother, a passably good saxophonist. "I heard you in November."

"You played here in November?" asked Tina, incredulous.

"A moment of lunacy. I hardly remember it." But he got up.

And so began the piano career of Tom Henderson. His repertoire astounded her. It ranged from World War I chestnuts to the latest from the big bands, tunes she had only heard in the movies. When he played *Moonlight Serenade*, her special request, the house fell silent. Jussi improvised a descant on the sax, and tears flowed freely in the dark.

"Your scotch is waiting," she said when he finished his set. "That's why you do this, isn't it? The free drinks."

"Singing for your supper. A time-honoured tradition all over the world."

It was easy to pretend that there was no war, and Tom was not a war correspondent but a pianist with a famous band, maybe Glenn Miller's. They were somewhere in America, in a city where the windows of the skyscrapers blazed with light and taxicabs went screaming up and down the streets. The Fennia was warm and intimate and blacked out except for a few candles, and the upstairs booths were very private. It was there that they sat in the evenings, and he pulled her to his chest so hard she could barely breathe and kissed her roughly, the taste of scotch searing her tongue. Their conversations were travelogues to destinations that had disappeared on November 30th.

"What would you do if the war ended tomorrow?" he asked. "What would you eat? What's the first thing you'd buy?"

"I'd buy a ticket."

"To where?"

"Wherever you were going."

"Do you know what I'd buy for you?"

"What?"

"Fancy hair combs, to hold back those curls that hide your pretty eyes."

"I'd buy you a piano."

"I think I'm too old to break into show biz."

"You could teach."

"Teach who?"

"Children." She wanted to say "our children", but couldn't find the nerve.

It occurred to her that her relationship with Tom, for all its make-believe and transience—she couldn't believe it would survive the war—was more real than her relationship with Paul. Part of it was the strength of their sexual attraction, which belonged to an adult realm as opposed to the infatuation with Paul that had somehow got stuck in adolescence. But there was more to it than chemistry. It was the giving of self, the union of two souls she'd dreamed of, the lack of pretenses and reservations. It was he who first called it by the name she only dared whisper in her bedroom. She was showing him some photos and came across one of her parents on their wedding day.

"They look so much in love," he said.

"And what do you know about love?"

"Not much. Why don't you explain it to me?"

She leaned over the tealight and whispered into his ear. "It's a rose, it's a fire, it's a symphony, it's a curse, it's the sun, it's the moon, it can stop the world and make the world go round at the same time. It can last forever or last a day. Does that help you?"

"Not really. Words just radiate around it, like light radiates from the sun."

"That's because love is the centre, where the light begins."

"So we're at the centre, the origin of the light." He seemed restless, as if he had entered some field of energy so intense he couldn't stand still or stand apart.

On other nights he would quiz her about the most elementary aspects of life.

"How exactly do they cook this cutlet? What are the bread crumbs for?" And they discussed the effect of coating on the tenderness of the meat.

"Does coffee really help a hangover?" And she tried to improvise an answer based on her observations from Midsummers long past.

It always ended with their litany of wishes.

"I wish I could see the Seven Wonders of the World," he'd say. "And all the other wonders. The kangaroos in Australia. The Eiffel Tower. Wait a minute. I've seen the Eiffel Tower. Scratch the Tower."

"I wish I could see Chicago. And the wide prairie sky."

Then he would kiss her and she burrowed into his shoulder in the dark booth.

"Of course," he whispered, "it doesn't matter if I miss out on a few Wonders of the World. I've already seen the greatest one of all."

"What's that?" Her fingers traced the curve of his throat and his thin collarbone. She knew the answer but it thrilled her every time.

"You."

8

Summa. A small town on the Karelian Isthmus, sleeping away a brutally cold winter. Normally it would have been of no interest to anyone but since the earliest days of the war, it had stood and stood, bearing the heaviest Russian attacks, blocking the road to Viipuri. Tom loosened the collar of the sheepskin coat he'd borrowed from Taylor. It had been minus twenty when he'd scrambled out of the Kämp at ten o'clock in the evening, but the thought of seeing Summa made him sweat.

In February the Russians hit the Isthmus again with new ferocity. At first the foreign correspondents were skeptical, but by the second week even the laconic words of the communiqués couldn't conceal the massive scale of the offensive. Rumours of a breakthrough multiplied until the exasperated government authorized two correspondents to visit Summa and verify that it was still in Finnish hands. Tom was one of them.

For this trip, a private car was provided. The driver sped along the snow-packed highway at eighty kilometres an hour. When the first half-hour passed and they hadn't landed in the drifts, Tom pried his fingers from the dashboard and scraped out a round opening in the window. Through it he could see cameos of the countryside, sometimes black and white, sometimes shades of grey and blue under a cloudless moon. He watched the trees flash by, spectral spruce and pine, standing unmoved by their passage, disinterested in a fleeting crate of humans. The trees stared them by, content to guard their lands. But the stars—bright and restless, raced along with them, riding above the trees. He tried to track them one by one but soon lost them. They rode along with you for a while, until their path suddenly diverged from yours. Except for the North Star. He could see it there, constant among the rest.

He dozed, and woke up stiff with cold as they climbed the rise of land that led into Viipuri. In the dead of night they crossed the castle bridge into the city, where not a light flickered. The sky to the southeast burned orange and a low rumble came from beyond the hills. He was whisked up the steps into a dark hotel. In the morning, there was time for a quick breakfast with his partner for the trip, Cam Hawkins, who had material-ized during the night. After an hour's drive, they left the car at the edge of a thick wood and followed their guide through the trees. Without warning they slid down a steep icy grade that ended at the entrance to the battalion command dugout. The slide was covered by snowy boughs hung on netting and even in the daylight you could pass it by at ten metres and never know it was there. A young captain greeted them. It was a fifteen kilometre journey to the front, he said, and far too risky by daylight. They would have to wait for the night; in the meantime they could speak to the men if they liked. A change in the front line had taken place the previous night. The company now resting here had manned the line since December, suffering heavy casualties.

They found a few of them leaving the sauna. One sergeant sat in the dugout for a while, speaking to them in halting English. Russian cannons lined up hub-to-hub. Red infantry coming in waves. Climbing over their comrades' corpses. No Finnish planes to defend the sky. The sergeant took a bite of hard cheese bread and muttered about the untested battalion that had moved up to the line during the night. Somewhat bleakly he hoped "those fellows" could hold. Tom gave him a cigarette and fumbled for his matches but abruptly the sergeant's words ended. He was fast asleep, his head on his chest.

At nightfall they continued forward in a horse-drawn sled. The forest around them sprang to life like a colony of nocturnal gnomes. Long convoys of sleds moved in either direction along paths that converged out of the trees, then diverged again. The noise of the guns intensified to drumfire and the woods shook and jumped with branches. A sentry stepped out from behind a spruce. They followed him through the drifting snow, crouching when he crouched, ducking when he ducked. More snapping branches, a blinding flash, thuds that rattled the ground. Every few seconds a snowburst obliterated everything in sight.

"Don't lose the sentry!" Hawkins whispered, hanging on to Tom's sleeve.

Tom nodded. Easy to say, but how to follow a track that disappeared before your eyes? How to find a path when every tree trunk looked alike, when around you the crash of shells ricocheted without direction, when the lay of the land itself seemed to be tilting? Tom had known bombs and shrapnel before but never a world like this one, a landscape without landmarks, as uncharted as outer space. He remembered the charming story Tina had told him in Berlin about the journey of the lost children. Here, stumbling through woods where the sky shifted with every blast, the story lost its charm and became a parable of survival. Not only survival of the body but of the spirit. He had felt lost for so long, in the bars of Chicago and the lonely meadows of his youth, in the capitals of Europe and the hotel rooms where his only companion was the scotch. He searched the sky for the North Star and reached inside the sheepskin coat until his glove touched the pocket watch. He wore it all the time now. As he clutched it hard and fast, all the old wounds of his life began aching, and along with them came relief to have found them. And to have found her. That's all you need, he thought. As long as you remember who you are and who you love, you'll overcome the primal terror of the wandering child, and clear a passage through the deadly forests of the night.

Finally they reached their destination, an advance command post a mile behind Summa. Under a hanging gasoline lamp they found a colonel who brusquely inquired about the men and anti-tank guns supposedly on their way. They had no answer, and the colonel turned away from them. Suddenly the dugout shook for several minutes, the lantern swinging wildly. He said that they could not go up to Summa that night and offered them tea and toast.

Dancing on Pins

1

Tom spent less and less time at the Kämp, instead spending the hours between press conferences at the Fennia, at the flat on Elisabeth Street, or walking around the city. The danger of air raids was always present but he knew where the bomb shelters were, and there hadn't been a raid of the magnitude of November 30th for a long time. The cold bothered him more than the bombs.

He liked the Fennia. There he saw the real Finns, not the public relations officers and military attachés of the Kämp. He learned how to read their moods by the tilt of a head, the flash of an eye, a tear fiercely brushed away, the tapping of a foot on the parquet floor. And the Fennia had a map of pins—a large wall map showing the battle zones, with pins stuck in it to represent the front, roundheaded dressmaker's pins that meandered across the Isthmus and up to the Arctic Ocean.

Since early December the pins had barely moved at all, except at Suomussalmi where they joyously jumped a little eastward after the Finnish victory there. People walked up to the map and stared at the pins, fingered them, sometimes ran their hand lovingly over a spot on the map. That must be his home town, Tina would whisper. Or that must be

153

her birth parish. Each one of those pins marks someone's ancestral farm, a mother's or father's or grandparent's handiwork, someone's church cemetery or childhood meadow. How much heartbreak can dance on the head of a pin? More broken hearts than medieval angels, she said, with a mixture of anguish and hilarity. Of course, the generals don't see the pins that way.

Tom began to pop into Fennia just to look at the map. He had more faith in its humble eloquence than in the plethora of rumours at the Kämp. Once in a while someone gazed at the map with a stricken look, then turned silently away. Those were the people whose beloved places had already fallen behind the pins, said Tina. The saddest were the Karelian evacuees who drifted through at times, in clothes that testified to their journey with stains, rips and mismatched gloves, hats that had been the latest fashion before leaking boxcars damaged them.

The patrons at the Fennia watched the map as they sipped their coffee, terrified the pins would move. It was their touchstone to the real war, the war behind the communiqués and the newspapers.

2

Up to this point, the Björnströms' food situation had held up fairly well, but there came a day when Selma said in hushed tones, "We're out of dried peas. And the potatoes are low. I've looked everywhere, but there's none to be had."

"Oh, no," whispered Tina, hoping her father would not overhear. He was half-reading, half-napping on the sofa, and the prospect of losing his weekly pea soup would dent his spirits, even though he would be too ashamed to admit it, knowing that the boys in the field needed such things far more than he did. She'd heard there was food to be bartered for in the countryside and thought of the farm where she'd gone with Paul the previous spring. Perhaps some of their crop was still in the larder.

Tom was slated to travel inland on a press junket and she decided to travel with him as far as the farmhouse. He agreed, and they boarded the morning train to the northeast. There was little opportunity to speak privately in the crowded car, but there was no longer much need for them to speak at all. It didn't surprise her in the least when he hopped off the train with her at her stop.

The day was sunny and not oppressively cold, and they were bundled up well. They walked down the main street to the post office. The postmaster was going home for lunch and had his horse and wagon tied up behind the building. He volunteered to take them to the farm and call for them early the next morning.

"Oh, we're not planning to be there all night," said Tina.

"You're not going out of here tonight, lady," said the postmaster. "Because I'm closing down now and I'm the only transportation." Tina cast a glance at Tom, who didn't understand the postmaster's words. Until then she hadn't fully faced the thought of spending the night with him though it had skittered around her mind all morning.

"Come along, then," said the postmaster, pulling on his overcoat. He locked up and they followed him to the horse and wagon. Tom helped her up and hoisted the gunny sacks she had brought on his shoulder. They spread them over their laps like furs and clucked at the postmaster as if he were the driver of a troika and they were racing on the steppes. He neither heard nor heeded them, but it felt like an arctic joyride nonetheless and the horse kicked up a respectable wake of snow.

"So you're going to see old Pauliina," said the postmaster over his shoulder.

"Yes," said Tina. The image of Pauliina came back to her, a fluttery little woman who refused to be called by terms of address normally used for the mistress of a house.

"Maybe you can persuade her to go and live with her daughter. We buried her husband two summers ago. While the boy Esa was here it was all right, but now that he's at the front she's all alone. Every morning I expect to find her frozen to death." He slapped the reins and the horse turned off on the side road Tina recalled from the spring, when it had been lined with lush green birches and aspens.

"We're almost there," she said to Tom.

"I've wanted to see this place ever since you told me about it," he said. "The old foundation. Three hundred years old."

"It's under a foot of snow now."

"We can dig out a patch of it. Maybe do a jig on the floor."

They saw smoke pluming out of the house and disappearing in the canopy of pines overhead. No pilot would spot the place even if he was crazy enough to want to bomb it. The February sun took the edge off the minus twenty degree temperature as they plowed through knee-high snowdrifts. In the spring when Tina had been here, the weeping birches by the lake had been newly in leaf and the chokecherries in full white bloom. She held her muff against her face and the cold filtered through its musty thickness and warmed her lungs like mild spring air. For a moment she forgot about Tom, overcome by the timelessness of the place, the circle of seasons that brought the snow and the cornflower and the melting ice, the constancy of existence here since a hunter first shot an arrow into the pines, since a farmer first burned a clearing to plant his crop. The foundation of the old house lay buried under the snow, a little to the left of the new house. Through war and famine, it had stood for centuries, an elegy to the strength of the human will to stay the course of ordinary life.

The old woman stood in the doorway, wrapped in heavy sweaters, her eyes twinkling under a woollen kerchief.

"Company for you, Pauliina!" shouted the postmaster as he turned his horse around.

Pauliina took a step forward and extended a mittened hand. Tina lowered her muff and the old woman gazed into her face.

"You've been here before," she said. "But not with this man."

"Pauliina, this is Tom Henderson. He's an American reporter here covering the war. We've come on a little begging mission. May we come inside?"

"Of course. A pleasure to meet you, Mr. Henderson. The only tolerable thing about this war is meeting new people. The train brings them every day to the village. I've seen them there, some pretty strange looking folk I must say." She spoke by turns to both of them though Tom plainly could not understand a word. Tina explained her errand, promising to pay whatever her asking price was for food she had to spare.

"We'll check the cellar later," said the old woman. "Surprising how much there still is down there. Of course, with everybody gone, I don't cook much for myself. I do have coffee on the stove. Business can wait."

And so they shook the snow off their boots and exchanged them for dry indoor felt slippers, and Pauliina brought a tray of coffee and pulla. The wood stove warmed the room and she kept up a chatter about the travellers passing through the village, the war, the postmaster's wife, and above all her son Esa, who was at the front. He was the last of her six children, the other sons having died in infancy, the daughters married.

"Wouldn't you be safer with your relatives instead of here alone?" asked Tina.

"This is my place, safe or not. There were Russians here during my grandfather's time and Swedes before that. They come and go. We stay."

She refused help in clearing away the cups and saucers. Stay warm by the stove, she said, then we'll look in the cellar. Instead Tina said they would go outside and look at the old foundation. This bemused Pauliina, but she offered stiff knee-high felt boots.

Tina and Tom stomped into the sunlit afternoon like schoolchildren at recess. At the bottom of the landing he stopped.

"There's your tree," he said. And there it was, a birch with a crooked trunk like the one on Elisabeth Street. It pleased her that he had noticed. They inspected the great old tree, which grew straight for two-thirds of the way before the main trunk tilted toward the house. A secondary branch forked horizontally away from the house.

They gathered twigs and began to brush away the snow from the perimeter of the foundation. The stones had been mossy green and overrun with wildflowers in the spring. Now, they stood bare in brute imperviousness. Tom was pacing on them, slipping and sliding, his boots filling with snow. Suddenly he reached for her hand.

"Let's do that jig," he said. He lurched toward her and they both fell into the drifts.

"That does it," she huffed. "You'll be the death of us. Now we'll freeze solid."

"Then let's go sit by Pauliina's stove again. She'll have more coffee and a hot lunch. How much do you want to bet on it?"

They stood and looked at each other, soaking wet in the snow. She felt a sudden exhilaration. The farm existed in a separate time and place. She felt things peeling away—the war, her duties, fear for Paul, her former life.

"If this were another lifetime we'd be together from day one, wouldn't we?"

"Yep. I'd be a jazz pianist."

"I'd be the waitress at your club. Every night I'd bring you your scotch and shoo the brazen women away from you. I'd wear a starched apron."

"They'd laugh you out of Chicago."

"For shooing women away?"

"For the apron." He rubbed her chin with a snowy mitten.

"That makes no sense at all," she said.

"Does everything have to make sense?" he said softly, as if he knew exactly what she meant. And she was sure he did. He'd always seemed to be tuned into her thoughts, from their first encounter at the Andalusia in Berlin.

Inside the house the stove was going full blast. A pot of coffee simmered on it and beside it a steaming soup tureen, and Tina recognized the scent of stewing turnips. Pauliina was setting out tableware with steady hands, her feet agile in a pair of shiny black T-strap pumps. She'd changed into a grey dress with lace at the throat.

"You can go down to the cellar before supper," she said. "Take as much as you like, an old woman can't eat very much. Soon it will be spring and Esa will come back from the war, and we'll plant another crop."

The cellar was behind the house on a slightly sloping rise of land. Its heavy wooden entrance was well protected by shrubs. Tom pried it open and held the candle as they looked down. The ladder was shaky and it was pitch black. He went first, feeling his way carefully at each step. Tina followed, carrying the sacks and holding the candle high, watching the flame dancing against the stone walls. They found themselves surrounded by bins and crates. Pauliina was well enough stocked to open a small restaurant. They began to fill the sacks with turnips, potatoes, beets, and dried peas. When they had enough munitions to make Selma happy, they made their way back to the house and while Tina helped Pauliina ladle turnip soup into bowls, Tom went out into the darkness to fetch more wood for the stove.

"No need for you to bother," said Pauliina. "The postmaster comes by in the mornings and brings in my wood. Poor man, having to live with that devil woman—"

A loud crash and a cry from outside. The ladle nearly dropped from Tina's hands.

"You stay here, I'll go and see," she told Pauliina. "There haven't been any Russian partisans around here, have there?"

"No, dear, calm yourself. I expect he's stepped into one of Esa's mousetraps. The postmaster did one day. My lazy old kitty can't keep up with the mice." She stroked a grey cat that lay dozing by the stove.

Candle in hand, Tina plowed toward the woodpile. Thrashing noises came from there and she saw scattered chunks of firewood and a dark form writhing in the snow.

"Tom! Tom, for God's sake, are you all right?"

A great roar, and then silence.

"Tom!" she reached him and bent down, the candle flickering in his face. "Speak to me!"

"Fucking mousetrap. It's OK now. Got it off. Lucky I was wearing those boots or my toe would be gone."

"Oh! Let me see. Are you sure you're all right?"

"No, I'm not all right," he said. As she bent over him he deftly snatched the candle and pulled her down into the woodpile. With his free hand he pinned her beneath him, showering them with wood chips and snow. "Look, I have a splinter in my finger." He held his hand in front of her eyes and grinned, the candle high in the other hand and licking at a nearby log.

"Oh! It's not funny. You scared me. And be careful, we could start a fire here."

His body lay full length over hers and he pressed his lips to her ear. "Some fires start by themselves."

She got up and shook herself, helped him re-fill his arms with firewood, and led the way back to the house.

After supper Pauliina brought out homemade currant wine. Frost was creeping through the haphazardly taped windows but the room was cozy and the wine was potent. She began to speak of her own wedding, which had been held in this room. "It was on Boxing Day, of course, when there were lots of leftovers," she explained. "Around here, most people are married on Boxing Day and born around Michaelmas. Dying is less predictable." She began to hum a song.

"My wedding waltz," she said. "The first waltz—*Carmen Sylva*. A foreign tune, but pretty, don't you think?" From somewhere she retrieved a garland, its ribbons frayed and its flowers dried into petals, and placed it on Tina's head. "My wedding crown," she said.

Tom stood up and took the garland and ceremoniously laid it on Pauliina's white hair. Tina watched, sipping her wine, as he bowed deeply to her and led her to the centre of the floor. They stepped into a waltz in flawless measure. Where on earth had he learned how to dance a country waltz? she wondered. Who taught him how to hold his arm out straight, to bend his knee on the second beat, to pull his foot back and glide in a circle? I want this man, her heart whispered. Forever.

Later Pauliina showed them to her guest room. No one had asked about sleeping arrangements and no one mentioned them now. By the light of the candle they sat on the edge of the double bed. The warmth of the stove was far away and they only removed their boots and sweaters before climbing under the covers. There they huddled like novice campers, pulling the massive feather bed up to their necks. Suddenly it was unbearably hot, and he was kissing her throat, her face, her hair. There was nothing between them now, skin to skin, and his lips and fingers covered her with the pleasures she had half-imagined, half felt, until she was conscious of only the ecstasy that swept over her and she threw off the heavy quilt and they came together naked in the darkness. But even as she reached the crest of it the buzzing started again—pregnancy outside marriage was a disgrace, pregnancy with your fiancé at the front was probably treason. She mumbled, "I can't—" and he drew back. She felt the hot rush of his ejaculation on her thigh and her mind spun in circles—that's not where it should be, you can't make a baby this way— and then her thoughts shut down and she drew him back and let the grandeur of her well-being sweep over her, the afterglow of a release her body had never known. She reached for his bare shoulder and felt it was shaking. Oh God, I'm so sorry, he whispered, I'm so sorry. Forgive me. No, it's my fault, she said. It's you who must forgive me. And he turned to her and kissed her face. No, it's my fault. I knew better than to let it go this far. But it was what I wanted, she wept. Yes, but you hadn't made up your mind, I know you, God how I know you, God how I love you.

The next morning the postmaster came at eight o'clock and drove them to the station. Just before they got separated on the crowded train, Tom whispered in her ear.

"You know you'll have to decide—about who's going to take you home from the dance."

You mean who's going to take me home from the war, she thought. It was the lens through which every act and feeling was filtered—it justified the sacrifices, from the ban on dancing to rationed food, and it patrolled the emotions, so that in the beginning she'd told herself that her relationship with Tom was for the good of the country, a notion soon discarded. But at Pauliina's farm she'd seen how clear things were if all she had to listen to was her heart. She'd never known you could love someone so completely. She loved every word he said, each one was precious and transformed into greatness no matter how banal. She loved his every lifted eyebrow and half-closed eyelid, his silences and his rants, his jokes and his profanities. She loved his strong arms and the softness in his eyes when he looked at her. And if these things had not been so she would have loved their opposites in him because her love transcended any external criteria and was her only standard and source of faith.

3

Taipale

February 11, 1940

Dearest Tina,

Crouching in a corner of the tent, writing on one knee, the earth convulsing. All hell broke loose yesterday. Bombers in the sky all day. This morning they started at 7:30 with artillery barrages, four hours now. Here in combat reserve we live in tents. They're dug half a metre into the ground and camouflaged but the bombers find them anyway. And canvas is damn useless against shrapnel. I'd be safer under a tree, but it's too cold. Can't light fires. In the tent there's a bit of human heat. We sleep in layers. The bottom layer is less comfortable but those on top take the splinters first.

The word is that none of our positions have been lost but all are under heavy attack. I have a bad feeling this time.

February 14

Resting in the deep woods, after two days in hell. I left off on the eleventh, near noon. Around one-thirty we got the call. Difficult march in soft snow, feet aching. Around three our battalion massed near the Captain's dugout. Learned to our horror that position Number One was in Russian hands. Ordered to recapture it. Too little time, too little preparation, broad daylight. Timing of our artillery support off. Tried to rescind the order but we were already on the move. There were two hundred Russians in Number One with a dozen automatic weapons. Started to roll them out, first grenades, then strafe like hell. For two hours we pushed them back. Then—God Almighty!—we ran out of ammo and grenades! At the height of the fray we had to pull back while a young ensign rushed back to HQ for more. Fell back to the entrance and took shelter near a burnt-out tank. Just as the ensign returned a Russian grenade struck him. His whole squad down. All of us withdrew. Casualties high. The bodies of the ensign and his squad couldn't be recovered.

At nine in the evening we reassembled, what was left of us. Same assignment: recapture Number One. Volunteers from other companies joined us. Under cover of night and with a decent artillery blast from our side we charged into Number One. Lobbed grenades for all we were worth and strafed, and by one in the morning Number One was ours again. This time we barely suffered a single casualty. Then came a moment that still haunts me. Total silence fell over the whole sector. The Russian guns died over the whole of Cape Hook. Two hundred Russians lay dead in Number One. At four in the morning Third Battalion arrived to take our place. They seemed stunned, climbing over the piles of dead Russians. Our own nerves shut down hours before.

Back at camp we had a sauna. My hands hurt—it was twenty-five below last night and I tore my palms into open blisters on the cold grenades. But it seems my efforts at Number One were appreciated. The Lieutenant came by this morning. Said he's recommending me for a medal of valour and a leave. I said what timing, I'd been meaning to ask for a leave because I'm getting married. He slapped me on the back and congratulated me. So, my darling, will you marry me? Forgive my stupidity that I didn't ask you before I left in October. This time the first thing I'll do is buy a ring. Then we'll go to dinner at the Savoy, and do what we should have done years ago. Tomorrow I'll be on my way home for a ten day leave.

And if all goes according to plan, I'll see you soon.

Your Paul

4

The train returned from the farm at nightfall and Tom walked Tina home, toting her load of vegetables up to the flat. He arrived at the Kämp just as the communiqué was being read. The affable features of Captain Zilliacus were haggard. He didn't stay to chat as usual, but turned on his heel and left immediately. Later, over an omelet in the dining room, Taylor confided that there had been a break in the Line at Summa.

"Of course, the Finns may yet be able to patch it up. They always have."

"Not likely," said Mitch Webster, joining their table. "They simply have nothing left. Their men are walking shadows."

They sat contemplating their scotch when Tina rushed through the door and up to their table, not pausing to remove her coat and boots. Tom stood up and took her arm.

"What is it? Is it—Paul?"

"No, no, we've just heard the most fantastic news!" She glanced at Webster and pressed on regardless. "Father just got off the telephone with a friend in Paris. The Allies have reached agreement on sending aid to Finland. They have troop numbers, set dates, everything—isn't it wonderful?"

The men looked at each other incredulously. There was indeed an Allied conference going on in Paris, but if such a decision had been made, it had not hit the airwaves yet.

"Well," said Tom, "tell your father his horse might talk after all."

"Whose cavalry are you referring to?" asked Webster.

"How reliable is this information?" Taylor leaned forward.

Tina frowned. "It's not official yet, but my father's friend is well placed. He wouldn't mislead us."

"The Allies couldn't come at a better time," said Webster. "It's pretty grim right now, Miss."

Taylor lit his pipe. "I sincerely hope your prayers are answered, my dear. But I fear you misread the motivation for the Allied offer. Their primary goal is to cut off the shipment of iron ore from Sweden to Germany. If they send an expeditionary force into Scandinavia, I can promise you only a small part of it will ever reach Finland. The rest will stay in Norway."

"With all due respect, Mr. Taylor, the will of the people of Britain—"

"Doesn't matter a whit. Everybody wants to help your country, my dear, but it's just not convenient at the moment."

A short silence. Her flashing eyes turned to Webster.

"What do you think, Mr. Webster? You've seen more wars than anyone."

"I think—your horse better get here on the double. Your country is up against the power of the mass. It's the purest example of the struggle between the power of the mass and the power of the individual I've ever seen."

"Interesting." Taylor puffed away on his pipe.

"If it weren't so depressing." Webster pushed away the plate in front of him. Lately he fell into lapses of silence and withdrew into his own world. Tom considered taking him aside for a heart-to-heart.

It took him a moment to notice that Tina was not at the table. Excusing himself, he took his coat and went outside. It was not a long walk to the tree on Elisabeth Street. He found her there, leaning against the scrollpaper bark of the gnarled birch.

"Why are they so negative?" she asked. "Especially Taylor. He's downright cynical. Webster is different. He feels things."

"Newspapermen are a cynical, cold-hearted lot. You should know that by now."

"Well, I won't let them spoil my hope—my certainty that the Allies will come." He held her until they both began to shiver and she ordered him back to the hotel. It was a mild February evening, an unexpected respite from the clawing cold. He lingered in the park by the tree she loved. A few drops of water still clung to its thin white bark. It would freeze again, he thought, but soon the sun would revive it for another summer. He knew he had spent too long in dark places. He'd taught himself not to invest too deeply in anything, since he didn't think he deserved a return. But maybe it didn't matter if you deserved a return or not, only that you bought a share. Now she had come into his life and this war had gripped him by the throat.

And there was more to it than that. Everything seemed clearer when he was with her. He remembered a time when he had his own moments of clarity, when he felt that some great understanding was close at hand. Those moments had stopped, but now he could feel the door creaking again, opening them up. He took a deep breath and touched the birch, whose twisted trunk was the path that led her home through all her stormy nights. Then he bounded down the street toward the hotel.

5

They call the tango the dance of lust, but Tina always thought of it as the dance of life. No matter how wistful the melody, the rhythm persists and at the end prevails, just as the heartbeat of life goes on. Her people loved the tango, and she believed it had to do with their bond to the harsh and beautiful land. It was a dance of the earth.

In February the war took a frightening turn. They all danced their private tangos, the music growing more melancholy but the beat still strong. As reports streamed in of huge battles raging on the Isthmus, of fresh Russian divisions moving up, the promise of help from the west was their beacon in the night.

First they had to know whether their neighbours, Sweden and Norway, would grant transit rights to Allied troops. The Finnish foreign minister travelled to Stockholm to ask once again if Sweden would allow passage. The answer was No.

Tina sat in the Fennia studying the map of pins the day the news came out of Stockholm. The pins had not moved since December. Now there was a break near Summa and for the first time they moved back, one tiny agonizing step; for the first time a general retreat was ordered from the Line. Then to read the terse words of the Swedish prime minister, denying Finland's request for troop passage—blood rushed to her head and her limbs would not sit still. She marched off in the cold twilight to the Kämp.

It was not difficult to find Tom. Every foreign reporter in Helsinki was at the phones that day, getting out the news of Sweden's refusal. Tom steered her to their favoured alcove and ordered her a scotch.

"This won't affect Stalin's thinking," he said. "He'll think, if the Allies want to send troops to Finland, they'll walk right over the Swedes. Just like he would do."

"Damn the Swedes!" she said, fighting back tears.

"You don't mean that," said Tom.

She reached over and expropriated one of his cigarettes, dragging deeply as she always did when under duress, then letting it burn away unheeded between her fingers. "The Swedes preach about their neutrality, yet they see nothing wrong with selling iron to the Nazis. What do they think the Nazis use it for? Making pots and pans? Pots and panna?" She said the phrase over and over, imitating the sing-song cadence of high-society Swedish. She took a sip of the scotch and straightened a wrinkle in the white tablecloth. "But to let Allied soldiers cross their soil en route to Finland would be an unthinkable breach of their neutrality."

"That's neutrality for you," he said. "Meaningless in peace and a joke in war. I guess sooner or later we all have to step into the ring."

"The ring?"

"Whatever game is in town. Aren't you being a little harsh? Look at the Swedish homes taking in Finnish children, the money collected, the volunteers. And be honest. Would you risk putting your country at war for the sake of someone else?"

"Oh, the international law book is on their side, all right. But there's another book, a book written by the human heart." She stopped. The truth was she no longer knew what to believe. The neglected cigarette stood precariously between her fingers, a fragile cylinder of ashes, and she gazed at it as if the fate of the nation was visible in its porous column. Then she felt a nervous convulsion, her body trying to shake free from its vise of tension. He went on with soothing words about the Allied offer, but she no longer heard. Instead she listened to the music coming from the back of the Kämp, where people were dancing.

She stood at the edge of the small dance floor. The music of the tango washed over her like rain over a parched field, a field of spring anemones, a field somewhere else, in someone else's life. The violins soared over the rhythm, the heartbeat pounded beneath. Tears streamed down her face. She didn't care that dancing had been banned for the general good. There was no general good. There were only moments and there was only Tom. She sensed him standing beside her. Something in her broke free and she was in his arms.

"Dancing is forbidden," she whispered.

"So is killing."

"Tonight I'm going to break all the rules."

"Here and now?"

"Here and now, and later in your room."

He really didn't know how to dance the tango, but they composed their own steps. He pulled her close to him and she arched her breasts hard into his chest. The scent of his shirt was unfamiliar. Some faint aftershave mixed with cigarette smoke. The skin at the back of his neck was hot. She ran her fingers along his shoulder blade and down the groove in his back.

And then, in the dim hallway light, she saw a face. Someone cried, "Paul!"— she realized it was her own voice, and at the same instant she tore away from Tom and rushed toward Paul. Where had he come from? Standing there in his army overcoat, his eyes deep in their sockets, staring at her. Before she could reach him he wheeled about and pushed his way through the drunken throng toward the door. Half-stumbling she ran after him. Tom had seen him too, and he rushed to the gramophone and ripped it out of the wall so forcefully it raised a shower of sparks. Hey, you can't do that! someone shouted, and he shouted back, I just did. Tina heard no more, for she was at the outside door.

She nearly lost her footing on the snow-covered steps and at the bottom of the steps she paused, scanning the dark Esplanade for Paul. How could he have vanished so quickly? The hazy moon gave just enough light that she could make out his dark form striding down the boulevard, already past the statue of Runeberg. He was almost at the corner and in a few more seconds would be turning it, to disappear into the side streets. She shouted—"Wait! Paul, wait!"

He seemed not to hear. The frigid air hurt her lungs but she shouted again. "Paul, wait!"

He slowed down, stopped and then leaned against the wall of the building on the corner. She ran, slipping and sliding recklessly over the cobblestones, clad only in a blouse, skirt and high-heeled shoes. The freezing harbour wind clawed her face but she hardly noticed. She stopped a few feet away from him and strained to see his eyes but he was too far in the shadows. He bent over and cupped his hands, carefully lighting a cigarette. Even a solitary match was a dangerous thing in the wartime night.

Seconds passed, then minutes. She couldn't think what to say to him; she knew he would soon turn and walk away. Before her racing brain had chosen the words, he muttered gruffly, "You're going to catch pneumonia standing out here without a coat."

Thank God, he was talking to her. "Then let's go back to the hotel or to the house, anywhere you want. Why did you rush off like that? What were you thinking? We were just dancing, Paul. It didn't mean anything. For God's sake, Paul, it didn't."

He said nothing, only dragged on his cigarette.

"Paul, are you listening to me? If you have some crazy idea there's something between me and Henderson, you're wrong, wrong, a million times wrong." She stepped closer to him, shaken by how easily the lie came to her lips. "Ever since we were children you've been the only one. How could you think—" The cold gripped her throat and she coughed. His silence crystallized into a barrier sharper than barbed wire.

"For God's sake, don't go; don't leave like this," she croaked.

"You never wanted to open your legs for me," his voice was so soft she strained to hear the words. "Didn't want tenement seed."

"What? What did you say?" Her thoughts circled wildly, broke in pieces and wouldn't connect. She could not reply. He threw his cigarette butt into the snow and straightened himself, hoisting his pack high on the shoulder. He muttered in her direction, as if admonishing a young and irresponsible sister, "You shouldn't stand there like that; this is no time for anybody to get sick." With that he turned and walked away.

She watched him, her eyes caressing the dusting of snow on the shoulders of his heavy army coat. She yearned to shake those shoulders and not let them go until he listened to her. Panic struck—after all these years, he's walking away from me, walking away in the middle of the night in the middle of this hideous war; tomorrow he might be dead or I might be dead. Dredging up the last breath from her battered lungs, she screamed at him.

"Fine! Be an idiot! You said you loved me! You wouldn't walk away like this if you loved me!" Another fit of coughing cut off her words. By now he was around the corner and she could no longer see him.

"Idiot!" She kept screaming, her throat so raw that every word was agony. "I don't care! Do you hear? I don't care!"

Words would not come any more. She stood alone and shivering in the indifferent dark, tears frozen to her cheeks. The arctic night found her bones and she began to shake violently. Her feet hurt at every step but she started to hobble back toward the Kämp. Maybe I'll die right here, freeze to death right on this street. Then he'll be sorry.

After only a few steps someone threw an overcoat over her shoulders and pulled her close. It was Tom, stepping out of a recessed doorway. She didn't ask how long he'd been standing there or what he'd heard. He half dragged her back into the hotel, paying no heed to the curious stares that followed them as she collapsed into the corner. He ordered a coffee for her and a double scotch for himself.

"He just walked away," she whispered. "Just like that."

"Never mind, tomorrow he'll be the same." His voice came from a distant place.

"You don't know him. It can never be the same."

He fell silent.

"We were just dancing," she whispered. "He thought there was something more. But there wasn't." She searched his face so fiercely that he turned his head away. "Was there?"

"No," he said, his eyes cloudy and mild as if he were looking at lotus blossoms on the water.

Good, she thought, he agrees. Then perhaps Paul could be talked over. She couldn't let him return to the front thinking she'd betrayed him. She would fix things with Tom later.

Music blared again from the back room, the gramophone had been reconnected. A woman in black leather, a famous correspondent, slinked from table to table with practised Hollywood style. The full scope of the wrong she had committed hit her. It wasn't just about Tom. She had come to the oasis, sought the company of strangers who didn't care if her people lived or died. She had deserted her post.

She pulled on her coat. Tom fell into step beside her and they walked in silence through the desultory snow. The city was clad in the black cloth of mourning, the whole country was a dimly lit church lost in common prayer, and the two of them had offended the gods with their selfishness. It was not the time for dancing. But she couldn't believe it was not the time for love. If there ever was a time for love, this was it. But she'd got that all wrong, too.

At the entrance, she took out her key and whispered goodnight.

"Tina—"

"Tom, I can't talk about it now. It's not your fault. But I just can't talk about it." Then she hurried inside with a clang of the gate. She didn't envy him the trek back to the hotel. He would head straight up to his room and reach for the scotch on the night table.

For her, sleep would not come, only tears. She didn't weep for her own lost happiness. She wept for Paul, returning to the front burdened by the weight of her disloyalty. Those we love always have to pay the price for our sins. Dear God, punish me, not him. Don't let my weakness undermine his strength. The prayer surprised her. She rarely embarked on one-on-ones with God.

6

Paul walked through the blacked-out streets until the pounding in his head let up a little. The darkness embraced him and he welcomed it as a dear friend. The bright lights in the hotel had bothered him, for at Taipale daylight meant danger and death. The soldier's best ally was the night and its coming was devoutly awaited. How they loved the night.

He had no clear idea of where he was going. It made no difference, as long as he was walking away from the scene he had just witnessed, away from her. He could not even think her name. His stomach was queasy and he was sweating the way he did under artillery fire. He came to the end of the street that led away from the Kämp and crossed the Senate Square. He passed the library, the Fennia, and the jewellry store where earlier that day he'd bought the golden band that now weighed like a stone in his pocket, bought it and waited while the jeweller engraved the date on the inside of the band. He had no use for the ring now, nor for the speech he'd rehearsed on the train; no use for the dinner reservation he'd made. What was the use of anything now? He still had several days' leave left and no idea what to do with it. He could visit his father in the country, but what would he say about—her? There was nothing to say about anything.

After a few minutes of aimless walking, he noticed he was heading toward the railroad station. Of course, he thought; where else to go but the war? There would be a train leaving soon for the east. They left continually, relentlessly bearing young men to the battlefields. He would go back where he was needed. Possibly, if he felt like it, he would get off and visit Kotka en route. It wouldn't be much of a detour.

As he neared the sandbagged station, the whistles of the wood-burning engines cut the air like tracer bullets. The great hall within was cathedral-dark and packed with soldiers, men and boys who stood, leaned, lay sleeping, or sat on their gear. Some smoked, some conversed quietly. These were veterans; they had seen friends and brothers blown to bits, they had shivered in the cold as the guns raged around them, they had mowed down advancing Russians with their automatic rifles, sometimes killed them in hand-to-hand combat. Many had bandaged arms, legs, or heads and a few leaned on canes. Paul felt at home. The familiar jolt of fear passed through his body as he thought of where he was returning, but he knew that was where he belonged. The memory of the hotel receded and whenever it returned, he pushed it away.

Lottas began to serve coffee out of the station restaurant and he left his pack and stood in line. The fragrance of real coffee reminded him of that other life that had ended when the Russians attacked, and now seemed to have ended all over again tonight at the Kämp. Then he heard the train puffing outside and rushed for the door. He was astonished at how many men rose up from the unlit corners and converged on the platform, lining up to board the cars, battered cars whose sides were pockmarked with bullet holes. In the moonlight the dented metal resembled a modern sculpture he had once viewed in a Helsinki gallery with Tina.

"So how many days did you manage to get in?" asked the sergeant who shared a seat with him, a seat he'd been lucky to get. Most of soldiers sat on their knapsacks or on the floor.

"Get in?"

"This is only my second day. Two days off during the whole bloody war, and they call you back. Pissed me off."

"What are you talking about?"

"Where've you been?" the sergeant tried a smile that ended in a sneer. "Haven't you heard? All leaves—all, no exceptions, were rescinded today."

"Excuse me, I have to stretch my legs." Paul stepped into the aisle, unable to listen to another word. He felt the same need to flee the scene that he'd felt when his father telephoned him at work to tell him his mother had died, that he'd felt when his ankle twisted on the track in Berlin. There had been nowhere to flee then and there was nowhere to flee now. In fact it was worse in the aisle, because he could hear conversation from every part of the car, and the name "Summa" came up every time.

"Somebody said just outside Summa, right?"

"A whole company just up and ran."

"Under vicious artillery fire. Molotov's got cannons lined up wheel to wheel."

"They ran after the Russians smashed Poppius to bits. They tried to keep up the fight on the ramparts but couldn't hold." Paul recognized Poppius as the name of one of the bunkers at Summa which had been under heavy bombardment since the beginning of the war. He was sweating, but there was no room to turn around, to take off his heavy coat. He forgot his personal woes, forgot the scene at the Kämp. If Summa fell, the road to Viipuri was open, and after that the road to Kotka and Helsinki.

"We were rationing ammo at the height of the battle!"

"Fucking politicians! Not enough sense to buy enough shells!"

"Mannerheim begged and begged. The old coot knew what to expect and they wouldn't listen to him. Now we're up shit creek, rationing shells in the middle of a war."

The voices raged on and every minute spirits grew higher. Defiance crackled in the air like icicles breaking off the eaves. Anger at the Russians, anger at the politicians, anger at the neighbours who did nothing but send their cast-off ammunition and woollen socks. Not long afterward, a song rose out of one corner of the car. Paul took a deep breath and leaned against the window. You can't lose a war with guys like these, he thought. So what if there was a break at Summa? The Reds would have a tough time getting any further.

They'd been ricketing along for about an hour, stopping at a few stations to pick up more troops, when suddenly the train came to a jolting halt. The doors flew open and cold air rushed in, along with the shouts of a railroad engineer. The track up ahead had been damaged by bombers. There would be a delay.

Paul hopped out to see where they were, and whether there was a station house nearby serving coffee. To his surprise he saw they were almost near the junction where the tracks turned south to Kotka and he knew beyond a doubt what he would do. He would go into town and catch the morning train. After all, he was still on leave and had received no official notification to return.

He lost himself in the darkness quickly, not wanting to fall under suspicion as a deserter. In the general confusion no one noticed him walking down the track, along the familiar road that led to his hometown. He hitched a ride on a passing truck and was soon in Big Park.

7

The night was clear and cold and the stars were brilliant. There was the Great Bear, Ursa Major, twinkling through the smoke above the harbour where he had watched it every summer and winter of his life. There was the North Star. Small fires still smouldered everywhere. Houses and buildings lay in ruins; wood burned like dry grass in this freezing weather. My beloved city, he thought. You've done nothing to deserve this. He continued walking. In the glow of the stars and the fires he could see docks in ruins, loading platforms floating among the ice floes, and layers of ashes where lumber in neat bundles had once stood. The scene at the hotel now seemed as distant as the moon. What did all that have to do with me? These are the streets of my town, this is what the bastards have done to it. My God, why have you deserted us? Wasn't that what Christ said on the cross? Or somewhere on Good Friday?

He walked the pitch-black streets toward downtown. The North Star kept its steadfast watch over the crippled harbour. He could see other stars as well; never before had they seemed so intriguing, so important. He began to sing softly, an old folk song every Finnish child learned at his mother's knee.

"Here beneath the northern star we make this land our home,
But on the far side of the stars, another home we'll own."

He walked the streets where he had lived most of his life; every wooden rowhouse, every spruce stand, every granite outcropping, was beloved and beautiful. Scenes from his former life tripped through his heart like early evening clouds. Finally he grew weary, and the cold numbed his ears and fingers; moreover, he knew there were Home Guards about and he had no wish to encounter one of them. It wasn't so much that he feared a reprimand for being out in the street, it was just that whomever he met would be someone he knew who would ask questions about him and Tina. He ducked inside a doorway and lit a cigarette, carefully shielding the spark with his hand. After a few drags he put it out. It was forbidden to show light in the darkness, and like every Finn he was instinctively law-abiding to the bone.

Taking a short cut to his father's house, he realized it was past ten o'clock and he had no key. The old man was in the country, and the neighbour who might have let him in would be asleep. Lind's store was just around the corner. The second floor windows were tightly blacked out but he knew Marita would be up. Suddenly he raced up the hill and walked into the courtyard behind the store. It had been three years since his last visit and he had never intended to come here again.

He knocked on her door quietly. After a minute she appeared in the doorway, dark hair framed by the candlelight in her room. He said, quite formally, "Good evening, Marita. I was just passing by. I'm on a few days' leave. I noticed your place and I thought, if there's one thing I can count on, it's that Marita will give me a cup of coffee."

She invited him in. Her eyes were shy but held a curious poise, as if she knew why he was here better than he did himself. She took his coat and made him comfortable in her only soft chair.

"I do have real coffee, Rio Mocha in fact," she said with modest pride.

"Well," he said, "This is my lucky night. You don't get Rio Mocha at the front."

"I'll just be a minute," she said, and brought a blanket. "You warm yourself. Wrap this around your feet." He pulled off his boots and lifted his numb feet onto a hassock. She turned toward her kitchen alcove but stopped midway there and faced him with flushed cheeks.

"Oh, how rude of me," she said. "I didn't even tell you what a pleasant surprise it is to see you."

If there was an implied question in her statement, the question of why he was here instead of with Tina, she didn't betray it. She placed her hand on her throat and ran her fingers through the lace at the bosom of her nightdress. Then she rushed to her cupboard, pulled out a tin and started measuring coffee into the red enamel coffeepot.

Marita was a Karelian. Small, lively, with a merry laugh and a delicate face, she was a butterfly of a girl and the best dancer Paul had ever seen. On Saturday nights at the island pavilions, he'd watched her; she never lacked for partners and she never tired. Her tiny feet barely touched the floor, especially during a polka. She was talkative but never pried into his affairs when she encountered him on the streets. He felt safe, knowing she would not pry now.

As they drank coffee, Paul studied her. He'd grown up with her; had known her just as long as he had known Tina. In some ways he knew her better than Tina. Their fathers had been friends and co-workers at the mill. The families had drifted apart somewhat when Marita's father had married an outsider, a woman from Karelia, Marita's mother.

She asked him about his leave, and he told her whatever came into his mind. They didn't speak about the war. Not on a cold dark evening, when it could be forgotten for a few blessed hours. She knew how it was at the front. She had a brother there. Instead they spoke about coffee and sugar, about the rationing, about the terrible winter. Slowly Paul felt his emotions reviving; he still could not focus on the scene at the hotel nor see Tina clearly, but the pain crept back into his heart as the warmth of the room thawed out his icy limbs. In agitation he began to smoke, and rambled about Summa and about the Russian guns until Marita began to fidget nervously. She whispered, "I have something else in my cupboard. Something you'd like even better than coffee."

Paul looked at her in amazement. "Vodka?"

"Brandy. Mr. Lind split his stock with us girls before he left for his country estate. He gave me the brandy. Said I was the quickest clerk he had." She smiled. "He said before this is over we'll all need a stiff drink. Shall I get it?"

"Well, you really are my guardian angel. There's nothing I'd like better. If you only knew..." He caught himself, before he said something about Tina.

"If I only knew how long since you've had a shot?" Marita rummaged in her cupboard and finally found the amber bottle, along with two small glasses. She handed him the glass and he swallowed the bitter stuff, wondering how long old Lind had nursed it in his store, and immediately felt better. His hands stopped their incessant movement, he put down his cigarette, his shoulders fell back against the back of the chair. He emptied his glass before Marita had two sips of hers. She refilled it.

"That's not necessary," he mumbled. "I don't want to go through your whole stock in one evening." Still he took the glass with no pretense of reluctance.

"I wouldn't mind. In fact I told Mr. Lind I didn't even want it. If you like it, you can have every drop. I know—" she paused, and Paul sat up straight, afraid she would ask about him and Tina. She continued, her voice a soft massage. "I know what it must be like having to go back there. I know you can't tell me about it, but I do understand."

"You're a very understanding girl, Marita," said Paul. "I've always wished I'd had a chance to talk with you more. I mean, we played together, but I haven't seen you much since then." He was on his third glass of brandy and fancied they were at a dance and he was making clever small talk. He moved closer to her, and stroked her shoulders and her hair, and then her small round breasts. He buried his head in her neck and pulled her to him. She led him to the little curtained alcove where she had a narrow bed.

The walls of the alcove were decorated with framed copies of his press clippings from the Berlin Olympics. He remembered those walls. And the bed, too.

"It hasn't changed much since you were last here," she said.

"Oh, that," he stammered. "I couldn't have been very good company."

"I wouldn't say that. You were pretty blue when you came, but when you left you felt better."

He recalled the visits hazily, as he did everything that had happened in the month or so after Berlin. He'd been drunk most of the time and stayed away from Tina, helping his father fix up the flat here instead. In Marita's bed he found the relief he could get no other way. He'd tried to forget that interlude, but here he was again. Another disaster, another visit.

"You are my Lady of Lourdes," he said, "or whatever saint it is that heals the sick."

He lay down and she snuffed out the candle. Then she came to him. It was not a large bed, but it was large enough.

"Do you remember the map, soldier?" she asked.

"Yes." Under the duvet his hands found them again, the neighbourhoods where he'd lost himself after Berlin, and the ice-pick edges of his bitterness had started to chip away and soften. His fingers traced the path from her nipples to the hollow under her ribs, then crossed at her navel, followed the groove of her thighs to the spot where she had guided him and showed him how to rub, hidden deep in her pubic hair. She arched her pelvis down and he entered her. Her strong, thin legs opened and locked around his waist. He remembered the feeling from three years earlier, as she pulled him inside her as if there was nothing else on earth she wanted, and he pushed into her until he could push no further, so hard and so long that she finally told him to stop. He lay back exhausted. She kept her legs wound tightly around him, and his shudders dissipated in her flesh.

"There's something I should have told you a long time ago," she whispered, her lips pressed against his temple. But she saw that he slept, and buried her face into his neck. "It can wait."

He awoke at four and clung to her small, warm body through the hours of the early morning. He couldn't sleep. This one night, when he was free at last of the carnage and his ears had stopped ringing, he should have been clinging to *her*, the other one; but he couldn't think of her, he couldn't allow her face to appear in his imagination. That would drive him mad, he was sure of it. He got up and went to the taped window; a grey dawn was rising out of the east. The wooden floor was icy. He lit a cigarette and sat down at the kitchen table, pulling a blanket around himself for warmth. His thoughts still whirled around her, the one whose name he couldn't say. Hadn't he always known it would end like this? He'd never truly believed she would be his. But tonight—why tonight? Could she not have given him this one night, out of all the nights they had known? No.

Marita woke, and in the white breath of the morning she silently fixed him some coffee and offered him all the food she had—sugar, bread, cheese, milk. The stove struggled to warm the frigid room. Paul didn't notice. It was a lot colder where he'd come from, and where he was heading once again.

He got his gear together and hurried out. There was no time to go and visit his father's empty flat, to put the money he'd carefully saved into the old man's cupboard. He gave it to Marita instead. Then he rushed to the station, Marita beside him. The platform was overflowing with departing soldiers and their kinfolk. She clung to him wordlessly and he took her hand.

Will you weep for me if I die? he wanted to ask her. Will you weep for me? But he didn't ask. And it was really *her*, the other one, of whom he wanted to ask that question. At the last moment, when the train had already pulled into the station, Marita reached up and kissed him, and thrust a small golden trinket into his hand. He looked down and saw it was a locket with her picture in it, very similar to the cameo of Tina he'd kept in his pocket since Berlin.

"Remember me," she whispered into his ear.

"I will. And you remember me." He kissed her deeply and then he turned to board the train, already loaded, hissing and spitting its impatience. Suddenly he wheeled and ran back to her. He fumbled in his pack and found it, the gold ring he had bought for Tina in Helsinki, and buried it in Marita's cold small hand. It would have yesterday's date inscribed on it, but that didn't matter. She will weep for me, he said to himself, and kissed her again. Then he jumped on the train; he was the last one on board.

8

Later, he rested in a warm dugout filled with twenty snoring men. The men slept the sleep of the comatose, aware they might not get another chance to sleep for days, aware this might be the last earthly sleep they would ever know. The small stove burned nicely, and the oil lamps gave off the familiar dim glow. They were still far in the rear but the explosions coming from the front shook the earth constantly. He inspected the walls of the dugout. It was solidly built. Only a few sprays of dirt hit his face during the hours he lay there dozing. Finally he got up, dislodging the bodies on either side of him, and crawled out. He went to the table. Someone's coffee was bubbling. Probably the night guard's, who was engaged for the moment outside, answering nature's call.

He lit up a cigarette, and rummaged in his knapsack for pen and paper. The guard returned and offered Paul some of his coffee. Silently he drank, and began to write. "My dearest Tina." The words came automatically, until he noticed them and stopped. He saw her again dancing with Henderson, as if nothing else existed. What else had she done with him? He'd pushed those thoughts out of his mind and gone running to Marita, just as he had after Berlin. But he'd been wrong about Berlin and perhaps he was wrong now. He felt calmer. He would sort things out later, when he got back.

He was still staring at the blank page when the alarm bell on the dugout wall rang and a voice rasped, "OK guys! Let's move!"

He folded the unfinished letter carefully into his backpack, between his mess kit and the notepad, so it wouldn't get crushed. Here, far behind the lines, the snow was deep and the night clear and starlit. Reluctantly the men shuffled into line, knowing they were being called up to relieve a company in trouble. Knowing how much trouble lay ahead this time. Markus softly sang his aria, the one he had sung to the exclusion of all others since Jokinen got hurt. As they strapped on their skis, Paul asked him, "You've never told me. That song you sing all the time now. What do the words say?"

"It's about a man awaiting his execution, reminiscing about making love under the stars."

Paul looked up. The stars seemed less brittle than before. Almost unnatural. Possibly what Tina's fashionable friends would have called surreal. He'd never asked exactly what the word meant. Was it this? Markus' voice warming up the sky with Mediterranean passion; the stars drawing nearer, draping a sparkling canopy over the frenetic nightlife of war, over the living and the dead who emerged from their burrows and dugouts, over a bazaar of resurrected lifetimes. Many of them would be cut short at daybreak when the shells crashed again, but for now there was life and starlight to last the night.

"Making love under the stars? Since when does a farm boy think about the stars?" They skied in tandem, Markus pulling ahead as usual. "Slow down, we'll get there. The war isn't going anywhere."

"*Stridea l'uscio dell'orto,*" Markus kept singing. "The creaking gate. There's a gate by the summer house where Elina used to sleep. I'd wait there and listen for the gate. For her footsteps. *Entrava ella, fragrante.* The bed was by the window and we could see the stars through the leaves of the apple tree, the scent of apple blossoms came through the window." His voice dwindled to a whisper. "I made love to her. Elina! Elina!" He cried out her name as if she were back at the last farmhouse, within shouting range, and then he collapsed into the snow.

"Get up, get up, you can't stop, you'll freeze to death!" Paul seized him by his sobbing shoulders and propped him back up on his skis.

"Never again! I'll never again—"

"Yes you will. You will, you will."

"Tell her." Markus leaned against his pole. "Tell her how much—"

"You'll tell her yourself."

He was already singing again, half in Finnish now. "Life never seemed so precious as at this moment," sang Markus, as he skied toward the orange glow ahead, and wagons of wounded and dead passed by in the dark.

We poor northern stiffs, thought Paul. We can't even talk about love without the aid of a foreign language. He kicked hard to keep up with Markus, who was gliding far ahead now, along the narrow road.

Going South

1

After the night of Paul's return, Tina avoided the Fennia and the Kämp and any other place where she might encounter Tom. She pushed him to the back of her mind, and tried to place her life back on the rails from which it had fallen. Her guilt was an all-consuming altar where she prayed for forgiveness from Paul, God, the nation, the world.

Her atonement began with work. She spent all her evenings at the Lotta headquarters, stuffing packages for the soldiers with medicines and newspaper-filled vests and socks. Dozens of pairs of thick, double-knit socks. One evening after packing boxes, when her legs refused to take another step and her hands ached with the cold, she stopped at the Fennia on her way home. It was nine o'clock, so Tom would be at the Kämp waiting for the communiqué. There was no danger of running into him.

The candlelight flickered over the map of pins. She hadn't seen it for days and when she looked at it now, she gasped. The pins had moved west, far west. At Taipale they stood immovable, but on the western Isthmus they were nearly at the gates of Viipuri. The cached hints in the communiqués hit home as she stared at the pins, those brittle guardians of her hopes. The newspapers still trumpeted great victories in the north and reporters toured sites where fresh Russian divisions were demolished—but never on the Isthmus. The fortunes of that tiny neck of land were shrouded in secrecy.

The waiter handed her the coffee cup and it wobbled precariously in her hand. She thought for an instant of dashing to the Kämp, finding Tom and borrowing a cigarette. Why did she never carry her own? What a silly genteel inhibition for a time like this. Instead she gulped down the coffee and hurried home.

The flat was silent, dark, funereal. In the kitchen she lit a candle and saw a thermos and a plate of sandwiches on the table. Her father was still out. There was no point in trying to sleep. Instead she found a pen and a writing pad and began to write a letter to Paul. She'd written several to him since the night he walked away from the Kämp, but had not received any back. This was understandable, she told herself, in light of the grim military situation.

For an hour she sat at the table, drinking coffee, deliberating whether Selma would wake up if she brewed a fresh pot, staring at the only words she had penned: "My darling Paul." An oddly artistic structure of crumpled papers lay on the floor beside her.

Her father came in so silently that when he materialized in the kitchen doorway, the outline of his bowler hat magnified in the candleglow, she nearly shrieked.

"Shh, it's only me," he whispered. "What are you doing up so late?" He tossed his hat and coat on a chair and sat down beside her.

She rubbed her eyes with her sleeve and moved farther away from the candle, so he wouldn't see her tear-streaked face. She knew the national credo: Finns don't cry. At least not in anyone's sight.

"Don't despair just yet," he said gently. "It's a long way from Summa to Helsinki. Be brave, my dear. Our sisu is all we have left."

Suddenly she hated the word, that national virtue they prized so highly. The determination that was so admirable, and so useless if you were small and alone.

"Surely you still believe the west will come to our aid," she said, whining like a cantankerous six-year old.

"The question now is time. Even if they come, will they get here in time to make a difference? The situation on the Isthmus could break up any hour like spring ice."

"If they don't come, we'll have to make peace on Stalin's terms."

"But we still have an ace in our hand—Stalin's fear that the Allies really will come. He'll never risk that. He'll sooner agree to an armistice. Until then we must keep fighting as hard as we can. As long as we can."

Her father always knew how to fold his cards. He was no happier about it than she was, but he knew how. She poured the dregs of the coffee for him but he already had a cognac in his hand.

"Are you writing to Paul?" he asked.

"Yes."

"What a pity you missed him when he came to town." Paul had stopped at their flat and visited with Selma before going to the Kämp. Tina had not found the courage to tell them what really happened that night.

"Yes. And I can't get a letter written to him. What am I to do, Papa? It's never been quite right between us, and now it's worse than ever."

"Why is it worse now?"

"Because he thinks there's something between me and Tom." There. She had to say it and she was sure he already knew.

"Is there?"

"Not—no." She hated lying to him. "Not now. But the point is Paul believes there is. And he believes I don't feel he's good enough for me."

"There was always a problem there with Paul," he said softly. "But it wasn't your fault. Or his, for that matter. The codes of society change much more slowly than individual ones. That doesn't mean we shouldn't try. Someone has to lead the way."

She had never seen it in that light. Her father was a historian, not a sociologist. He tracked changes, he didn't plan them. Had this been some social experiment?

"Is that why you saved him, all those years ago? To see what would happen? To carry out some test? You should have left him in jail. He would have got out on his own eventually." She was nearly shouting at him.

"No, Tintti, no," he said, using her childhood nickname. "Please don't say such things. As God is my witness, and at this particular moment you know I wouldn't say that lightly, all I ever wanted was to help him. There was no design, no plan. How could there be? Hearts always go their own way. Just remember, my dear, that perfection only exists in the realm of the ideal. We mortals have to make do with less. And the creator didn't make the universe static, but in constant motion. Human life is the same. A design we must keep reworking again and again."

So she and Paul had some difficult needlework ahead of them if they were to stitch together a life for themselves. This compounded her misery because for weeks now she thought she had found the perfect design, only it was with Tom Henderson.

"I'll make it right," she said, straightening her back. Her eyes were dry and her mind set. "If I could just write this letter."

"Leave the letter," he said. "It won't reach him."

Her tears obliterated another page. She cried because she was ashamed to be squandering her emotion on personal sorrows and because she was doing exactly what she had counselled Tom not to do—trying to bury her guilt and regret. You must face them, she'd told him. Let them back into your life. But to let Tom back into her life would be a force she couldn't handle. For him she was prepared to forget everything else, her country, her family, her betrothed, herself.

She couldn't share any of this with her father. He patted her hand. She put away the pen and paper and blew out the candle.

2

Dusk was falling as Paul slid into the Captain's sandpit, clutching a message from his Lieutenant. The days were getting longer as February turned into March, more time for the Russians to attack, less time for the defenders to attend to their needs in the safety of darkness. The line hadn't broken at Taipale, but they had abandoned most of their original positions after they were overrun by the Russians, retaken at great cost, overrun again, and finally so badly pummeled they were written off as indefensible. The new line consisted of little more than grenade craters, and the battalion command post was now an old quarry they called the sandpit. Its depth varied from three to four metres and its front ridge had been hastily fortified to serve as a dugout with enough space for a handful of men to warm up and thaw out. Outside, the cold continued fierce and killing. Minus thirty, minus forty degrees.

"You look familiar. Have you visited my offices before?" asked the Captain, accenting the word "offices" and casting a derisive look around the sandpit.

"No, sir. Not the inside. I was on the outside, the night we first arrived." Paul's company had been diverted to this sector during their march to Cape Hook, then ordered to retake Number Three in the dead of night, across swampy terrain unfamiliar to officers and men alike.

"You're from the company that lost all its machine gunners in one hour."

"Yes. They went down like dominoes. And then we came back here and christened this place our new headquarters with our sweat and blood."

"You've been listening to that poetry-writing Lieutenant of yours, son. You're waxing eloquent. Here, take a look at the eloquence out there, under the Taipale moon." The Captain gave him his field glasses. The sandpit offered an excellent view of almost the whole Taipale sector. Because the trees that surrounded it had long since been razed by artillery fire, you could see the fields to the south and southeast, and also across to the Russian side. The landscapes were from two different planets. The Finnish side was churned up and cratered as if struck by meteorites; the Russian side was thickly wooded with its winter postcard charm intact. For weeks now the lines had been mere tens of metres apart. Sometimes they had shared the same trench with the Russians, one at either end.

"No matter how this turns out," the Captain said, scraping ice off his beard with thick-mittened hands, "what I've seen here is so humbling I can't describe it. I thought I knew a thing or two about courage. I could eke it out of almost every man under my command. What I see here is something else, something no commanding officer can touch, because the soul doesn't take orders."

He spoke of the young lieutenant who had retaken Number Five with two squads after it was lost to the Russians. That night a strange cry echoed over Taipale, the Finnish battle cry, "Battalion forwa-a-rd!" The lieutenant had used the word "battalion" to make the Russians think there were great numbers coming at them. Around midnight the flares went up at Number Five. It was in Finnish hands again. But by noon the next day it was lost under massive artillery fire. The same men died there in the morning who had so joyously recaptured it hours earlier, the young lieutenant included.

The Captain shook his head. He motioned Paul to follow him into the dugout. "How long is it since you've had real coffee with cream, son?"

"I can't remember, sir."

"Just before dawn my adjutant went to the rear to see what was holding up the rations. He came back with a can of milk. Here. Chew these coffee beans and wash them down with the milk. Almost like the real thing, eh?"

"Almost." Paul chewed. Mixed with the milk and saliva, the beans softened and warmed up in the mouth just enough to evoke the memory of the Fennia on a March afternoon.

"Out of the eight hundred and forty men this battalion had when it came here, barely three hundred are left. That's counting the new guys. Kids, most of them students from the cities, some didn't even know how to load a rifle. And over there, sitting in our old positions, are two Russian divisions, maybe more. Armed to the teeth."

A sergeant straggled in, pulling a weight behind him. The weight was a limp soldier.

"Who is it?" asked the Captain.

"One of the new guys."

The new guys were a green replacement battalion that had arrived in mid-February. Thrown hastily into battle, they were chewed up, then re-deployed; some were sent north, others were still here.

"Is he dead?"

"No, sir. I found him halfway to the rear. He left his post."

Silence. They all knew that desertion meant punishment, perhaps a court martial. Except that such niceties of discipline had been forgotten here long ago and the only relevant question was life or death. The shell-shocked ones, the frozen ones, the stammering and quivering ones, all could be molded back into shape. If not for war, then for peace. Only the dead were beyond reach.

"Here, give him a smoke," said the Captain. He lit a cigarette. The soldier took one drag, then his head dropped again. "Not many pleasures left out here. Can't even jerk off because of the cold and the fatigue. Smokes are about the only one and this guy can't even enjoy that. Wake up, soldier, don't sleep." They shook him like a rag doll.

"Take him to the rear, find him a spot somewhere," said the Captain.

Paul tried to steady his nerves, tried to control his hands. He'd frozen them during a night siege in the swamp. They ached and he kneaded them automatically, trying to revive numb joints.

"I'd better get back," he said. "The Lieutenant is expecting me."

The Captain hastily scrawled a note to the Lieutenant and gave it to Paul.

"I'll come with you," he said. "I tour the foxholes every night. Check that the boys are awake. Can't let the cold kill my boys."

They crawled into the open foxholes and shallow trenches, patting the men on the back, shaking those who had dozed off, offering words of encouragement. The men rarely responded.

"I noticed the change in them in the latter part of February," said the Captain. "That's what days and weeks of sleeplessness and exhaustion does to human beings. They're already past every limit of human endurance. Automatons who remember precious little of life except how to avoid death, some not even that."

3

"Please, gentlemen, one at a time. One at a time." The placid cheeks of Captain Zilliacus began to sprout points of red and beads of sweat crept along his hairline. There were reporters draped on every chair and sprawled over the floor, some sitting cross-legged at his feet, and they seemed not to hear him as they continued their barrage of questions. Where exactly is the line on the Isthmus now? Where is the replacement battalion?

"I said one at a time!" Zilliacus shouted. There was a momentary silence. No one had ever heard him shout before. The questions resumed with somewhat more decorum but Zilliacus now seemed to have gone deaf, for he stared at the communiqué and gave no answers, and instead began to read announcements about bus times and briefings for the rest of the week.

Tom wedged his way out of the room from his spot near the door. He always left early. The nightly scene in the press room was becoming too painful. The Finnish authorities had been skimpy with information all along, describing even the greatest of victories in laconic phrases. Now details were even harder to pin down from the short statements and terse references to unfamiliar new battlegrounds, place names that had to be ferreted out with magnifying glasses from maps of Karelia. He under-stood that this new level of obfuscation was an ominous development and preferred not to join in the conjecture about what was really happen-ing. They would find out soon enough.

He avoided his colleagues, even Taylor. It seemed to him he'd joined a different race while they were waging the press war in the Kämp and he was no longer one of them. But the people he wished to be with had disowned him. Or at least she had. And she was the key to the life he'd so joyfully embraced. Now he could only fall back into his old routines, lying on his bed with the whiskey by his side, re-living the scenes from only days before that were lost to him now. He saw his life as a series of disjointed acts in a bizarre play where each curtain was a finale and the next one rose over a different production. Other people were able to connect the phases of their lives into a whole; he knew only how to sever them. And this loss was the greatest of them all, because he had given himself so completely, pinned his hopes on it so fervently despite the unlikeliness of the scenario. Perhaps because of the unlikeliness. It was too unlikely to be real, and so it felt more real than anything else. But now he saw it as the last of the illusions he had reached for and lost.

And yet the scent of her skin would not leave his fingertips, and the contours of her mouth seemed to be embedded in his pillow when he buried his face in it. There had been nothing illusory about her, or about the brief but spectacular lifetime he'd lived with her, modest by anyone else's yardstick perhaps, but breath-taking by his.

He spent less time sending out the war news and more time looking around at the nation he had come to love. He saw no panic, only the same stubborn optimism that hadn't wavered since November. It struck him that the Finnish papers, heavily censored, were deleting the adverse news from the Isthmus, focusing on victories further north. This was a necessary diversion, he knew, to maintain morale in a tiny country where the slightest crack could bring down the whole house of eggshells. He wanted to talk it over with Tina, with her father; wanted to ensure that they had plans in place in case the worst came to pass. He wasn't sure what he would say if he did see her. Would he try to maintain the pretense they'd begun after Paul left, when she'd insisted he deny there was anything between them? Maybe. Denial was not new to him. What he could not accept was never seeing her again.

Sometimes he imagined what might happen when Paul came back. She would have to choose between them. Why would she choose a foreigner over a man she'd loved for years? Perhaps he'd only been a surrogate for Paul anyway. Hardly an unusual phenomenon. Yet he didn't believe it. What she'd felt for him was real and fully his, only his. But her guilt had overwhelmed it. He understood guilt and he understood her. She would have to wrestle with it now, before she could choose.

He was determined to be there when the time came for her to choose. He would fight for her love. Those words, which a few months ago he would have ridiculed, were now the focus of all his hopes. He felt no ill will toward Paul. On the contrary, he remembered how he'd been drawn to him because he reminded him of his own youthful self. It was not surprising that they both loved the same woman.

He slipped into the Fennia almost every evening, directly after the press conference. It was a sullen and deserted place now. No one noticed or cared when he sat down at the piano, playing tunes that suited his own mood. He played for himself and also for the others, for those he imagined were sitting in the dark listening to him, those he had loved. He played his mother's favourites, and *Mademoiselle from Armentieres* for his father, who had lost a cousin at the Somme. Then *Nola* for the farmer's daughter, and finally, endlessly, Tina's beloved *Moonlight Serenade*.

4

Paul leaned into the side of the foxhole as tightly as he could. He couldn't remember when he'd lost track of time. Every day and night was the same now. He never slept, only fell into trances where his mind dozed while his body stayed tense and awake. He dreamed, frequently about Tina, sometimes seeing her in the arms of the American, sometimes as they used to be last summer and the summers before that. Sometimes he saw Marita in his dreams and mixed her up with Tina. His father and long-dead mother visited him and often he was at the starting line in Berlin again.

He tried to remember how it felt to be warm. Summer warm, with the heat from the rocks and the sun soaking your skin. Sauna warm, when the heat from the walls and wooden benches seared you with its smoky, eye-burning breath until you poured water on the rocks and steamed yourself into a sweat. Or whiskey warm, that started burning in your throat and chest and spread through your body from the inside out. And sex warm, the heat of Marita's skin next to his.

They'd been living in the craters and foxholes ever since they abandoned the old positions to the Russians. Night and day, no relief, for days, for weeks. No, it couldn't be weeks. It was impossible to think. The fatigue had shut down his brain. He barely recognized the men, even the ones he'd known since the war began. Their numbers grew fewer daily, hourly. How few he couldn't say, because they lay scattered across the open cratered fields, and because their faces had changed. The ruddy cheeks were grey, bruised, white from frostbite; the eyes had lost their colour, icicled beards and eyebrows gave them all a manic cast. Every rag and scrap of clothing had been bound, tied, stuffed, and folded around their heads and bodies to keep out the killing cold. Knit ski masks and grey-white hoods covered the helmets of those who still had helmets, until Markus joked that they looked like arctic bulls.

If only he had water. It was impossible to get water to the front lines except during the night, and most nights no one could stay awake that long. A few times drivers made it through with water jugs. But the drivers were becoming scarce.

And the cold would not let up. You had to keep an eye on each other, keep each other awake, try to wiggle frozen toes, watch for signs of hallucinating, keep your thoughts going when all your brain wanted to do was sleep. The body went on, eating, loading rifles, shooting, following instincts and routines—but the spirit began to look inward for shelter from the storm. Paul looked around the foxhole. There was Lampinen, collapsing into stupor.

"Wake up! Wake up!" They rushed over and shook him, and propped him against the wall of the trench.

"Wake me up when I'm dead," he muttered.

"Just think of us as angels," said Paul.

"Fucking angels. Leave me alone," said Lampinen, but he opened his eyes.

Now the Russian infantry was coming again. The drumfire let up while they charged across the black field of churned up earth and snow. The machine guns mowed them down, methodically, resignedly. The first wave stopped fifty metres from the line and took cover in the pockmarked field. They seemed to lie there a long time, firing dispassionately toward the Finns. Then there was a pause. The artillery stopped and their loudspeaker began to blare, although grenades still whistled through the air.

"Afternoon concert," said Markus. Since the beginning of the war, the Russians had bombarded them with propaganda from their loudspeakers. If you could endure the first deafening strains of the *Internationale*, what followed was a medley of popular Russian waltzes and folk songs.

"I hope they play *White Acacias*," said Paul. "That's the finest Russian waltz of all." It had been his mother's favourite.

"I'd rather hear Tchaikovsky," said Markus.

"Send a request."

Markus didn't answer. A grenade splinter had come from nowhere and blood streamed from a cavity where his ear had been a moment ago. They lowered him gently to the bottom of the foxhole, trying to find level ground. There was nothing soft for a pillow so they tugged off his felt boots and lay them under his head. Markus wouldn't be walking out of here, and his multi-layered socks would keep his feet warm enough. A more serious problem was the lack of gauze or any clean cloth for bandaging. Lampinen finally took his knife and cut the sleeves off his snowsuit. They were encrusted with dirt on the outside, but the insides were relatively grey, and they wrapped Markus' head carefully with the cleanest parts of the sleeve against the wound.

"It's not that bad, we'll get you out of here and to the medics," Paul said. It was much worse than he let on, but there was no use saying so. Markus looked at him with clear, sad eyes. "Don't talk," said Paul, as if the other were about to begin a chat. "Save your strength."

"Someone should sing for him," said Lampinen.

"I will." Paul burrowed into the frozen side of the foxhole and in a hoarse whisper began to rasp into Markus' remaining ear. It was surprising how many Italian lyrics he had learned in four months. His cracked lips struggled with the task as he mouthed the words to *A Lucivan de Stelle*, then stopped. It shouldn't be a song about dying. Markus was not going to die. He began *O Sole Mio* instead, thinking of the sunny hills of Tuscany. The words stuck to his dry palate, trapped by his frost-encrusted lips, until finally the "m" broke free in a sudden burst of breath.

The Russians' pause extended into the late afternoon, and the battleground froze in a static tableau punctuated by popping grenades. The men in the foxhole sucked their cigarette butts to the end and chewed up the last of their coffee beans. Thirst was something they no longer bothered to complain about but Markus, blood oozing through the cloth around his ear, began to mumble, "Water. For Christ's sake, please, water."

The medics would not come until after dark to take him away, nor would any food or water be brought up to the line. It had snowed overnight and there was a two-inch snow cover between the lines, only ten metres away, fresh snow, nearly white. Paul fastened his mess kit to his coat and checked that his helmet was secure. It would make a good bowl. He'd have to dash back to the foxhole in a crouch, in order not to spill the snow. But he'd make it. After all, he was a runner.

"Where are you going?" asked Lampinen.

"To the well."

He was gone before Lampinen and the others grasped what he'd said and snapped out of their torpor to shout after him, "Come back! There's no well out there!" Paul began to dive his way toward the snow, leap-frogging from crater to crater. The afternoon sun was low in the sky and there would be little fighting left that day, but the guns had not been put away. Halfway to the snow, a Russian machine gun caught him, and he felt a fire in his midriff and the hard blow of the earth as he fell. Then silence. He lay on his side, watching his blood seep over the rock, amazed at how red it was, and how healthy looking. This is good blood, he thought. His eyes scanned the pale sky above him and the mangled remains of the forest that had once stood here. He had fallen directly beneath the jagged shard of a blackened tree. The tree focused with perfect clarity and he studied it avidly. Was it the corpse of a pine? He imagined how it must have looked before the guns found it, its wide-tufted boughs riding proudly above the hills. The pines of Karelia were famous. Then his eyes filled with tears as he saw it—the tiny, ragged piece of white bark still clinging to the trunk. It was a birch after all! That's why he felt so much at home. As if he had come home. "I am proud to die on the same field with thee," he spoke to the birch in the familiar "thee", as to one beloved.

He knew he would never get up again. The pain now intensified with every gasp. He almost lost consciousness, then the shock of the realization that he was dying revived him. So there would be no time. No time to untangle the chaos that had overcome his life, no time to mend the rift with Tina. Pain convulsed his body, then suddenly eased. He was leaving the realm of the living, the earth whose colours and contours he had loved and pleasures he had embraced. Please God, forgive me and let me go with her. And let me go in summer. He shuddered and something let go, and instantly he was with her, sailing in the islands on a day in July. The waves sparkled and the sunlight danced. She was with him, and he drifted further and further into the brilliant sea.

5

Rumours of peace had been circulating in the Kämp for days. The situation of the Finns on the western Isthmus was known to be desperate and the Allied offer of aid now deemed to be too late. On the twelfth of March, Swedish newspapers printed a report that the Finnish Parliament had voted to accept the Russian peace terms, and the foreign correspondents erupted in frenzy. The nervous Finnish government, striving to preserve secrecy around the still-ongoing negotiations with Moscow, reacted by sending inquisitors to the Kämp to find the source of the leak.

The first real harbinger of peace was not an official statement but rather the news that the State Liquor Stores had closed their doors. The correspondents stayed up all night sprawled in the hallways and lounges of the Kämp, huddled around their radios. Confirmation that a truce had been signed came in the early hours. For the details of the settlement they would have to wait until noon, when Foreign Minister Tanner would make a radio broadcast to the nation.

The Kämp was in a carnival mood, sensing the great story about to break. Tom slept in his room for a few hours in the morning and decided to listen to the noon broadcast at the Fennia. He wouldn't understand many of the words, but would see the truth in the faces around him.

The café was packed and tense as the clock approached noon. He studied the people around him, the usual collection of office workers, store clerks, and a few well-dressed ladies. At one table close to him sat three men in uniform, one of them a senior officer with a bandaged shoulder. The faces he saw were serious but not despairing. It occurred to him that he probably knew more of the real state of affairs than they did. When the radio was turned on, the café fell into a deep silence. The foreign minister began to speak, his voice breaking several times. The faces in the room told Tom all he needed to know. Shock paralyzed them in unison, all struck by the same hideous blow; tears trickled unheeded or were absent-mindedly brushed away. He knew he should be at the Kämp, ready to jump at the translation of the speech as soon as it was made available, queuing up for the phones. None of that had the slightest importance to him. He thought of Tina, and wished more than anything to comfort her; and he thought of Paul, of whose death he had learned from Taylor only a day ago. He wanted desperately to talk to someone, but there was no one at the Kämp he wanted to see. Not even Mitch Webster was around any more, having gone back to London weeks ago.

The speech ended and morbid silence continued. No one moved. Tom would not look at the faces around him, feeling it was an intrusion into their grief, until he realized that his face must look exactly the same. One of the junior officers finally walked up to the map of pins, pulled them out and stolidly lined them up where the new border would be. Almost all of Karelia was behind the pins now—the Isthmus, Viipuri, the area north of Ladoga. Even Taipale, which had never fallen.

Two women in black walked up to the wall, and in one savage swoop tore the map down to the floor. A mother and a sister, Tom thought. Or a young widow.

He lingered over his coffee as the patrons shuffled out mutely, as from a funeral. He didn't know where to go, although he knew he must eventually return to the Kämp and fulfill his duties. In the nearly empty room, the trio of officers still sat at their table. They were looking at him, at his yellow press armband. The officer with the bandaged shoulder began to question him in a toneless voice.

"You are American?"

"Yes."

The officer pulled up a chair. "An American reporter?"

Tom nodded. The officer, a captain by rank, stood up and seized Tom by the collar with his good arm. In alarm, the others began to pull him away, but the captain didn't let go. He pulled Tom up to his own height and whispered, his face only inches away: "You promised. You promised you would help. And what did we get from you? A couple of old planes! Some joke! Some bloody joke!" The grip on his collar grew tighter, and Tom had difficulty breathing. Then, just as abruptly as he had gripped him, the captain let him go and returned to his table. He collapsed into his chair and sobbed, shoulders shaking violently. The junior officers looked away with tear-streaked cheeks. These were soldiers known for their refusal to weep even when suffering the most grievous wounds. But no wound had ever been as grievous as this one.

6

Tina sat at the kitchen table, staring at the newspaper. "Peace Made on Harsh Terms! March 13, 1940." When she tried to read it the same rage flared up in a vicious flash. She put down the paper for a moment; her heart slowed down, the whizzing in her ears faded and her brain began to find its normal pathways, this way and that way, like putting a drawer in order, getting the cutlery to stop jumping. Then she looked at the page again.

This was the rage that peace brought. Peace. Such a joyful word in other vocabularies. For her it was very different. On the day the peace terms were announced, she went home at noon to listen to the foreign minister's speech on the radio with her father. In offices and factories, in dugouts and field hospitals, everything stopped. The voice on the radio broke many times and the nation listened, transfixed in horror. The Karelian Isthmus, gone. Viipuri, gone. North Ladoga, gone. Hanko, leased to the Soviet Union for a military base. At this Björnström's face turned white and Selma rushed to get him a glass of water. Hanko, only seventy miles from Helsinki in their backyard. His cousin lived there, in a white oceanside house.

The Finnish people did not understand, in that first hour of trauma. Their army had not been defeated. Only days ago the papers told of great victories, of Allied plans to come to their aid. They thought they had earned a just peace. Instead they were blindsided with a sledgehammer. Those were Tom's words, later.

Björnström got up and turned off the radio, and looked at Paul's photograph in its black frame on the bookshelf. He turned the photograph sideways, as if he couldn't bear to look Paul in the face. He walked slowly back to the sofa. Oh, Papa, thought Tina, such blows shouldn't fall on old men.

She and her father sat immobile but Selma moved like a priestess. On the bookshelf there was a small Finnish flag mounted on a miniature silver flagpole. She took the flag out of the shelf and lowered it to half-mast.

"There, professor," she said. "The Finland we knew is dead. God only knows what will rise in its place."

It was a cold March day. Winter still gripped the country and snow lay on the ground, but sitting in the apartment would have driven them mad, so Tina and her father went for a walk around the city. Everywhere flags flew at half-mast. Every face wore the same stricken look. The air raid wardens were still at their posts, and Tina half-wished the sirens would wail again so they could fight to the death.

She left her father at the Kämp. The main floor was a zoo of correspondents, but she knew he had his private rooms where he could find the details he sought from people the reporters never saw. She didn't want to go home. She wanted to share this tragedy with her countrymen and from habit she walked to the Fennia. It was nearly empty. Tables had not been cleared, the waiters shuffled about aimlessly. You could pour yourself a coffee for free and no one cared.

The map of pins lay crumpled on the floor. Someone had ripped it from the wall, and most of the pins had fallen off or been torn out by angry hands. Tina knelt down, scraping her knee on the wooden floor. She smoothed the paper and scrutinized the Isthmus—there it was, Taipale. None of the pins at Taipale had moved. She carefully tore that section from the map, making sure the pin at Cape Hook stayed put. This was the one small victory she claimed that day, Paul's victory and that of his comrades at Taipale and all the other battlefields that had held to the end, and the ones that had bent but not broken. It wasn't much, but her knees were a little stronger as she rose. She folded the torn piece of map into her handbag and wandered out of the Fennia.

7

Björnström knocked on the door of Tina's bedroom softly, one morning a few days after the armistice. When she saw his face she knew immediately what he'd come to tell her. She'd been expecting it, the news of Paul's death, ever since the night at the Kämp. When it actually came she couldn't deal with it. Her heart began to race and wouldn't slow down. She was dizzy and it seemed her lungs couldn't draw air any more. When her father's cognac and Selma's hot soups failed to calm her, their family physician came to the flat and gave her sedatives. For four days she lay in bed, lost in a sleep without dreams.

Finally one evening she raised herself on her elbow, turned on the bedside lamp and looked at the paper her father had placed there when he told her of Paul's death. It was a poem, written by the Lieutenant, Paul's company commander. Paul's father had sent it to her.

"To my men
All the trees here lean westward
Bent by the constant eastern gale;
How painful it is to send you
Into that searing wind.
How patiently you obey me
And how silently you die."

She decided then and there that if Paul could get up and face the Russian guns every day, she could get up and face the rest of her life. That night she arose and dressed, and walked into the living room like a human being again, to Paul's framed picture on the bookshelf. She promised him she would devote herself to serving what remained of her country with what remained of her heart. As she sat on the sofa her father came and sat beside her.

"I'm glad to see you're up again, Tintti. I was so worried about you."

"I can't talk about him, Papa. I understand now why you didn't talk about Mama."

"I should have talked more about her to you. You were so young when she died, you lost your memories of her. I should have shared more of mine. But we are selfish and we avoid pain."

"Does the pain ever go away?"

"Not completely. It changes you, but that's what life does. If it doesn't, you haven't lived. As for Paul, grieve because you miss him, not because of what might have been. Live for him instead. Love as he would have loved."

She rested her head on his shoulder.

The three of them made the trip to Kotka on a sunny March day for Paul's funeral. He was laid to rest outside the red-brick cathedral, where a military cemetery had been created for the war dead of the city. His father was there, mumbling that he would rather have buried Paul in the family plot beside his mother and younger brother Markus.

Tina stood bareheaded in the March sunshine as the rites were read. A cool wind blew up from the sea, through the groves of Big Park. She could see the apple orchard from the church hill, as she stood by the gravesite of the boy who had stolen an apple for her a lifetime ago. Her tears fell on the roses she carried, roses she'd unearthed in a Helsinki shop, wilted but fire-red. She still loved Paul, despite what had happened with Tom. How could you explain it? She had never stopped loving him, but something bigger had come along, something that eclipsed everything else, a star from another universe.

One afternoon she saw the Lieutenant, whom she recognized from his photographs in the newspapers due to a volume of poetry he had published about his experiences during the War. He was sitting alone in a restaurant, clearly a broken man though not an old one. She went up to his table and introduced herself and they spoke for a while about Paul and the others. Markus survived the war, but lost most of his hearing. This seemed to bother the Lieutenant a great deal. You can't listen to Puccini very well with a hearing aid, he said.

Not long afterward Tina received the velvet bag of chess pieces in the mail. The Lieutenant had brought them out of Karelia, and since she was the first family member, as he imagined, whom he encountered, he sent them to her. A few months later she read that he had died, one of the victims that the war killed slowly.

A Karelian Spring

1

The Finns had lost so much and paid such a great price that at first the peace felt more unbearable than the war. That was before they knew how desperate the military situation on the Isthmus had been, how close they had come to catastrophe. Gradually, they understood. The peace was cruel, but there had been no other choice; and they still had their country and their freedom. Truncated, battered, bloodied, but still there.

Most of the foreign correspondents conjured themselves out of Helsinki as quickly as they'd appeared. The glamour of the war dissipated overnight and the Finns were left alone to clean up the mess—resettling half a million Karelian evacuees, rebuilding shattered cities and towns, learning how to live again as a nation.

And there was the return of the soldiers. The survivors, men from the abyss who had given everything and found it was not enough. Exhausted and silent, they trickled back to their homes. They sat on their porches during the long spring evenings, trying to remember the routines of civilian life. Each in his own way and his own time tried to put the war to rest. Some never did.

Tina watched them as they returned. Even the outwardly healthy ones were different now. They might tell a story from the trenches or even a joke, but they fell silent again far too quickly. As if they were waiting, still listening for something. What? The rumble of the artillery, the whine of grenades?

Others, broken in body or spirit, had difficulties adjusting to peacetime. The Lottas helped here as they had throughout the war. Gunilla continued to work in that capacity in Kotka and once again Tina decided to go there. Her emotions were reeling. The only thing that was clear to her was the need to devote herself to her country, and especially to the returning soldiers.

Also, she still couldn't face seeing Tom again. She'd heard that, unlike most of his colleagues, he was still in Finland. Now that Hitler was invading Norway he would surely leave to cover the larger war. When she returned to Helsinki he'd be gone and she'd never have to think about the night they danced the tango, when Paul came back.

Kotka had suffered great damage and a corner of Gunilla's mansion had been shattered, which workmen were now furiously trying to rebuild. The yellow house was drafty and cold and filled with voiceless weeping. Tina listened to it through the long spring nights. Sometimes it came from afar, the high-pitched wailing of a woman floating through the morning hours; sometimes it seemed to come from inside her mind. At night she listened to the voices and in the mornings she went to the Lotta office and tried to sort out the problems of local veterans, a strange name for boys who were mere months older than when they left their mothers' firesides in October. There were pay discrepancies, lost belongings, lost jobs, medical problems. Every day she waded through masses of paperwork and listened to their stories—stories told haltingly, indifferently, often angrily.

One day a young man came in who looked vaguely familiar. He had wavy dark hair and looked like he'd once known how to navigate a dance floor. Now, his grey eyes were dull and glanced about in exasperation. Gunilla referred him to her as a difficult case. To make matters worse, his right arm was in a sling.

He presented his papers to her and she stifled a gasp. It was Mika, Marita's brother. She hadn't seen him for years but he clearly remembered her.

"What may we do to help you?" she asked. "If it's a question of back pay, you must take it up with the army. If it's accommodation, we can arrange it."

"No," he said, drawing some papers from his pocket with a clumsy left hand. "It's—I just don't know how to take care of all this."

"All what?"

"My sister Marita. She worked in Lind's store. I don't know what to do about her affairs."

"What do you mean?"

"You didn't know? She was killed in a bombing raid at the beginning of March. I buried her yesterday but now—"

Slowly he explained. He was her only sibling, and their parents were dead. There was a grandmother living in Karelia who should have long since been on a refugee train out of there. He didn't know her present whereabouts, as he hadn't been close to his family. Now he must dispose of Marita's estate and empty her apartment, deal with legal matters, find his grandmother—and he had a useless right arm.

Tina decided to take Mika in hand. They walked over to Marita's flat, a pleasant simple room. Marita didn't have much in the way of material possessions, but it was still a good day's work to sort and pack them. Mika, with his bad arm, would never get it done and there was no one he could turn to for assistance. Besides, she'd decided she would do it the moment she recognized him. She had the address of his Karelian grandmother tucked away in a drawer and hadn't forgotten the promise she made to Marita. Sending Mika back to the Lotta office for boxes, she began to look around.

She opened the drape leading to the sleeping alcove and was thunderstruck to see framed newspaper photos of Paul on the wall. Marita had never gotten over her childhood crush on him, then. Somehow it seemed embarrassing and she carefully took them down, removed the frames, and folded them inside her bag. There was no need to share this secret with the world. It would remain between Marita and herself, this love for the man who now lay under a white cross in the church cemetery.

She removed the bed linens and folded them into a pile on the mattress. Marita had embroidered everything, even her pillowcases. Inside the chest of drawers she found a pillowcase with the needle still in it. She had been sewing initials into it, intertwining them in a lattice of roses, red looping M's and blue curlicued P's. Tina sat down on the edge of the mattress, suddenly hot with a discomfort that flared into panic. She glanced at the night table beside the bed. A framed photo sat there, a photo of an old woman wearing a peasant kerchief, sitting on a swing in a cornflower-blue field. At her knee was a fair-haired boy about two years old. His eyes looked out gleefully and the eyes were very familiar. She had seen those eyes in another child's face, long ago in an apple orchard. There was no question in her mind whose child this was.

She pulled open the drawer in the night table. A few toiletries. A small pile of papers she was afraid to look through. But one letter caught her eye. It was dated December 1939 and written in an unsteady, old-fashioned hand.

"Dear Marita, greetings from the farm. All is well here so far. Our boys seem to be holding the Russians off. Many of them have marched by here. Fine looking soldiers with fine guns. We are well. The boy had a cough, but I've kept him indoors and he is better now. Thank you for the money. Don't worry about us. Just watch yourself. It's the cities that are getting bombed. Do you at least have food to eat? If not, come here. My larder is full, we got the vegetables in before the men left. The cow is doing as well as can be expected in this terrible cold."

Tina heard the creak of the door as Mika returned, dragging in several cardboard boxes with his good hand. Composing herself, she set the boxes out and labelled them for clothing, dishes, bedding and miscellaneous. You supervise and I'll pack, she told him. But first sit down. Let's have a cup of coffee before we start. Marita has a little real coffee here.

As they sipped on the coffee, Tina went to the alcove and brought out the photo of the little boy. Mika didn't know who it was and had never heard of a child living with his grandmother. It must be one of the neighbour's children, he said. They have a whole yardful of them. Of course, they come in handy for looking after the farm. They helped out Grandma, too, since Grandpa died. Yes, it must be one of theirs.

Packing up Marita's belongings didn't take very long, and they were finished by evening. Tina made arrangements for the shipment of the boxes to Mika's address in Helsinki. They should have been sent to the grandmother, but her farm was in the ceded territory. Marita had been in the habit of storing her important papers and valuables out there. They couldn't find her birth certificate, for example. It would be with Grandma, said Mika, wherever she was right now. He thanked her for her help and hurried to catch the train to Helsinki. He hoped a message from his grandmother would be waiting for him there.

Tina waited for two days before calling him, ostensibly to check on the arrival of Marita's belongings. They wouldn't be there yet, but she could wait no longer. She had to know if the grandmother had been in touch, she had to know where the little boy was. Then she had to arrange to see the boy and talk to the grandmother, and she had to do it alone. That much was clear to her, and not much else. But when she reached Mika, he was very worried. Not finding a message from his grandmother, he'd called the evacuation centre she would have logically come through on her way west. He managed to talk to an evacuee from her parish. The old woman had refused to leave the house. The last time the neighbours had seen her, the military were trying to get her moving. The soldiers, newly freed from combat, now struggled to assist civilians relinquish their homes as well as evacuating themselves, their wounded and dead. The Russians had given Finland two weeks for the process.

That evening Tina boarded a train heading east one more time. Gunilla gave her blessing for the trip and a letter of introduction to the local Lotta executive, though Tina didn't tell her the reason for this sudden need to travel to a chaotic evacuation zone. Neither did she tell her father the reason when she hastily called him, except to say she was looking for someone and the address and name of the hamlet where she was going, just outside the newly drawn border in Karelia. To his frantic questions, she answered that he'd have to trust her judgment, although she privately shared his fear and had no idea how her mission would turn out or if she would even be allowed to reach her destination. All she knew was that the one thing she could still do for Paul was to ensure that his son was in safe hands.

2

So far Tom had successfully fended off the pleas of his editors to leave Helsinki. Show me the greener pastures and I'll go to them, he wired. For now there were only rumours of Hitler's plans for Norway, of Allied plans for Norway, and the expectation that something would happen in France. Or conversely, there would be another Munich and the whole thing might still blow over. In the meantime he'd covered the peace in Finland from every conceivable angle, and in the absence of real action elsewhere it sufficed. To himself, he rationalized his stay with the same reasoning he'd used during the lull in November—Taylor was still here. That had been his bellwether then, and he looked to it now, having long since concluded that the Englishman had more intimate relations with the Russians than he let on.

Sitting in the Fennia on a cold March afternoon, staring at the blank wall where the map of pins had been, he had to admit that Taylor had nothing to do with it. He was still here because he had to see her again. At least once. And it was more than that. It was because in the few months he'd been here, he'd become too deeply entangled with the affairs of this small nation to make for an easy parting.

He wanted to visit Paul's grave. He wanted to apologize, to say the words he would have said had Paul lived. But just as with his father, death had the last word. Above all, he had to see Tina, even if there was nothing that could be said or done, nothing that could right the wrong they had so carelessly created. It had been a massive wrong, but in truth he could not call it a heinous one. If she would not love him, perhaps she could explain it to him. He was not yet accustomed to self-examination, after so many years of indifference to his own happiness. His present life was intolerable, but he had no wish to sink back into his old one, either.

He returned to the Kämp in the early evening and filed yet another story about Karelian evacuees. The clerk gave him an urgent phone message from London. His editors had booked passage for him to Norway. The message ended with the words, "Get back to the real war!"

Taylor was sitting in the nearly empty lounge, nursing a scotch.

"Saw Björnström today," he said as Tom sat down. "Seems he's setting off on a bit of an adventure. In search of a lost daughter." Taylor paused, with a sly glance at Tom's face. His eyes froze when Tom came toward him, fists clenched.

"Don't mess with me, Taylor! Tell me what you know."

"All right, calm down. It seems she's disappeared. Yesterday she left on some goose chase to the evacuation zone, and now there's no trace of her anywhere. The old man is frantic and was on his way home to pack his bags and take the first train east. You know the Russians are taking over the ceded areas in a few days. This is no time to be wandering about in the vicinity. Once they close the border, it will stay closed."

"But she wouldn't be alone and she wouldn't be lost. She's gone out there before, her aunt works in one of those refugee centres—"

"The aunt has lost track of her. Utterly so."

Tom got up abruptly and paid for his drink, which had yet to arrive. "There's a night train to Karelia, right?"

Taylor leaned back and waved his pipe in the air, plumes of smoke whirling around his head. "I say, old chap, don't be bloody ridiculous. Just what purpose do you imagine your presence might serve in this foxhunt?"

Tom slumped into his chair and closed his eyes. Naturally Taylor was right. What purpose indeed? But he should be the one going out there, not an old man with arthritis and a bad heart. If he did nothing else in his life, he would do this. The answer suddenly took shape as he gazed at the Englishman, whose pipe-puffing elegance had barely wavered since Berlin. He would go on this foxhunt in Björnström's place, but he would go armed.

"The useful presence in this foxhunt is not mine but yours, Taylor. If Tina is by some chance stuck in the Russian zone, that's where you come in. Don't pretend you don't know what I'm talking about."

For an instant Taylor pretended, then gave it up. "Do you understand what I'd be risking?"

"Your whole career and maybe your neck, if you were ever found guilty of treason against His Majesty. But why would that happen? Why would I betray you? Do I care about your loyalties?"

"No. Screw king and country. Your memorable phrase from Berlin just came back to me."

Tom smiled to himself. This was proceeding exactly as he had hoped. In truth he had no plans to expose Taylor, but it was crucial that Taylor himself believed him completely. "If anyone should be afraid," he continued, "it's me. Once your Russian friends realize I know who and what you are, it's me they'll want to rub out."

"No need to worry on that score. I can hide the trail quite easily. In any case, the Russians have so much on their minds right now they wouldn't notice. All right, Henderson. Call me once you get out there. If you need to get into the Russian zone, I'll arrange it."

"How can I thank you?"

"You can't. Just don't mention my name."

"Will we ever meet again, old buddy?"

"Not for a while. Who knows?" He studied Tom's eyes intently. "So what do you think of me, then, old chap? You who despise all ideologues and 'isms.' "

"I think you have the right to be crazy. And I have the right to say so."

They looked at each other in silence for a moment. In the wake of the storms they had weathered, a slender willow of friendship still swayed in the wind.

"Think about this carefully, Henderson," said Taylor. "About your career, everything you've built up. Listen to your editors, go to Norway. The action is just beginning in Europe. This is no time to go soft in the head, or rather, soft in the heart. You always pay for that down the road, you know."

He knew, but he also knew you paid the other way. In the end it was just a question of which price you wanted to pay. He'd made his choice without a second thought.

They downed their scotches a little more pompously than usual, and then Taylor walked him to the door, talking quickly. "Björnström will be at the station. He's a stubborn old coot but he knows this trip is too much for him. And he trusts you implicitly. Just make sure you get all the information you can from him, the exact address in the Russian zone where she might be. If you have to go in there, someone will be at the checkpoint waiting for you."

"A Russian guide dog? Do they speak English?"

"He will. But Henderson," he puffed feverishly at the worn pipe, "don't play games with these chaps. One dead American will fit in nicely in the pits where they're burying all the Red soldiers the Finns killed off. And no one will know what happened to you. I always knew this girl would be your destiny. By the way, you're on your own with the Finnish military. I have no influence there."

He would solve that problem when he came to it, thought Tom. Right now, he had to get to the station before Björnström got on the evening train.

He found the old man on the platform in the station.

3

Tina had never lived on a farm until she found the old woman, Marita's grandmother, and the boy. It was a tiny cottage, a crofter's plot of Karelian field and wood, some distance from where the actual fighting had taken place. The old woman clung stubbornly to her horse and her chickens and her cow, and to little Pauli. When Tina walked up to the cottage, a black and white dog rushed out, barking furiously at her in the stillness of the morning.

The weather had turned mild. Yellow grass poked through the melting snow and willows were budding. Water dripped from the eaves of the cottage to the brown earth of the flower beds below. The old woman fretted about spring seeding and her grandson Mika who would come to help her with it any day now. She utterly ignored Tina's entreaties to leave now, now, before the Russians came.

At least they had begun to converse. At first, Tina had found it impossible to talk to her, but on the second day she started to chatter as if they were old friends. Since then, they had lived this strange existence, Tina determined not to leave without the boy, the old woman determined not to leave at all. If pressed too hard, she would simply point across the melting brown field, to where the church spire stood unblemished—for the war had not even come close to here—and she would sweep her arm toward the cemetery behind the church.

"My family," she would say. "Two hundred years in this parish."

And the talk of leaving would stop. Even when Tina took her by the arm and showed her the long lines of wagons and people on the main road, trudging west toward the Finnish heartland, away from the hazy eastern horizon where the devastated borderlands lay, she was unmoved. She turned her head away, pointedly refusing to watch the exodus of her neighbours and friends.

"Marita will come back for her son," she said. "We have to be here when she comes."

She did this often, lapsing into forgetfulness or denial, Tina couldn't tell which. Then she had to be gently reminded that Marita was dead.

"Marita is not coming back," said Tina. "She'd want us to take little Pauli to safety."

"We are safe here. God does not suffer harm to come to those who have prayed for His grace."

They walked about the thawing fields, inspecting the trees, counting the birds that came to feed by the stable. The cow had suffered terribly from the cold, said the old woman, but she had survived. A bird with a rosy breast landed on the feeder and pecked at the seeds.

"Oh!" the old woman clutched her chest.

"Grandmother!" Tina panicked. "Are you all right?"

"Do you see it? The red-breasted nightingale."

Never much of a bird-watcher, Tina could not comment on the identity of the visitor, who had already flown away. The old woman took her elbow as they continued to plod through the soggy field.

"It's a sacred bird," she said. "You city folk know nothing of these things. When Christ hung on the cross, the crown of thorns hurt him greatly. His forehead bled—" she swept a bony hand across her eyes, "—and this bird took pity on him and plucked the thorns from his brow, easing his suffering. Some of our Lord's sacred blood spattered on the bird's breast and that's why its descendants have red breasts."

Another afternoon they trooped down the road through slush and mud to where a trail led downhill to a rivulet. The stream, confided the old woman, descends into the great lake, Ladoga, the sea of Karelia, mysterious and deep and always cold. Ice still floats on its waves in July. The seal lives there, a denizen of the ocean, hundreds of miles from salt water. On summer evenings you can sit on the shore and hear the bells of the monastery twenty miles out on an island in the lake. She'd gone there once in a boat, and nearly drowned when a wall of fog suddenly enveloped them and the boat had run into fierce waves during a squall. But when they came out of the mist the golden crosses and cupolas of the island gleamed before them, and the scent of its apple trees and lilacs floated over the water. A flock of white Karelian swans rose out of the lake. She'd been a young woman then, it was the time of the tsars. We will go down to the lake soon, she said, to a place where little Pauli can play in the water.

So it went. The wagons disappeared from the road, and even the soldiers vanished. God help us, thought Tina. The Finnish army is gone. Paul was dead, she could do nothing for his son, her own life was in ruins, her country had nearly been crushed. It was easier to give in to despair. She would stay here with Paul's boy, even if it cost her life.

Ah, little Pauli. He had won her heart from the moment she saw him. This was the child she should have had with him. The joy that should have been theirs. She could not find it in her heart to blame Marita. The only one she blamed was herself. It was her fault that Paul had turned to someone else. She had not been loving enough, she had made him feel unworthy. And then the final insult, to come back from the front and find her dancing with Tom. She picked up the cheerful little boy and cradled him, kissing his unruly straw-coloured hair. Hair just like his father's.

On the third day the old woman began to talk about the boy's parentage. They'd watched as the last wagons creaked along the road, and she'd pointed out one in particular.

"Those people—" she said, "have spread the rumour that Pauli is not legitimate."

Tina froze. What did the old woman know about the conception of this child?

Instead of going to the stove to brew coffee as she usually did at that time in the afternoon, the old woman went to a chest of drawers and pulled out a small box, and placed it on the kitchen table. She then returned to the drawer and fished out a large bundle of letters. These too she placed on the table.

"Look at the ring," she ordered. "They took this off poor Marita after the bomb killed her. I didn't want it buried with her. I knew it would be needed, and I was right."

Tina opened the box and took out a gleaming golden band. Her hand shook as she held it up to the light.

"This was the ring he gave to Marita," confided the old woman. "See. Read the date. That must have been the day they were married."

Tina squinted and looked inside the band. There was an inscription there, all right. Suddenly she was afraid to read it, afraid it would bring back the full trauma of that February evening.

"Read it," prodded the old woman.

She had to read it: February 17, 1940. Had it been the seventeenth of February when Paul came and found her dancing with Tom Henderson? It must have been. So Paul had bought this ring, with the intention of proposing to her that evening. This was her wedding ring. After the bitter scene at the Kämp, he'd gone to Marita and given her the ring. Why not? At least he could be sure she would treasure it.

"Do you see that?" demanded the old woman. "Is that not proof that Paul and Marita were married? That little Pauli is a legitimate child?"

"Yes," she said dully. There was no use arguing with her about years and dates. To the old woman, the ring was absolute. Tina looked away to hide her tears.

Resolutely the old woman put the ring back in its box and stowed it away in the drawer. Then she went to the stove, filled the coffeepot with water and lit the burner. While she waited for the water to boil she pulled out the coffee mill and set about grinding the beans. As soon as the water came to a boil, she spooned in the coffee and removed it from the heat, letting it simmer, letting the grounds settle.

"Never let the coffee boil too long once the grounds are in," she said to Tina by way of instruction.

The scent of coffee filled the small, silent room. The boy dozed on the sofa, and the old woman covered him with a blanket.

That evening, after the boy and the old woman had fallen asleep, Tina found the courage to look through the letters. Most of them were from Marita to her grandmother, but she had seen one bundle stamped with army postage bearing painfully familiar handwriting with a note attached saying Paul Salmi requested these be forwarded to Marita in the event of his death. Why had Paul not forwarded them to his father? She suspected the answer was in the contents. She set about reading them, steeling herself to discover what Paul had been thinking in the trenches. But when her eye caught the name on the very first letter, she stopped in horror. It was addressed to her but had never been mailed. Sifting feverishly through the pile, she saw several beginning "My dearest Tina". Had he not had time to separate them or had he not wanted her to see them? In any case, Marita had received them and sent them to her grandmother, obviously believing this was the safest place for her treasures. What cruel irony that was, too.

Tina got up and went to her purse. The old woman would never know, if she opened a window. She had to have a cigarette. On the trip out to Karelia, she had bought her own package. Using a saucer as an ashtray, by the light of one dim candle, she poured a mug of lukewarm coffee and began to read.

Taipale

February 2--, 1940

My dearest Tina,

This war has made old men of us all. In my quiet moments I contemplate things you should contemplate in old age, when there is no longer a future, only the past. No more dreams, only regrets. Regrets about the hours and days when life was real and breathing, and you sat watching it pass by. What do they call them, sins of omission? The words of love I never got around to saying to you. The way I let my bitterness over Berlin poison my dreams. And the other kind of sins, the things I did. Please forgive my terrible words that night at the hotel. No matter what, I should have remembered that I am a civilized human being. You were right. I loved you and yet never had the courage to propose. All these wasted years! The best years of your life and mine.

I stopped at a jewellry store when I got into Helsinki and bought a ring. I was very nervous. What I saw at the hotel seemed to confirm what I always feared, that our childish affection was a burden on you, that I should set you free. You deserve the most accomplished husband the world has to offer. I don't blame you for being impatient and I wouldn't blame you if there had been something between you and Henderson. I thought if I had succeeded in Berlin it would have changed everything. But that was a pipedream, too. No gold medal would make a difference. I realize that now, thinking about the medal they gave me for valour. What I've found here is greater than any medal.

We kept our promise. That's all the heroism I'll ever need.

Don't be sad, my love. I am at peace. Scared, frozen, starving, but at peace. I will always love you, no matter what. Perhaps nothing more was meant to be.

I must confess something else to you. I went to Marita's bed after I left that night. Can you forgive that? And I must confess I was with her once before. After I came back from Berlin, when I believed you'd want nothing more to do with me. Marita is a nice girl, I think she loves me. I gave her the ring. You'll have to forgive that too.

Give my regards to Henderson. I bear no grudge against him. Tell my father I wish I'd been a better son. Do you see what I mean? How old I've become? How can I walk out of here and be young again?

Keep a candle in your heart for me.

Your Paul

She sat for a long time, smoking until the cigarettes were gone, lighting up crumpled butts. The candle burned out and she puttered in the dark, looking for another, hoping not to wake the old woman and the boy. She would figure out how to camouflage the smoke later, although she realized how ridiculous it was, sitting here in a lonely cottage in Karelia, waiting for death or something worse, waiting to hear the enemy knocking on the door to kill or enslave her—how ridiculous to worry about cigarette smoke. But she was always a stickler for doing the right thing. Smoke was not good for the lungs of the very young and the very old. She cried and laughed, and cried again. She read the letter over and over until she knew it by heart. She heated up the coffee and rooted in the cellar, coming up with a bottle of some unidentifiable liquor. At times it seemed that Paul was sitting across the table from her, smiling benignly.

"How can you ask for my forgiveness?" she said out loud. "It was I who wronged you, at the most crucial moment of your life."

The night outside the window grew colder. The universe rolled on, and the lights of the stars struggled against the northern blackness. It's a hard sky, she said to the few stars she could see, but don't give up. Don't give up on us here at the edge of the world.

Exhausted, sick from too many cigarettes, dizzy from the liquor, her senses numb, she could not move a muscle. Going to bed was out of the question. But slowly a balm seeped into her heart, calming the raw nerves and closing the open wounds. Paul, from beyond the grave, was giving her a final gift from some other existence of which she knew nothing, offering her the first drops of the wine of absolution.

She heard stirring upstairs. The boy was an early riser. Looking east, she saw a tentative softening of the indigo night. She resolved even more firmly to repay Paul the only way she could—making sure that his son, the son he knew nothing about, was safe. The old woman would just have to come around to her point of view.

4

By the end of the next day Tina had won her over. Perhaps she finally believed her stories of what would happen to them when the Russians came. They will not let you stay here, Tina said. They will take us all to Siberia. Do you want Pauli to die in a work camp? At suppertime the old woman finally snapped to her senses and agreed to go, the danger of their isolation crumpling her face in fear, her thin wrinkled arms clutching the boy fiercely. Tina knew they were fighting against time. They had not seen a Finnish soldier for days. No one had come back for them. We must leave in the morning, she said firmly. We will pack the wagon and hitch up the horse. The sleepy old nag in the stable did not look capable of anything more strenuous than chewing hay, nor did the cow. But they had to try.

The March sun was afire in the western sky when she saw the column of brown figures approaching from the Viipuri road. Only God can help us now, she thought. The Russians are here.

The old woman already had the boy bundled up in three coats and had stuffed a large black carryall with her most important possessions, including the box with the ring. If we leave now we can outrun them, she said. For a moment Tina wondered if she'd lost her senses. They were utterly helpless. No, insisted the old woman, there's a way along the back roads that will keep us ahead of them if we leave now, now, this very instant.

But it was too late. Someone was on the front stoop, testing the door. They both clutched the boy and cowered in a far corner. It didn't take long to break the flimsy lock and three dark figures swept in. Two were in brown coats and heavy boots and began to systematically check the room. The third man lit the lamp on the table and the room danced with light around him. It was Tom.

It could have been a few seconds or an eon between the moment Tina recognized him with a gasp and he silenced her with his eyes. The Russians who accompanied him went through the house methodically and quickly, rifles in hand. Satisfied that there were no mines or booby traps or weapons, they prepared to leave.

"Well, Vasily, are you happy now?" said Tom genially to the shorter, stouter of the two, whose collar twinkled with stars. Tina saw that this was a political officer, one of the infamous commissars. Those who stayed in the rear and prodded his countrymen forward with a gun. She had read about their cruelty.

A grin spread across his broad face as Vasily stared at her breasts under their thin pullover. "I am always happy, Mr. Henderson," he said in thickly accented English. "But I think tonight you will be a happier man than Vasily. Good night, ladies. We will be here in the morning to escort you and Mr. Henderson to the new Soviet-Finnish border. Please be ready." With a bow he left and closed the door.

After the Russians left there was a stunned momentary silence. The boy clung bashfully to his grandmother's skirt, turning his face away from the stranger. Tina searched for a word, one word, but found none. Meanwhile, the bravado Tom had shown for the Russians crumbled. He slipped off his overcoat and slumped into a chair.

"Do you have anything to drink?" he rasped.

Tina brought him a glass of the liquor from the cellar, while the old woman watched in speechless wonder. He downed it at a gulp, then looked at the three of them.

"Perhaps you should introduce me," he said, with a modicum of poise now.

They went into action, brewing coffee and bringing out bread and cheese and more liquor. Then they all sat around the pine table and talked. Soon enough everything was clarified, from Tom's brief account of his journey and his meeting with Tina's father at the station to the identity of little Pauli, which she explained briefly and painfully. When the old woman went for more coffee, Tom grew serious. They had to start packing immediately and be ready to leave at dawn. The Russians did not fully trust him despite his high-level clearance for this peculiar mission and there was no room for the slightest misstep. He had with considerable difficulty persuaded Vasily to leave them unguarded in the house. In the end, Vasily had been swayed by the comfort of the large farmhouse close to the village as a more suitable lodging place for an officer in the Red Army. But Tom was sure they were being watched, nevertheless. His instructions were strict and simple. He had permission to come to this house and this house alone, and take its occupants back to Finland with him within twenty-four hours. The house was now the property of the Soviet state. They could take only what they could carry, and would ride in an army truck to the new border. The old woman burst into tears at hearing she would have to leave the cow and the horse, but

Tom assured her she would at least be permitted to take the black-and-white dog that slept under the porch.

For the next hour they worked, unearthing every suitcase and bag in the house, combing the rooms for anything of value. Tom helped the old woman in her distressing chore, communicating with her in a way that amazed Tina, while the boy dashed about in high excitement and had to be removed from underfoot at every turn. Tina prepared a supper of potato stew and kept the coffee hot. The vegetables would have to be left for the Russians, but there was no reason to leave the coffee. The early spring evening yielded another soft sunset, and after they were done the old woman took the boy and went outside to tour her land and buildings for the last time.

For the first time since the night at the Kämp, Tina found herself with Tom. They sat on the back porch, listening to the small sounds of the evening, the dripping of water from the roof still coated with snow, the newly mild air strangely empty.

He didn't look at her but he began to speak. "I'm so sorry. About Paul. About the war, about the peace, about everything."

She glanced at his stricken face in the twilight. Strange that she should be the one comforting him. Someday she'd talk to him about Paul, but not just now.

"It's all right," she said and saw that his shoulders were shaking. She reached to touch his arm, but suddenly the boy ran up, the dog at his heels, and the old woman following slowly behind with tear-streaked face. Tina had never seen her cry before.

"I'll put little Pauli to bed, grandmother," she said. "Have another cup of coffee."

"No. It's too late for coffee." The old woman never had coffee after eight o'clock. It was plain that she wanted this night to be like all the others, the eighty years of days and nights she had spent here. There would be no change in routine that would acknowledge it was the last night. She continued her journey up the stairs and to her room.

Tina put the boy to bed and returned to find Tom still sitting on the porch. It was dark now and she saw lights in the village. The Russians had moved in. Fury reclaimed her and she tore a cigarette from Tom's pack, refusing to let him light it, and dragged heavily on it as she glared at the village. Vile bastards, coming here and taking people's homes and lands. Driving old women from their beds.

"I hate them," she said under her breath, not wanting him to hear. He was here by the Russians' leave, after all. "It won't end this way." But he heard, and seeing her gaze toward the Russian lights, stood beside her. A fresh moon flickered through thin grey clouds, and the snow still ran in rivulets from the eaves.

"Why are you still here in Finland?" she asked. "Aren't there more important places for you to go?"

"No."

She waited and listened for the voice crying in the night, the disembodied wailing that had been her constant companion for weeks, but it was gone. He pulled her to his chest and she wept softly into his shirt, but they were ordinary tears, the kind she could feel on her face, like spring rain.

"I love you," he said. "That's why I'm here."

"I love you, too. More than you can imagine."

His mouth was on hers, on her throat, in her hair, caressing her face. He pulled her further into the porch, into a corner to a pile of rag-woven rugs she had helped the old woman drag out of the house, intending to beat them in the yard the next day. His hands slid under her sweater and he kissed the bare flesh of her stomach. The rugs tumbled down and covered their bodies and he rolled down her brown stockings. The corner was fragrant with the scent of damp pine and cedar. He wrapped the rugs around them tightly, a cocoon to keep out the chill, to keep out everything. Afterwards she felt amazed and slightly ashamed that the surge of life could replace the stench of death so quickly.

5

She woke just before dawn. Shivering, jittery, anxious that they should be ready when the Russian escort came. Tom still slept soundly beside her on the narrow cot in the spare bedroom where she'd brought him at midnight. Gingerly she swung her feet to the wooden floor, searching for her shoes; not finding them, she crept barefoot down the stairs. There she stopped cold, fear in her heart. Someone was on the main floor. She could hear movement, the noise of things being dragged, clanks, bangs, and rasping breaths.

Could the Russians have come already, in the middle of the night? No, that was unlikely. If they had, everyone in the house would have been thrown out by now. Still, it could be a dangerous intruder—perhaps a deserter, a thief.

She lowered herself to see into the living room. The old woman was moving about, as agile as a twenty-year old girl, mop and bucket at her side, scrubbing the floor and the walls, dragging all the furniture into the centre of the room. She mopped and swept round the edges and up to the ceiling, and around the window frames. Tina rushed down the stair.

"What on earth? What are you doing, grandmother? Why are you cleaning the house for the Russians?"

"Don't be ridiculous. It's not for them I'm cleaning it."

"Then why?"

The old woman drew herself up, straightening her back as far possible, standing at attention beside her mop like a cadet.

"If you give a gift to your country, it should be like new."

Then Tina noticed the canister of gasoline in the corner. How had the Russians missed it? It must have been hidden in some secret place, but there it was. And neatly beside it a box of matches. It was a sacrifice that many evacuees had made, this burning of the family home so it would provide no comfort to the invader. She stared at the old woman in awe, ready to receive any order from this unlikely general. The destruction of her home and her life here was her gift to her country, and it should be an immaculate one. Tom would never believe such a thing until he saw it for himself in the morning. Here was the soul of her people, right here in this room.

But the thought of Tom reminded her. "Grandmother, we can't do this," she said. "Your house is Russian property now. We can't destroy it. They'll punish us, maybe kill us."

"I will take the full blame. It's my house. No Russian will ever sleep in my bed. They can kill me if they like, it makes no difference now."

Tina was speechless. This was not the frightened wisp of a woman she had cajoled into leaving. During the night, her tears had dried.

"Let me help you," she said, and together they finished the cleaning. Tom will think of something to placate the Russians, she thought. In the meantime they would finish this ritual. She poured gasoline around the furniture just as she saw the first rays of dawn in the east. But the old woman pocketed the matches. She and she alone would light the flame, when the time came. It was useless arguing with her.

By the time Tina had roused the boy and dressed him in the clothing laid out the night before, Tom was downstairs, berating the old woman in a mixture of English and the few Finnish words he remembered. They sent the boy out to get the dog before he asked too many questions about the strange alignment of furniture downstairs. Instructing him to be quick and wait at the front door, Tina shooed him out the back through the kitchen and walked into the gasoline-scented parlour. For a brief moment the room flooded with light as the sun rose brilliantly out of the east, then just as quickly dimmed when a cloudbank of grey rolled in from the north.

There was the sound of an engine in the front, and she knew the Russians had come. She looked out the window and saw Vasily swinging down from the cab of the truck. "Quick," she said in both Finnish and English, "Get out of here. He mustn't see this. Go. Meet him on the walk." The boy was already skipping on the wooden sidewalk, the dog jumping up to meet the visitor. She and Tom took all the baggage they could and dragged it to the truck, prompting Vasily to snap his fingers at the driver to help with the bags.

"Good morning, my friends," he said. "Lovely day to travel. Not too hot. You see how well we treat you, we give you porters who need no capitalist tips."

Several more soldiers materialized and stood around the truck, rifles cocked. "Travelling companions," said Vasily. " Makes the trip more pleasant. Where is the baba?"

Their bags were hoisted into the back of the truck and the driver started the engine. Vasily swung the boy over his shoulders and deposited him onto the platform, and tossed the dog up after him. The old woman emerged from the house, black kerchief tied neatly around her head, carrying her black bag and almost running in her high-necked laced shoes. Vasily smiled broadly at her but his eyes widened in surprise and then in fury when he saw the first licks of flame shooting through the cracks and windows, and the wooden house went up like a tinderbox, smoke billowing into the morning sky.

"You!" Vasily sputtered. He turned and glared at the old woman and Tina. "Bourgeois swine! Traitorous dogs!" A tirade in Russian followed, his English lexicon of insults apparently exhausted. The soldiers closed in with guns pointed at their heads, while the boy screamed in the truck. Tom reached for her hand but Vasily stepped between. He pushed Tina to one side, and glared again at the burning house, now crackling and sparking in all directions, casting sparks as far as the road and the truck.

"Get in the truck, American!" barked Vasily. "I promised to return you to your masters. But these others—" he spat disdainfully toward the women "—these are enemies of the Soviet people, and will be treated accordingly. March! March to the village, whores! And take the brat with you!"

Tina felt the end of a rifle at her shoulder blade. The old woman wailed in terror, her cries mingling with the screams of the boy, who had been roughly thrown out of the truck and tossed into her arms. Tom was standing perfectly still, eyes hard as granite. Please think of something, Tina prayed silently. Aloud she said in his direction, "Go with them. Don't worry about us. They'll put us in a camp and eventually send us back. There are others trapped behind the border too." She'd heard of small enclaves of Finnish civilians who had not made it out of Karelia. But secretly she did not believe they would ever see their fellow prisoners. Vasily was too angry. They were non-entities whose presence here was not officially acknowledged. Even her father would be helpless, if she survived the firing squad. Lost in these thoughts and cradling the sobbing boy, trying to watch the old woman and keep her from a quick death, she suddenly noticed that Tom was digging in his pocket and speaking soothingly to Vasily, whom he had steered off to one side.

"What does it matter about the house? It's only one of hundreds they set on fire. No one will blame you. Tell them it was a rat-infested health hazard, it had to be destroyed. Why cause unnecessary trouble for yourself? What's one old woman's action to the might of the great Soviet state? It means nothing. Hardly worthy of your attention." Something gleamed in his hand as he spoke, its golden brilliance deepened by the fast-burning fire behind them. Tina recognized it instantly. It was his father's pocket watch. Vasily gazed at it intensely and his frown disappeared as he weighed the situation. To a Russian, even an officer, the watch was worth a great deal.

The heat and sparks from the fire threatened the gasoline tanks in the truck. Vasily made his decision. He snatched the watch from Tom's hand and shoved it into a breast pocket. He turned to the women and motioned them into the truck. Once again he was the suave cavalier. After a few words to the driver, he selected one soldier to sit in the back with the passengers and another to ride in the cab.

The soldiers rearranged the boxes in the back of the truck and squeezed the boy in and propped up the old woman's suitcase for her to sit on. Tina waited for Tom to climb up with her, but he did not move, just stood and gazed into her face. Vasily paced impatiently at a short distance from them, still muttering and frowning.

"Tom, we should hurry. He might change his mind," she said.

"I have to go back to Leningrad with Vasily," he whispered. "They have their rules and they have to account for me. I can't be left to my own devices. That's the kind of deal you get from the devil."

"No! Oh, make them change their minds!" she said, terrified at this unexpected turn of events.

"Don't worry. You'll be safe. And I'm booked on the morning train west from Leningrad. Meet me at the Fennia tomorrow night at eight o'clock."

"All right. But be careful," she said as bravely as she could. "And Tom—I can never thank you enough for this. Never."

"You're the one who told me to always wear the watch."

"And now you've lost it. Your father's gift."

"Maybe I don't need it any more. Maybe my father would be pleased. Finally you got it right, he'd say." She couldn't hold back her tears, and he dabbed lightly at her wet cheeks. "Hey! You're my wishing star, remember? Keep shining."

"I will. Until the universe blacks out."

He kissed her on the forehead. "At least until the Fennia tomorrow night."

"Until tomorrow night," she whispered, and hoisted herself into the back of the truck. Vasily nodded to the driver and the truck's engine sputtered and roared. Tina watched as Tom approached the irate Vasily and took him by the shoulder, and walked away with a wink back at her. They got into the black officer's car that would take them to Leningrad.

The truck lurched along the dirt road away from the farm. Behind them the fire spread higher. The old woman sat stoically on a suitcase, her arm resting on the side of the truck. She stared at the burning house until they reached the main road and it disappeared around the bend, only the orange and black glow still visible in the sky.

The boy had forgotten his terror and began to play with the dog. The rolling hills of Karelia passed by, empty of their ancient masters, here and there dotted with camps of Russian soldiers. Tina gazed at the pine stands and the greening fields, the church spires and the farmhouses. They belonged to the invader now and the bitterness would endure, but she still had a country to cherish. There would always be a white cross in the cemetery to remind her of life's hard truths and consequences. And she had accomplished her mission. Paul's son was safe.

Above all there was Tom, who had brought her the greatest happiness she'd ever known, greater than she knew existed. With him she could face anything.

They reached the border at high noon, and the sun dutifully broke through the clouds as they crossed to the Finnish side.

6

The next evening she rushed to the Fennia at seven, to be sure they got their regular table. On the second floor, the orchestra was back in business and couples filed up the stairs to dance. They would do the same, she thought, but only after the finest dinner the café could purvey. She ordered cutlets and spring vegetables, and a bottle of champagne. Over the next hour she commandeered every spare candle, re-arranged the place settings a dozen times, and drilled the waiters on the timing of the courses. At seven fifty-five on the dot a double scotch arrived at the table and was placed in the seat of honour. At eight the headwaiter took his position by the door, ready to hang up Tom's overcoat.

The music rose louder and she watched couple after couple trip lightly up the stairs, girls in short summer frocks and young men in top hats, who took positions on the landing and surveyed the crowd on the floor.

At eight thirty the waiter abandoned his post, shrugging his shoulders.

"It's all right," Tina told him. "He's been delayed. You know what the trains are like these days."

"Yes." He added ice to the champagne bucket and poured her a glass of wine.

At midnight she drank as much champagne as she could without keeling over. The orchestra was in full swing upstairs. It was American jazz night and a hundred dancing feet eager to escape the war kept up a drumfire that shook the floor.

"It had to be you," someone sang.

At three in the morning the music wound down and they began to pull up the chairs. Tina paid her bill, pulled on her coat and trudged home. Halfway there she began to run, struck by the thought that he'd called and left a message with Selma hours ago. But Selma met her at the door, silently took her coat, hugged her and turned down the covers of her bed as she had done when she was a child.

There was no message the next day, nor the next, or any other day of the thousands she waited through since then.

Epilogue

But I forget.-- My Pilgrim's shrine is won,
And he and I must part, so let it be,
His task and mine alike are nearly done;
Yet once more let us look upon the sea.

Lord Byron

For weeks Tina haunted the Fennia and the Kämp, searching for anyone who might know about Tom, asking after messages or phone calls. None ever came. March turned into April and April into May, and then into a summer as hot as the winter had been cold, but her heart remained trapped in a permafrost of grief.

Her only happiness now came from the boy. She received consent from Paul's and Marita's kinfolk to formally adopt him, and in the rush to relocate evacuees, the papers went through without delay. Meanwhile, the war turned fierce and irrevocable—Hitler took Norway, Denmark, Holland. Stalin made threats in Finland's direction at every turn.

That was when Tina made her decision. The war had already cost her two people she loved and she was determined it would not cost her a third. She decided to take the boy to Toronto where her mother's cousin lived.

With the help of her father, she booked passage on the last American shiₚ leave Finland, the *American Legion*, sailing out of the Arctic port of Petsamo in July 1940. She begged her father and Selma to come, but they declined. Both of them wept unabashedly at the station when she boarded the train to Lapland with the boy in tow.

She has photos from the ship that brought them to Canada. One was taken at a party given by the ship's staff. The boy is wearing a conical paper hat, the first party hat he'd ever seen. Another shows him eating a banana for the first time. Simple things. But they were proof that she'd made the right choice. Children should not have to clear away rubble and play amid undetonated mines.

Through the long years that followed, she still hoped for a message from Tom. Slowly, in agonizing incremental moments of clarity, she became resigned to the fact that she would never know his fate. She looked out across the waters of Lake Ontario and eastward to the Atlantic, to the convulsions that were ripping out the entrails of the Old World. There was no chance to search for one missing name among the millions, one soul out of the multitudes lost in the battlefields and death camps and gulags in the slaughterhouse that stretched from Normandy to the Urals.

Taylor became a celebrity journalist with clearance to ride westward with the Red Army as it mopped up after the retreating Nazis. He wrote some of the first accounts of the death camps in Poland.

Björnström lived for a few years after the war, not a broken man but much saddened. Tina spoke to him frequently by telephone. He took fierce comfort from the fact that the Finns remained a free people when so many others did not. The horse did talk, he muttered over his cognacs; it didn't say much, but it said enough. After his death, Tina persuaded Selma to come to Canada. For their home, they eventually chose the West Coast, a place with natural beauty and unlimited opportunity. And winters without snow.

Gradually she told the boy about his parents, and about her relationship with his father. She said little about Tom but as he grew older the boy seemed to fill in the missing pieces for himself. He grew up strong and smart and had a brief running career that died a natural death when he decided to concentrate on his medical studies. He became a doctor and married a fine girl. They had two daughters who have grown up and left home. The younger one has Marita's dark hair and dancing feet.

Tina is awake again, watching the moon on the water. The leaves of the birch beside her window rustle. When she hears the rustling of the leaves and closes her eyes, she is once again at the Fennia with Tom. She talks to him every day and he answers, from the place in her heart where he still lives.

Outside her window the sea turns the colour of blue growing old, then dying. She knows the water rippling in the shade of the cedars is the Pacific Ocean, and in daylight she can recognize the hemlock and the holly fern of the rainforest. But at twilight she sees only the sentinel spruce marching down the cliff to the sea, taking her to a sterner world far away, a world of dark streets echoing with angry voices and harsh footsteps, the stench of death sweeping across the loveliness and pride of Europe.

She plays a tango on her stereo and shivers. Strange that a dance from the balmy south should make you cold, she thinks, but life does that, laughs at you at every turn as if to say, see what a fool you were to think it would all make sense in the end. The sea is dark now, a canvas of indigo with ebony streaks like the spills of blue-black ink on her writing paper in school, pages and pages of spilled ink. There is only one small glint of silver on the water. Perhaps the reflection of a candle in a window somewhere, a beacon for someone making their way home.

The Winter War that began with the Russian invasion of Finland on November 30th, 1939, lasted for 105 days. The armistice of March 1940 did not bring lasting peace to Finland, only a year's interval until the next war, which the Finns simply called the Continuation War. Their dream of staying neutral was put away, as neither Stalin nor Hitler would allow it. When they resumed their struggle with Russia in 1941, it was under very different circumstances but the end result was the same: they lost Karelia again. However, Finland was the only country bordering Russia to maintain her independence after World War II.

CPSIA information can be obtained
at www.ICGtesting.com
Printed in the USA
BVHW040831230922
647618BV00006B/392